THE LADY OF THE LAKE

THE LADY OF
THE LAKE

Peter Guttridge

This first world edition published 2019
in Great Britain and 2020 in the USA by
SEVERN HOUSE PUBLISHERS LTD of
Eardley House, 4 Uxbridge Street, London W8 7SY.
Trade paperback edition first published
in Great Britain and the USA 2020 by
SEVERN HOUSE PUBLISHERS LTD.

British Library Cataloguing in Publication Data
A CIP catalogue record for this title is available from the British Library.

ISBN-13: 978-0-7278-8967-6 (cased)
ISBN-13: 978-1-78029-665-4 (trade paper)
ISBN-13: 978-1-4483-0363-2 (e-book)

All Severn House titles are printed on acid-free paper.

Severn House Publishers support the Forest Stewardship Council™ [FSC™],
the leading international forest certification organisation.
All our titles that are printed on FSC certified paper carry the FSC logo.

Typeset by Palimpsest Book Production Ltd.,
Falkirk, Stirlingshire, Scotland.
Printed and bound in Great Britain by
TJ International, Padstow, Cornwall.

For my much missed big brother, Michael.
(1945–2018)

'Sweet were the days when I was all unknown,
But when my name was lifted up, the storm
Brake on the mountain and I cared not for it.'

(*Idylls of the King*, Tennyson)

'Other women cloy the appetites they feed but she makes
hungry where most she satisfies.'

(*Antony and Cleopatra*, Shakespeare)

PROLOGUE

A heron alights on a high tree branch, closing its wings with a fast flutter that sounds across the large pond below. The heron watches the turbid waters with its sharp eyes.

Among the mass of marsh marigolds there is the occasional splash as carp come from the muddy depths to the surface to snatch at the hovering dragonflies and flitting pond striders. Shafts of sunlight poke down between the trees in the woodland round the pond.

The pond is placid because there is no wind and the springs that feed it are little more than slow trickles. They never have been more, even when the Romans first dammed the springs to create this pond and the watercress beds beyond.

But now there is this gentle ripple, working its way towards the small island near the middle of the pond. A naked man has lowered himself from the bank into the water. He wades gingerly into deeper water, stirring up silt. Stirring up something else. As he starts to swim towards the nearest cluster of marsh marigolds, behind him an outstretched hand slides up from the water and points at the sky.

Oblivious, a few yards away, the naked swimmer floats on his back, eyes closed, basking in the sunshine.

Another splash as another carp surfaces. The heron takes flight.

ONE

The call about a dead body in Beard's Pond, Plumpton Down came into Haywards Heath police HQ around eight in the evening. Just around the time Detective Inspector Sarah Gilchrist and Detective Sergeant Bellamy Heap of the Brighton division were leaving a post-meeting meal in a chain restaurant in the town's thriving restaurant area. They'd been having the meal with police officers from Lewes and Haywards Heath, following an afternoon briefing there about county line drug trafficking in rural areas and how they could use Norfolk's Operation Gravity, launched in 2016 and deemed a success, as a blueprint for their own approach.

'Going country' – drug gangs recruiting teenagers as drug mules – had become an epidemic in the UK. Some fifteen hundred drug trafficking routes were known to exist, including a number coming out of Brighton and spreading all across Sussex. Of particular concern was the potency of cannabis, which had doubled across Europe in the past decade, both in cannabis resin and herbal cannabis. Levels of Tetrahydrocannabinol, or THC, the main psychoactive part of cannabis linked to psychosis and mental illness, had doubled to seventeen per cent in cannabis resin and doubled to ten per cent in herbal, supposedly healthier, cannabis.

Police at Lewes District were taking the lead in the county. However, Lewes was notoriously short-staffed thanks to the draconian police cuts of recent years so Gilchrist and Heap had been seconded there for three months. Both Haywards Heath's and Lewes District's only murder investigation officers were on leave, so Gilchrist and Heap offered to check out the dead body and report back.

As they drove out of Haywards Heath on the Ditchling Road, Bellamy Heap said: 'I'm not sure whether Beard's Pond is a large pond or a small lake. Such a stretch of water in the Lake District might be called a tarn.'

'Thank you for that clarification, Bellamy. I'm sorry to say that while I regret the loss of anyone's life, I'm pleased we have a potentially meaty investigation.' She saw his glance at her. 'Oh, come on, Bellamy. Aside from this county line stuff it's not exactly all go out here in the country is it? Did you see the Lewes daily briefing this morning?

'A woman's emotional support guinea pig died of fright when somebody rehearsing for Lewes Bonfire Night set off a string of fireworks nearby. Catnapping is on the increase and there's a worry it's going to spread to dogs – that gang needs to be found and pronto.' She nudged Heap's arm. 'I'm serious, Bellamy. British people can cope with any kind of horrors inflicted on humans – especially Johnny Foreigners – but harm to a pet is a hanging offence. And there is a positive epidemic of pet-snatching in Sussex. Do you remember when it happened in Kemp Town? Owners forced to pay hundreds of pounds in ransom?

'But we do need to be on the lookout for some hard man with Lewes connections who escaped from Wandsworth prison by climbing over the outer wall on a rope ladder dropped by a drone.'

'He's probably halfway across Spain by now,' Heap said.

Gilchrist looked out of the window absently then turned back to Heap. 'How's Kate? You know she and I are having a girls' night out tomorrow night?'

Kate Simpson had been Gilchrist's best friend for some years. She still was, really, but they'd seen much less of each other in the past couple of years since Kate and Bellamy had become an item. Recently Kate had given up her flat in Brighton to move into Heap's spacious flat in Lewes.

Gilchrist glanced at Heap now with fondness. He was a small, unassuming man who looked like a teenager, down to the blushing when he got embarrassed. But she knew there was steel in him and all the good qualities that made a decent man. If only there were another man with his qualities out there, she found herself thinking. Then: *Gawd, Sarah, stop being maudlin.*

Heap looked serious.

'I know you're having a drink, yes, ma'am. I'm pleased. Kate's finding it very difficult. The failure of her Channel Swim and the suicide of her mother coming so close together.'

'The swim wasn't her fault though,' Gilchrist said. 'The weather conditions turned atrocious – the pilot of the support boat did the right thing to turn back.'

Gilchrist and Heap had both been in the boat as Kate's supporters. Fat lot of support Gilchrist had been once the boat got into what the pilot called 'very lumpy' water. When she wasn't throwing up over the side – or, given the wind, more usually over herself – she was curled into a ball under a blanket groaning. Bellamy, of course, capable as he was in every field, or so it seemed, was fine. He must have a Teflon stomach.

'When is her mother's funeral?'

Gilchrist had never warmed to Kate's mother on the couple of occasions she had met her. One of those well-preserved, well-turned out, stick-thin, chilly and remote older women Brighton did so well, although they were pretty much ghettoized in the huge old apartments of the Regency squares or up around the Seven Dials.

Kate's mother had not, of course, had anything to do with Kate's Channel swim attempt, except to comment, typically, on how much weight Kate was putting on. She only ever huffed when Kate explained umpteen times that Channel swimmers needed a bit more blubber to function effectively in the chilly waters. You were supposed to eat a lot.

'The funeral is in three days,' Heap said. 'So she's keeping herself busy with the arrangements. Then there is her father, of course.'

Kate's father, William Simpson, had been a corrupt politician, involved in suspect activities for which he'd never been brought to account. An ex-government spin doctor, he now made a substantial living as a public relations consultant for various dubious dictators and states around the world. Kate's mother had left him unexpectedly as part of the fallout of the notorious Milldean Massacre some years earlier.

Kate had a fractious relationship with him. Oddly, his name had come up in the murder investigation Gilchrist and Heap had concluded a few months earlier. Not as a suspect but in some potentially suspicious business dealings involving the West Pier that had come to nothing.

'I can only imagine what she's going through,' Gilchrist said. 'Does she at least like living in Lewes?'

'Being waited on hand and foot you mean, ma'am?'

Heap had a lovely big grin on his face. Gilchrist barked a laugh.

'That's not exactly—'

'She seems to be liking it, ma'am.'

Gilchrist often forgot Heap's pawky sense of humour. *Pawky* – she so liked that word. She'd come across it when she was about twelve and reading all the Sherlock Holmes short stories. Holmes had referred in passing to Watson's *pawky* sense of humour.

Ma'am. She'd once tried to persuade Heap to call her Sarah but it hadn't taken. He'd stayed with *ma'am*, except that now he used it all the time as a kind of acceptance he was being silly. She read his use of it as respect – quite right too – and affection.

'You continue to take care of my friend, Bellamy, or you'll answer to me.'

'I intend to, ma'am,' he said. They were driving now down to the roundabout in the middle of Ditchling Common. The Downs filled the near horizon, their soft, undulating lines looking impossibly English. 'The whale-backed Downs,' Heap murmured.

'That sounds very poetic, Bellamy,' Gilchrist said.

'Kipling, ma'am. He lived down this way for a few years.'

'I like Kipling.' She lowered her voice and gruffly half-sang, half-spoke: 'I'm Louie, King of the Jungle, yeah, Louie that's my name.'

Heap giggled. It was an odd sound to come from Mr Sobriety and it made Gilchrist laugh too.

'I'm not sure he actually wrote the songs in the *Jungle Book*, ma'am.'

'Get outta here,' Gilchrist said. 'Next you'll be saying T. S. Eliot didn't write *Cats*.' Heap shook his head.

'I think I've burst enough bubbles for one evening, ma'am.'

They turned left at the roundabout and wiggled down onto lengthy Spatham Lane, which would bring them out eventually right underneath the Downs on the Lewes Road.

'I like walking on the Downs,' Heap said as they came into sight again. 'It only takes five minutes to get onto them from my house.' Heap lived in Lewes, near the prison, which somehow seemed fitting for a policeman who was so devoted to his job.

'Have you walked the South Downs Way yet?' Gilchrist said.

'Not yet but I intend to. Have you, ma'am?'

'I'm not much of a walker. I wouldn't mind cycling it.'

'Not in Lycra, I trust,' Heap said.

Gilchrist bridled.

'What? You think I'm too fat for Lycra?'

Heap flushed and stammered, clearly startled by the speed of her angry response: 'N-not at all. I merely meant that, personally, I dislike anyone wearing Lycra in the countryside. Those garish colours are such a vulgar contrast to the natural greens and browns all around – especially at this time of year.'

'Well, I agree,' Gilchrist said. 'I'd never dream of wearing something gaudy. I got you there though.'

'You did, ma'am.' Heap looked relieved. 'Lot of cyclists on the Downs, mostly up from Brighton,' he said. 'Sadly, they are usually going at speed so can't appreciate the beautiful scenery they're passing through. Give me walkers and horse-riders every time.'

'I get it, Bellamy. Enough said.'

They pulled on to the Lewes Road and turned left. Soon the road went under a canopy of trees and curved sharply at Westmeston church. As the road straightened, they passed on the right the V of trees planted on the side of the Downs to commemorate Queen Victoria's Jubilee. On the left were field after field of vines.

'All these vines,' Gilchrist said, 'everywhere you look.'

'It's taken the local farmers long enough to realize what the Romans knew 2,000 years ago – this is the perfect land for planting vines. The wine industry is flourishing.'

'It's like being in Tuscany,' Gilchrist said, remembering her one holiday there.

After Plumpton Agricultural College and the Half Moon pub the road got even more winding. Beyond Novington Lane, Heap turned left into a narrow, tree-canopied lane. They turned right again into a driveway. There was a sign that stated *Access to Plumpton Down House Only*. A white-painted five-bar gate in front of a cattle grid swung away from them as they approached.

They drove slowly along the narrow, curving driveway, over regular speed bumps, past sheep grazing on unfenced meadows either side of them. They nudged patiently along when the sheep were in their path, waiting for them to move out of the way.

A bright yellow digger was parked some ten yards from the road, its bucket half raised, beside the thick base and exposed roots of an old oak that had come down in some storm. The oak's big trunk lay on the meadowland, branches already sheared off and piled high either side of it.

There was heavy woodland off to the right as they approached another five-barred gate and cattle grid. A police car was squeezed into a passing place on the left and a policewoman was standing beside the cattle grid. There was a roll of police tape on the ground beside her.

'Ma'am,' she said, leaning down to Gilchrist's window. 'I'm PC Duffy. There is parking just up the drive a hundred yards on the left at the far edge of the lake. There's a gate there onto a path you need to follow for a couple of hundred yards where my colleague, PC Malcolm, is with the person who found the body. And there is the body, of course.'

Gilchrist pointed down at the tape.

'I wasn't sure what to do ma'am,' the PC said. 'There are people driving to and from the house quite regularly. There is no other way out or in. I didn't know if they should be prevented from going about their business given the body was discovered over towards the far end of the lake.'

Gilchrist nodded.

'Leave it for now.' She looked to the left as Heap drove slowly forward, rattling over the cattle grid. Behind a low, Victorian iron railing and a sparse hedge of trees and bushes there was a long stretch of water, fringed by another wood. She couldn't see the far end of the lake. There was a passing place at the end of the 100 yards with a police car already there.

There was a *Private: Keep Out* sign on a well-made narrow gate. A chain and combination padlock hung off the gate post. The wire fencing either side of the gate was sagging. Gilchrist reflected it would be easier just to climb over the fencing than go to the faff of fiddling with the padlock.

They both put on wellingtons then went through the open gate onto a partly overgrown path beside the lake.

'Wow,' Gilchrist said looking across the lake. 'This is a little hidden delight. I had no idea it existed.'

'Nor I, ma'am.'

They reached PC Malcolm, a portly, chalk-faced man in his forties. The dead body lay face up on the bank of the lake. There was a deep slash across the neck but no blood. Neither was there any bloating, as would be normal if the body had been in the lake for any length of time.

'If you haven't already, please call for SOCO and Frank Bilson, the pathologist,' she said to the policeman after they had made their introductions. 'The person who found him is still here, I understand?'

'Yes, ma'am,' PC Malcolm said. He pointed to a stand of trees some twenty yards away, a veiled expression on his face. 'He's over there. His name is Donald Kermode.'

Gilchrist and Heap walked towards the stand of trees. As they neared Gilchrist saw a police thermal blanket lying on the ground. Then she saw a man sitting on a tree stump looking out at the lake. He was bare-chested.

'Mr Kermode?' Heap called. The man swivelled towards them on the tree stump. Not bare-chested: stark naked.

'That's me – and you are?'

He was a man in his fifties with receding curly hair and a paunch. Gilchrist noticed the cold water and the chilly morning hadn't done him any favours down below the paunch.

'I'm DS Bellamy Heap,' Heap said. 'Would you mind getting dressed?'

'I would if I could but someone stole my clothes.'

'Someone stole your clothes?'

'I believe I just said that. Yes. While I was swimming somebody thought it would be a jolly jape to steal my clothes. So I had to run off like this to get a signal – there's no phone signal to speak of here.'

'They took your clothes but not your phone?' Heap said.

Kermode looked at him sharply.

'I never leave it with my clothes. I hide it under my towel on the bank where I get in.'

'You didn't see who took your clothes?' Gilchrist said.

'Of course not – otherwise I would have chased them with a big stick.' He saw her instinctively glance down. 'No, not that little acorn. Why, Detective Inspector, I believe you have a dirty mind.'

Gilchrist flushed, not daring to look at Bellamy Heap. Ever the gentleman, he came to the rescue.

'Do you always swim naked?' he said.

'Don't you?' Kermode said.

'Not in a public place.'

'But this isn't a public place. It's a private lake.'

Gilchrist gestured.

'With a road running by it.'

'A private driveway.'

'I thought this lake was part of the Plumpton Down Estate,' Gilchrist persisted. 'Forgive me but why are you swimming in it?'

'What, you don't think I might be the owner of the Plumpton Down Estate?' He gave a ferrety smile. 'Quite right. Major Richard Rabbitt is the owner of the estate. He's the one lying dead over there with his throat cut.'

'You know him?'

'I've been to a couple of his magic lantern shows.'

Gilchrist couldn't help but look blank. She looked at Heap. He was clearly also in the dark but was hiding it a bit better.

'You're going a bit fast for me, Mr Kermode,' Gilchrist said. She pointed over to the corpse. 'You're certain that is the owner of the Plumpton Down House and Estate?'

'Well, as I've already told PC Plod over there, I've never seen the major with his throat cut before and without his terrible wig but I've seen him a few times. Either when he does his magic lantern shows – he's very proud of his collection of slides . . . *was* very proud of his collection, I should say – or when he is gracious enough to open his estate up for us peasants to come and have a look around.'

'You didn't like him?' Gilchrist said.

'Well spotted – I see why you're a detective inspector. But don't be jumping to any conclusions. I just happened to be the person to find him.'

'Why don't you like him?'

Kermode snorted.

'You're not from round here, are you?' he said.

'You clearly are,' Gilchrist said, trying to hide how much this man was pissing her off.

'Man and boy,' Kermode said.

'In that order?' Gilchrist said. She was aware of Heap giving her a look. Not succeeding at the hiding thing, then.

Kermode turned to her.

'Clever. Major Richard Rabbitt. Dick by name, Dickhead by nature. Fancies himself as lord of the manor. Squire Rabbitt or some such title. If people still wore hats he'd expect them to be doffed. He'd probably want people to tug their forelocks too but that has frankly always sounded rather rude to me. My first inclination was to leave him floating in the pond but that would have been terrible for Nimue. So, unwillingly, I had to touch him.'

'Nimue?' Heap said, frowning. 'You mean the Lady of the Lake? You believe in tree and water spirits?'

Kermode snorted.

'You're too clever for your own good, Mr Policeman. I mean the actual owner of this lake and woodland. Her name is Nimue.'

'Rabbitt doesn't own it?' Gilchrist said.

'He does not – causing him much gnashing of teeth. He's wanted to add this lake and wood to the estate for years – coveted it ever since he got here. And coveted Nimue too, probably.'

'You're a friend of Nimue's?' Heap said. 'She lets you swim here?'

'Yes and yes,' Kermode said.

'What's Nimue's full name and can you give us a contact for her?' Gilchrist said.

'Nimue Grace.'

'Agh, okay,' Heap said.

Gilchrist frowned. 'The actress who used to be a movie star?'

Kermode looked pained.

'If I might give you a note: never use that construction to her face. Once a movie star always a movie star.'

'Is she still working then?'

Kermode shook his head and pursed his lips.

'Second note: never ask an actress if she is "still" working. As far as they are concerned, even though all fear they will never work again, and many haven't worked for years, they are always available for work and hoping someone will "still" want them.'

'Does she "still" live in the same house?' Heap said. He tossed Kermode the blanket. It fell neatly into his lap. Kermode smirked.

'That depends on which house you mean.'

'The one near here under Plumpton Hill?'

Kermode nodded.

'Can you tell us how you found him?' Heap said.

'I arrived for a swim around seven p.m. I went for a swim around 7.10 p.m. I saw the body around 7.20 p.m. I hauled it out around 7.30 p.m.'

'Did you see anyone when you were arriving or when you were swimming or when you came out of the water?'

'I didn't but obviously there was someone here since my clothes were stolen.'

Gilchrist looked back at the dead man.

'OK, Mr Kermode, thank you,' Heap said. 'The constable over there will get your details and someone will be in touch to take your statement. And I'll arrange for you to get a lift home.'

'Naughty Nimue Grace?' Gilchrist said to Bellamy Heap as they walked back through the wood. 'It's her lake?'

Heap got on his iPad when they got back in the car.

'According to the Land Registry, ma'am,' Heap said, 'it's owned by a Vivien Nimue Grace. So, yes.'

'She was gorgeous. That body. I hated her.'

'Ma'am,' Heap said.

'You've seen her films?'

'Not lately,' Heap said. 'But some of those early films still stand up. Good actress.'

'Good actress? Bellamy, are you serious? She had two expressions and when she'd exhausted them she took her clothes off.'

'She was certainly not backward in coming forward with the nudity, ma'am.'

'But you think she's good, Bellamy. I'm surprised. Admit it, it's the nudity you like.'

Bellamy blushed. Inevitably. Gilchrist took pity on him. 'She's a bit of a recluse these days, isn't she?'

'Well, she hasn't gone the full Bardot, ma'am, but she does keep to herself. Doesn't do interviews or public appearances. I just looked her up on IMDb and she hasn't done any films for a while – and never has done telly. She does theatre now and then. I saw her not so long ago at Chichester doing a Strindberg.'

'Gone the full Bardot? IMDb? Doing a Strindberg? Bellamy, what is this strange, new language you're speaking?'

'I like to try and keep up. But with regard to the last, I just meant she was performing in a Strindberg play.'

'You try to keep up. Really. I thought you were the Jasper Rees-Mogg of the police force.'

'I don't think his name is Jasper, ma'am, and, if I may say, I'm rather offended at the comparison. I'm a member of the Film Club at the Depot in Lewes.'

'Well, excuse me. I was trying to be funny, Bellamy, and I don't know that throwback's first name. But my apologies if I offended you. Where does she live?'

'Plumpton Hill Cottage. It's a mile or so away from this lake by road. Few hundred yards as the crow flies.'

'Do crows fly in a more direct line than any other bird?' Gilchrist said.

'I wouldn't know, ma'am, but it's certainly worth exploring further.'

'I thought they were the birds that if they left the Tower of London something bad would happen.'

'Those are ravens.'

'What's the difference?'

'Again, I wouldn't know – twitching is not my area of expertise.'

'You know I'm resisting the obvious jokes.'

'I'm grateful, ma'am.'

'It will be too late to call on Grace tonight by the time we've been up to Rabbitt's house and spoken to the people there,' Gilchrist said, looking at her watch and up at the sky. 'Let's do it first thing tomorrow.'

They drove on up the drive. There were fields of grazing sheep and llamas. Gilchrist looked again. Llamas in an enclosure looked totally out of place in this English pastoral landscape. Still, it could be worse – she'd heard about at least two ostrich farms in the vicinity.

The Georgian mansion loomed up at the end of the drive ahead of them. Their car crunched across the gravel inner drive and they pulled to a halt outside the large porch.

A woman answered the high double doors. Middle-aged, statuesque, with thick, curly grey hair cascading over her shoulders. Gilchrist introduced them and she stepped back and ushered them into the huge foyer.

'I believe you've been informed that Major Rabbitt is dead,' Gilchrist said. 'We're sorry for your loss. Do you mind me asking you who you are?'

'Tallulah Granger.'

'You live here? Work here?'

'Both.'

Gilchrist's attention was drawn to an enormous construction taking up about a quarter of the foyer beside a grand staircase. It was a not-so-miniature village. With a Georgian house and grounds and lake and woods. It was made of Lego.

'That's impressive Lego. There are children here who did it?'

'The children aren't allowed anywhere near it,' Granger said.

'Does it represent Major Rabbitt's estate? He commissioned it?'

'Richard made it. Lego is his relaxation.'

'I read about a government minister who did that. But I thought Major Rabbitt's hobby was magic lanterns?'

'He has time for more than one hobby – and hobby horses. Yes, this is the estate and the Downs. Have you seen Brighton and Hove football stadium?' She pointed at an arena on the Lego recreation of the Downs. It was indeed the shape of the local club's stadium.

'It must have taken ages.'

'He is very detail obsessed. Was.'

'Have you worked for him long?'

'No one works for him long so I've been here longer than anybody else.'

'Bad boss?'

'The worst.'

'So why have you hung on?'

'I'm his sister.'

'OK,' Gilchrist said slowly. 'When was the last time you saw your brother?'

'A week or so ago. Roughly.'

'He's been away?'

'Not that I'm aware of.'

'You've been away?'

'No.'

'But I thought you said you work for him? And you live here? Yet you haven't seen him for a week.'

'Yes and yes and yes. But this is a twenty-bedroom mansion. He occupies the left wing; I have a room and an office in the right wing, where all the Airbnb rooms are that I administer. That's my function.'

'Does he share the left wing with anybody? Is there anybody I should be talking to?'

'Nobody regular. He likes to pick and choose.'

'You seem to have a cynical view of your brother.'

'Yes, well, I've been stuck with him all my life. Plus he got the inheritance. According to him he was doing me a big favour employing me and letting me live here.'

'Why did you allow that?'

'You don't know me well enough to ask that,' the woman said.

'This is a murder inquiry. I'm afraid there's scarcely any limit to what we might ask. But, OK, is there anyone close to him we should be talking to?'

'His ex-wife.'

'And she is?'

'*Leessell* Rabbitt. Spelt L-i-e-s-l. She has a café on Lewes High Street. I forget the name but it's between a posh shop and a second-hand bookshop.'

'And her name is pronounced *Leessell*?'

Granger nodded.

'You mentioned children – your brother's?'

'Two boys,' Granger said. 'Aged eight and nine. Away at boarding school.'

'Do they know yet?'

'I was waiting until I heard more of what has happened from you people.'

'Well, Mr Rabbitt has been murdered. Perhaps the boys should be taken out of school and brought home?'

'Not by me. I can't stand the little brats.'

Gilchrist frowned.

'OK then. We'll contact Child Services here to inform the school and we'll tell his ex-wife. Does Mr Rabbitt have a current partner?'

'I wouldn't know who that is. You could ask his secretary, Rhoda. Rhoda Knowles.'

'Is she here now?'

'She went home upset when she heard the news. Lives in Plumpton Green.'

Heap made a note.

'Even though you haven't seen him for a while do you know if he has a regular routine?' Gilchrist said.

'Like clockwork. I told you, he's a bit obsessive compulsive. He needs routine.'

'Does that routine involve visiting the lake?'

'Nimue's lake? Not that I know of. She's one that got away, incidentally. Way out of his league and didn't need his money. I don't know about you but I'd also be put off by any man vain enough to wear a toupee but cheap enough to buy a terrible one.'

'Are there any other siblings?'

'No. There were just the two of us.'

'Do you know of any business partners?'

'Not partners, exactly, but there are people he is in business with.'

'For this estate?'

'No – this is all his. He has other business interests.'

'Any names you could mention?'

'He keeps all that stuff pretty close to his chest. But there's a property guy who owns a lot of flats in Brighton. Moroccan I think. He actually lives on the farm next door to Nimue Grace. They're up to something together.'

'Nimue and this Moroccan man?' Gilchrist said.

'No! My brother and him.'

'Up to something?' Gilchrist said. 'As in something criminal?'

'Just a turn of phrase,' she said. 'But you can bet it will be underhand and will be taking advantage of people. But then doesn't all capitalism do that?'

'I don't have an opinion on the matter,' Gilchrist said. 'Do you have a name for this person? And any indication of what they might be up to?'

'Said Farzi. And I expect they are buying some property together. Or land. I think they both might also want to squeeze Nimue Grace out.'

'Out of what?'

'Out of the area. Get her home and her land.'

'I see. Do you have a particular reason for saying that?'

'Snatches of overheard conversation.'

'And the other person?'

'That spin doctor as was. William Simpson.'

'Him again,' Gilchrist muttered.

'What?' Granger said.

'William Simpson. Again, would you know what kind of business?'

'Again, undoubtedly underhand.'

Gilchrist nodded.

'Thank you very much for your help so far. I'm sure we'll be back with more questions later. Is it possible to see your brother's part of the house.'

'I believe a search warrant is customary,' Granger said.

Gilchrist let the surprise show on her face.

'Well, this is to help us find out who murdered your brother.'

'We all want to do things by the book, I'm sure, DI Gilchrist. It won't take you long to get a search warrant and then we can move ahead very quickly.' She held out her hand. 'I look forward to seeing you again soon.'

'Well, that was odd,' Gilchrist said when they were back in the car. 'How suspicious was that suddenly?'

'Very,' Heap said. 'I'll make the calls and get us back in there tomorrow. Where now?'

Gilchrist looked up at the darkening sky. 'I think we call it a night and make an early start in the morning.'

Gilchrist and Heap went back to the lake at eight the next morning. It was another blustery day and Gilchrist imagined hang gliders floating above the Devil's Dyke, a couple of miles further along the Downs. As they came onto the pathway beside the lake a duck came out of a stand of reeds leading four ducklings in a line.

'Very *Swallows and Amazons*,' Heap said.

'Why a canard?' Gilchrist said.

'I didn't know you liked the Marx Brothers, ma'am.'

Gilchrist frowned.

'You have totally lost me, Bellamy.'

'You're not the first person to tell me that, ma'am. I thought you were referencing the Marx Brothers film where one of them mishears the word "viaduct" as "why a duck?".'

Gilchrist thought for a moment. 'Do you think you needed to be there, Bellamy?'

He laughed. After the giggle, she was now surprised at how high pitched his unfettered laugh was. Almost girlish. 'I think so, ma'am,' he finally said.

'So why is it called a "canard"?'

'You mean a fabrication?' Heap said. 'A lie?'

'Yes. Or to put it the way of your Marxist friends: why a duck?'

Heap laughed again. At a lower octave. 'I believe it comes from a French journalist – I don't remember his name – who published a story about a breed of cannibalistic ducks who ate each other until only one remained. A little like "I am the captain of the ship". When the journalist admitted he had made the story up – for its time it was what is now lazily called "fake news" – voila, a "canard" was born.'

'Bellamy, that was admirably clear but, as usual, you lost me at one bit. What captain of what ship?'

'The *Nancy Bell*, ma'am. A poem/song by Gilbert, of Gilbert and Sullivan fame,' Heap said. Then, to Gilchrist's stupefaction and delight, he began quietly to sing: 'Oh, I am a cook and a captain bold, and the mate of the *Nancy* brig, and a bo'sun tight and a midshipmite and the crew of the captain's gig.'

She laughed. 'You actually sing in tune! Are you an am-dram type, Bellamy? *Pirates of Penzance* and all that?'

'I had my moments at university,' Heap said.

'I'm sure you did, Bellamy. But I don't want too much

information. And I still don't see the connection between "canard" and Nancy Whatsit.'

'Shipwrecked boat, ma'am, everybody ate each other until there was only one left who had eaten all the other ranks and positions on the boat.'

'The clouds part,' Gilchrist said as they arrived opposite Frank Bilson, who was in waders in the shallow water by the island. Actually, island was putting it a bit strong. It was a strip of land only some twenty yards by ten. There was a tree house on it that looked a bit the worse for wear.

Bilson followed her gaze then waved cheerily.

'*Swallows and Amazons*, eh, Sarah?'

Gilchrist shook her head. 'So I gather. I wasn't much of a reader when I was a kid. What exactly are you doing?'

'Who was that contaminating the crime scene with his singing?'

'Bellamy – and he sang very well.'

'The young man did indeed. I was tempted to join in – I'm a light operetta cognoscenti myself – but even I didn't feel it appropriate in the circumstances.' He gestured to his surroundings and the body still lying on the bank, but now covered with plastic.

'What are you doing?' Gilchrist repeated.

'DI Gilchrist! It's not like you to pry. But if you really want to know I'm looking for a set of dentures.'

Gilchrist glanced back at the body.

'He wore dentures?'

'His top set. Back in the 1930s my parents both had all their teeth out at the age of eighteen. It was the custom then, if you were poor, to avoid disease. Not sure how French kissing worked when you encountered two sets of false teeth.'

'I don't think we need go there, Mr Bilson,' Gilchrist said.

'I hear you, Sarah. Sadly. I've already found the wig floating on the surface. But this lake is very muddy – the carp I think.' He tilted his head. 'I wonder what connection someone who carps has with these carp here.'

Gilchrist burst out laughing. She couldn't help it, even though she was at a murder scene.

'What's so funny?' Bilson said, frowning.

'It's already been that kind of morning,' she said. 'Ask Bellamy. He'll know. He knows everything.'

'Yes. That young man probably does.'

Gilchrist walked over to another part of the bank and looked across the lake. It had been a dry summer and the water was low. Gilchrist could see the roots of all the trees on the opposite bank. There was a sagging wooden edifice of some sort between the trees. Gilchrist peered more closely. There was something white beneath it.

'Bellamy,' she called. She pointed across the lake then down the path. Bellamy joined her and they walked in single file along the track, through trees and across dry stream beds. The lake petered out at a kind of dam with a dry stream bed threading through the trees beyond it to Beard's Lane and through a funnel beneath the lane. They crossed a couple of railway sleepers laid down as a bridge.

The track on the other side was more overgrown but clearly seen. Gilchrist avoided some droppings.

'You probably know what animal that's from, Bellamy,' she called behind her.

'Deer, ma'am.'

'You're bionic aren't you, Bellamy? Half human, half computer search engine.'

'I do have an implant in my brain, ma'am,' Bellamy called back.

'You admit it! It all begins to make sense now.'

'Yes, ma'am. It's called a good education.'

She stopped and turned to see his smile. 'Well, and being a swot, obviously.'

Heap bowed his head. 'Obviously.'

They reached the broken-down wooden structure. Gilchrist grabbed on to a tree and leaned out to look down at the white containers. Each was about the size of a three gallon can. They were all attached to a huge knot of thick rope. Heap got down into the water. The water was shallow but he hadn't taken into account the mud. The water eddied around the top of his wellingtons. He pulled at one of the containers.

'What are they?' Gilchrist called down.

'No idea, ma'am. Very thick plastic. Soldered closed at the top as best I can see. We need a cutter before we can tell more.' He bent down to peer at the knot of rope. 'Three frayed ends here, ma'am. I'm no expert but looks recent.'

'So some containers have been removed. Do you think it's anything?'

Heap shrugged.

'No idea. Judging by the exposed roots here, the lake is low and these containers are usually totally submerged. Maybe they slow release chemicals into the lake or something.'

'Wouldn't they float?'

'Depends what's in them, I suppose.' He tried to lift one of the containers. 'Too heavy or just too tightly bound, I'm not sure which.'

She reached down her hand to Heap and hauled him up. She nodded towards the trail by the lake. 'Let's finish the circuit.'

Within a hundred yards they reached a high brick wall tangled with creepers and climbers. There was an arched doorway in the middle of it. The door had been removed at some point. Gilchrist ducked to get through. Heap didn't need to.

They were back at the police tape at the cattle grid at the entrance to the lake. Heap chatted for a moment to the new policewoman on guard there and then they walked back along the driveway to their car.

'Let's go up to Plumpton Down House to execute our warrant then go and introduce ourselves to Nimue Grace.'

Tallulah Granger wasn't at the big house and nor was Rabbitt's secretary, Rhoda Knowles. Nevertheless, they were directed to Rabbitt's wing of the house. Cluttered and tidy at the same time. Gilchrist had never seen anything like it. Pile upon pile of folders, charts, maps and plans.

'OK, well I wouldn't know where to start here, Bellamy. Would you?' Heap shook his head. 'Call Sylvia Wade and get her to get a team up here. Make sure we sequester any phones and the computer.' She looked around. 'Where is the computer?'

Heap was at a large, not-quite-so-cluttered desk. He indicated a dust-free rectangular outline in the centre of the desk.

'Tallulah made good use of the few hours she insisted on,' Heap said.

'Indeed. We need to track her down.'

*   *   *

They drove back down the drive, past the lake and onto Beard's Lane. They threaded their slow way along the narrow, tree-canopied lane they were becoming familiar with.

'Parts of this lane – the straight parts – are an old Roman road underneath the Downs,' Heap said. 'It wiggles a little now but was essentially as straight as a die until it hit a big bend below Plumpton Hill.'

'What's a die?' Gilchrist said.

Heap didn't answer for a moment. Then: 'If I may say, we have been having particularly testing conversations this past couple of days.'

Gilchrist laughed.

'I'm in a curious mood, Bellamy. Be grateful I'm not my usual miserable self.'

'Ma'am. I understand it to be the plural of dice – or vice versa, now that I think of it – so I have no idea how that links to something straight. There is a die used in a printing process, I believe but, again—'

'All right, enough now, Bellamy. I'm sorry I encouraged you. Will you look at that?'

They came round the big bend in the lane. To the left towered the Iron Age fort, Plumpton Hill, and directly below it a conglomeration of Victorian buildings with a long-walled garden running down a slope to an orchard and then a wood.

'Plumpton Hill Cottage, ma'am.'

'If that's a cottage, I can't imagine what a mansion looks like round here,' Gilchrist said.

The entrance into the private drive was a hundred yards further along the road, opposite a cluster of Victorian brick-and-flint cottages.

There was a combination lock on the gate at the entrance to the drive. Heap got out of the car and pressed a buzzer beside the gate. A light voice answered. Heap said who they were and the person – Heap wasn't sure of the sex – gave him the combination of the lock. Heap fed it in and the gate slowly opened. There were speed bumps on the drive so they had ample time to enjoy the view of the orchard on the left with the steep hill in the near distance behind it and a fenced off wood on the right.

'It's a deer!' Gilchrist said excitedly. 'Over by that far wall.'

'Lots of wild deer around here, ma'am. They can be a bit of a pest because they like to eat saplings.'

'Small price to pay for beauty,' Gilchrist said as she craned her neck to examine the deer as it stood perfectly still, watching them.

'Ma'am, do you mind my asking: don't you get out of Brighton much?'

She laughed. 'I do not but I will once I've bought my bicycle – and my Lycra.'

They parked by some outbuildings and walked through a small, paved garden to a rustic front door. Heap tugged down on a bell pull and there was a loud clanging inside.

The door opened after a minute. An etiolated young person stood before them. Gilchrist wasn't sure if it was a woman or a man.

'I'm Francis. You spoke to me. Ms Grace does have company but she will receive you.'

Francis ushered them in. She or he indicated a corridor. 'If you go down there to the drawing room, Ms Grace will join you in a moment.'

The corridor went through two airy rooms and opened out, down a couple of steps, into a book-lined drawing room with a high ceiling and floor to ceiling windows. There was a fireplace big enough to walk into and a boudoir grand piano with the lid up and music on the stand.

'Wow,' Gilchrist said again, walking over to the long bay window that looked out onto the extensive walled garden.

Heap wandered over to an ample sofa in front of the fireplace. On a table beside it was a pamphlet called *The Hassocks Blockade: A True Account*. Most of the cover was obscured by a card attached to it by a paperclip.

There was a copy of a leather-bound edition of Tennyson's poems open on the sofa with a bookmark laid across the open pages. They were two pages of *Idylls of The King*, Tennyson's celebrated poem about King Arthur and Camelot.

Gilchrist could hear voices from the terrace. She looked to the left as Nimue Grace rose and left her guest and hurried past the window. 'Well, I never,' Gilchrist murmured to herself.

'Sweet were the days when I was all unknown,' Heap read

from the open book. Then a voice, from the French windows. Heap looked up. Nimue Grace was framed in the doorway, the light a halo around her head, looking every inch the movie star, even in jeans and a baggy sweatshirt.

She repeated: 'Sweet were the days when I was all unknown. But when my name was lifted up, the storm brake on the mountain and I cared not for it.'

Heap nodded. 'Nimue is quite a character for Tennyson, ma'am. But you don't like fame either?'

'It's nice to meet a cultivated copper,' Grace said, smiling a devastating smile. 'But "ma'am"? I've only ever been called "ma'am" once. In a dreadful Western I did for the money with Robert Duvall in Canada. And what an ornery individual he turned out to be.'

'Good actor,' Heap said.

'You think?' she said, an eyebrow raised.

'I'm getting my critical judgements questioned a lot today,' Heap said, flushing a little. 'You'd know better than me . . . Ms Grace.'

'You'd imagine so, wouldn't you?' she said, coming into the room and holding out her hand. He noted how long her fingers were. 'But, as William Goldman famously said: "Nobody knows anything in Hollywood." Call me Nimue, please.'

Heap took her hand but before he could reply Sarah Gilchrist came over from the window.

'DS Heap isn't very good at informality, Ms Grace,' she said.

Still holding Heap's hand, Grace turned to look at Gilchrist.

'You neither, it seems. Please – Nimue.'

She let go of Heap's hand and held her hand out to Gilchrist. Gilchrist took it. Grace had a firm handshake.

'We need to maintain a little formality at least at first, Ms Grace. I'm Detective Inspector Sarah Gilchrist.'

Grace gestured to the various sofas and chairs in the large drawing room. 'Please, sit wherever you like. Coffee will be here in a moment.' Gilchrist and Heap followed her instructions. Grace moved the book from the sofa to a side table and perched on the arm of the chair to the left of the huge fireplace.

'I must say your arrival is inconvenient. I have a guest for coffee. Will this take long?'

'It might,' Gilchrist said. 'I didn't realize you knew Bob Watts.' She pointed out of the window. 'Your guest.'

Nimue Grace frowned. 'You know him too?'

'An old friend,' Gilchrist said, flushing a little and cursing herself for it. It had only been the one night, for goodness sake. 'And our police commissioner.'

Grace took that in.

'Ah. I obviously didn't know the former but nor did I know the latter. We've only just met.' Grace had clearly noticed Gilchrist's blush. 'It's nothing like that.'

'None of my business,' Gilchrist said, overlapping with Grace saying:

'I won him in a raffle, actually. Or rather he won me.'

'None of my business,' Gilchrist said again.

'I didn't say it was,' Grace flared. 'Perhaps you should go and say hello or he should join us before you tell me why you're here?'

Gilchrist pondered for a moment. 'After.'

Grace raised one of her trademark thick eyebrows. 'It must be serious.'

'We're here for a sad reason, Ms Grace. A man was found dead in your lake yesterday. A man called Richard Rabbitt.'

Grace tilted her head. 'Where in the lake?'

Gilchrist glanced at Heap. Odd question. 'I believe in a shallow lagoon between one part of the shore and a small island.'

'Whoever found him was trespassing then,' Grace said. 'The lake is private and that is a couple of hundred yards inside my wood.'

'He was found by somebody called Donald Kermode,' Heap said. 'Do you know him?'

Grace rolled her eyes.

'I don't know him but I know *of* him. The restraining order didn't hold then?'

'We only just caught the case,' Gilchrist said. 'We're trying to catch up. Restraining order?'

'A stalker. They come along from time to time. Not as often as they used to but those with long memories . . .'

'He said he had permission from you to be in your lake.'

'He doesn't. Nobody does. I assume he drank the water?'

'Excuse me?' Gilchrist said.

'Was he naked?'

'Well, yes,' Gilchrist said.

Grace turned her mouth down.

'What did you mean about him drinking the water?' Gilchrist said.

'He knows I swim there naked. He used to spy on me without my knowing. And then he began swimming there naked because, well, he knew my naked body had been in the same water. And drinking the water for the same reason. If he'd known I peed in it too he'd probably have been even more excited.'

'People do that kind of thing?' Gilchrist blurted out.

'Pee in a lake? I can't imagine I'm the first. And this one is mine.'

'No – I meant the other,' Gilchrist said.

Grace smiled and gave a little twist of her head. 'You have no idea. If I told you about some of the weird shit . . .' She tossed her hair. 'I'm one of many Hollywood women on a website devoted to our thick eyebrows. It's affiliated to one about our hairy armpits – Julia Roberts and I were the poster girls for that for years but we've probably been superseded by younger actresses now. My feet get a look in on a foot fetish site – and are rated "beautiful" on Wikifeet – which is odd because I've got dancers' feet: buckled and bunioned.'

'Wikifeet?' Gilchrist said flatly.

'Yeah the site where some Alt Right person posted fake photos of some Democratic politician's feet a while ago.'

'Fake feet?' Gilchrist said.

'Photoshopped. The toes were the wrong length or something,' Grace said. 'Anyway, Peeping Toms are kind of the least of it – they're no different from paparazzi anyway.' She frowned. '*From* or *to* with different? I never know with that construction.'

'It seems to be either these days,' Heap said.

'Thank you, sir,' Grace said, favouring him with another of her killer smiles. 'I've always had Peeping Toms bothering me here. Admittedly, it's not as bad as when I first moved in, when one or more of them would steal my underwear from the washing line pretty much every time I put it up there. It's probably my fault. I was a bit of an exhibitionist when I was young and before I realized how I was presenting myself.'

'The passions you inspired, Ms Grace, were outside your control,' Heap said, flushing as he said it.

Grace looked at Gilchrist and Heap then smiled. 'I won't write my autobiography. The minute it's published, creeps will come out of the woodwork and sell their stories of sex with Naughty Nimue to some tabloid. Plus I've probably missed the boat. Tell my Warren Beatty or my Jack Nicholson stories and most people these days will have no idea who I'm talking about.' She saw Gilchrist's look. 'Not that I did with either of them. On principle really. But it turned out I fell for the less obvious Lotharios.'

'We'll follow up on the restraining order,' Heap said, his face now a constant pink. 'But did you know Major Rabbitt?'

'In the biblical sense? Certainly not, though not for his want of predatory trying. He was a lech, a bully and a creep and I'm not sorry he's dead.' In one effortless move she slid down from the arm of the chair into it, lifting her legs and raising herself to tuck her feet beneath her as she did so. She smiled a big, unfettered smile. 'Oops. I guess I've just made myself a suspect. My big mouth again.'

Gilchrist couldn't take her eyes off her. She'd met actresses before but never a bona fide movie star and she could see the difference. Without doing anything, Grace exuded a charisma. Corny as it sounded, her skin seemed to glow. Even without make-up – and Gilchrist couldn't see any – she looked luminous. And then, of course, there was her beautiful, thick red hair.

Grace saw her examining her face and looked down with a small smile. 'It's the freshly fucked look.'

Gilchrist didn't need to look at Heap to know he would be blushing. Grace gestured to her face. 'That's what cinemato-graphers and still photographers call it. It looks so natural and full of life. It's hard to fake.' She looked sardonic. 'But I guess I'm a better actress than people recognized since I haven't been. Freshly fucked, that is. Or even not so freshly, actually.'

Gilchrist glanced at Heap. Yep.

'Oh dear, there I go again,' Grace said. 'That's why I don't do interviews anymore – well, one of the reasons. I'm too frank. Can't help it. Always been the same. In Hollywood I was famous for *oversharing*.' She said the last word with an exaggerated American twang. 'Which is another way of observing what you are now observing – once I get started I can't stop gabbing.'

Gilchrist was enthralled by Grace's low, intimate voice. She didn't want her to stop talking. *Pull yourself together, Sarah.* She glanced at Heap.

'Did Major Rabbitt visit your lake regularly?' Heap said.

'Not that I know of. It's private. Nobody is supposed to go there. That's partly because of the duck breeding. When I first bought the lake people were letting their dogs swim in it and traipsing through the wood. I didn't really mind but then people kept leaving rubbish down there and I got fed up with it so put locks on the gates. And now we've encouraged more ducks we have to be careful of the dogs.'

'When was the last time you were at the lake?' Gilchrist said.

'A few days ago. There was a time when I didn't go there much at all. I created an idyll for children but then I didn't have any.' She grimaced and suddenly her face looked tragic and ten years older. 'It was too, too painful.'

'When was the last time you saw Major Rabbitt?' Gilchrist said gently.

'Months ago – I can't really remember.'

'How often do you go to the lake?'

'Couple of times a week for a swim, if I'm here. A couple of times a month with my woodsman. In the summer, if I'm not away, I go with a few friends for picnics. Yes, I do have friends – carefully selected – contrary to the tabloid narrative about my reclusiveness.'

'And you've never bumped into Major Rabbitt during those visits?' Gilchrist said. 'As I understand it the driveway to his house passes briefly between the two halves of your wood.'

'That's true but I only ever use the driveway when I'm going into the other part of the wood. The watercress bed side. Or what used to be a watercress bed. If I'm swimming I use a hidden entrance on Beard's Lane at the far end of the lake. I park there and go into the wood from that side because it's more private and people like Mr Kermode don't realize I'm there. I hope. And I swim at the end of the lake furthest from the drive.' She gestured to her body. 'I do swim naked, you see. And, despite my reputation for always taking off my clothes in films, I'm actually quite private. Prudish even.'

Nimue Grace was a very beautiful woman. She was in her forties but didn't seem to have had any work done on her face. Gilchrist was certainly looking for it, perhaps because she wanted to find fault with someone who naturally looked so perfect. There was a small scar or puckering near one of her ears but that looked to be more an accident than surgery.

'When I'm not around it's mostly fishermen and teenagers who trespass these days – although somebody did once rig up a camera in a tree to catch me swimming. Not Kermode that time. But these days, if I don't find empty cider cans and used condoms by the lake I'm happy.

'And the fishermen are wasting their time. The lake is very slow moving. It can't sustain a habitat for any fish other than carp because there isn't enough movement. Carp though, they like the mud. Which makes them inedible. As are the giant freshwater clams we found when I originally had the lake dredged. It was reckoned they were seventy years old but nobody really knows.' She looked beyond them both up at Plumpton Hill.

'That was quite a time. When I bought the lake it looked like a field of grass. It was covered with Parrot's Feather weed – this alien invasive species from South America that has spread since it was introduced to the UK, for reasons beyond me, in 1960. Left uncontrolled it would have killed the lake in the next two years. The carp were in there because a fishing club that once owned the lake had stocked it with them. But they proliferated and were adding to the lake's problems – it was becoming eutrophic.

'Nature scientists and archaeologists all queued up to see what we might find there. The Romans first created the lake and the watercress beds in the other part of the wood. There was a medieval village somewhere round here. The military was camped in the area during both wars – the Canadians actually billeted in Plumpton Down House and Danny House over near Hurstpierpoint. So there were all kinds of possibilities. They got me excited too.'

She stood. 'But there was nothing except the clams and the carp.' She looked at Heap. 'So, yes, I'm the Lady of the Rather Disappointing Lake. I'll be impressed if you can come up with a joke or a sarcastic comment I haven't already heard a dozen times from anyone who knows their Arthurian stuff. My parents were hippies. My father was a poet – wanted to be a poet – my mother an actress. Wanted to be an actress.

'They were living in a shepherd's hut in Wales when the Monty Python gang passed through to shoot a few scenes for *Monty Python and the Holy Grail.*' She spread her hands. 'Well, I was conceived when my parents were working as extras. My dad had got obsessed with reading all the early Arthurian stuff – Chretien de Troyes, Wolfram von Eschenbach, Malory's *Morte D'Arthur*, of course.'

'And my mother wanted to call me Vivien, the other main name for the enchantress, because she adored Vivien Leigh. Well, to be honest, I think she fancied herself as Vivien Leigh. But my dad was in his Celtic phase, even though he wasn't Welsh. So I got stuck with Nimue as well as Vivien.

'I wanted to change it when I decided to be an actress because nobody ever knows how to pronounce it – you do very well, by the way. And I didn't want people to think I was one of those wanky actresses who gives herself a silly name just to be different. You know, Lisbeth instead of Elizabeth or naming yourself after a country or state or a city like India this or Dakota that or Paris the other.' She smiled. 'Sorry, I talk too much. Anyway, Equity already had a Vivien Grace.'

'It's very interesting,' Gilchrist said. 'So is your mother still acting?'

'She never really did. It was a dream.'

'Is she still alive?'

'Very much so,' Grace said, with an expression on her face Gilchrist couldn't immediately read.

'She must be so proud of your acting achievements.'

'You'd think so, wouldn't you?' Grace said, the same odd expression on her face. She saw puzzlement flit across Gilchrist's face. 'Mother and daughter stuff,' she added. 'You probably have the same.'

Gilchrist nodded, thinking not of her mother but of Kate's. 'I think we all do.'

Grace gestured to the open French window. 'Do you want to say hello to your friend?'

She led the way onto the terrace where Bob Watts was sitting with a cup of coffee in front of him, fiddling with his phone. He looked up and stood up. He both grinned and looked embarrassed. 'Sarah. Bellamy. An unexpected pleasure. Why are you here?'

'I think they wanted you to explain what you were doing here,' Grace said, a mischievous lilt to her voice.

'Ha! Well, I won Ms Grace – Nimue – in a raffle.'

'Lucky you,' Gilchrist said.

'Indeed. Morning coffee at her lovely home.'

'Which must now extend into lunch,' Grace said. 'Because he hasn't really got his money's worth this morning.' She turned to Gilchrist and Heap. 'Would you care to join us, since you're all acquainted?'

'We can't, ma'am,' Heap said. 'We need to get back to your lake. With your permission. And we'll probably need to dredge it.'

'Oh, good – if you find a rather colourful necklace it's mine – it came off my neck once when I was having a swim.'

Watts raised an eyebrow. 'Ms Grace – Nimue – was just extending an invitation for me to swim in her lake whenever I wanted.'

'Because Bob was just telling me about his aborted Channel Swim,' Grace said. 'But, having recognized his name as the chief constable here when I first moved down, I realize I have yet to learn about that.'

'That was a long time ago,' Watts began, before Grace interrupted with:

'And besides the wench is dead.' She saw their blank looks. 'Sorry, once an actress . . .'

'We need to be going, Ms Grace,' Gilchrist said. She turned to Bob Watts. 'Enjoy your lunch – and you too, Ms Grace. We may be back with more questions later. We'll call first – shall we call Francis, your, er . . .?'

'My gender curious/gender fluid au pair?' Grace said with a sardonic smile. She shrugged. 'I know – this brave new world that has such wondrous creatures in it. But, yes, please, call first. Not that I'm going anywhere. I never go anywhere. I'm like Norma Desmond in *Sunset Boulevard*, except I never watch my old movies. I never watched them when they were new, for that matter. Can't bear to see myself blown up on a big screen.

But, like Norma, I have a dead body floating in my pool.' She shrugged again. 'Unlike her, I didn't put it there.'

'Where now, ma'am?' Heap asked as they drove back onto Beard's Lane.

'I think we should go and see Mrs Rabbitt in her café in Lewes. Don't you?'

'I do.'

Gilchrist settled herself in her seat. 'Nimue Grace is not what I was expecting at all. I like her.'

'An enchantress,' Heap said.

'I wouldn't go quite that far,' Gilchrist said. 'Charismatic, certainly.'

'In the Arthurian legends, I mean,' Heap said. 'That Lady of the Lake thing. She enchanted Merlin and was Lancelot's protector.'

'So that's what you were talking about earlier – all that Wolfram this and Malory that. I thought all the Lady of the Lake did was stick her hand up out of the water holding Excalibur for King Arthur.'

'Actually, I'm hazy now on the story but I think Arthur pulled it out of a stone first then, years later, chucked it in the lake when he was going to Avalon. She caught it and took it down into the watery depths.'

'Watery depths indeed.'

The café was halfway along the High Street in Lewes. As Granger had indicated it was between the last remaining antiquarian bookshop and a shop selling very little, laid out exquisitely on long shelves. Gilchrist had been in that shop once and come out bemused, asking just one thing: *why*?

The café was quiet, just a couple of people. A young man picked at his phone, a young woman was on her laptop with her headphones on. There was a woman behind the counter doing calculations on an iPad.

'Liesl Rabbitt?' Heap said.

'And you are?'

'DS Heap. We phoned ahead.'

'Oh, yes.'

'Is there somewhere quiet we can talk?'

'I'm on my own this afternoon. The girl who should be here

has phoned in sick. Typical English girl. We can talk here. If it's about Richard I don't care who hears what a shit he is.'

Liesl Rabbitt was a broad-faced, fake blonde with a full figure and full make-up. She had the frozen look of somebody who had had too much Botox. Gilchrist wondered where she was from. She had a kind of all-purpose Eastern European accent. As if Rabbitt could read her mind, she said: 'I'm Albanian-Greek and I see things as they are.'

'I believe you've been informed that your ex-husband was found dead this morning,' Heap said.

'That weakling. Yes, I'd heard before you phoned. He's still my husband, actually – so that's going to work out well for me, isn't it?'

'I wouldn't know about that, Mrs Rabbitt.'

'Well, I would. He got what he wanted from me, whenever he wanted it. Now it's payback, even with the prenup.'

How romantic, Gilchrist thought, but didn't say. 'Be that as it may,' she did say. 'When did you last see your husband?'

'Is that like that English expression I've never understood: when did you last stop beating your wife?'

'No,' Heap said shortly.

Gilchrist saw the expression on his face. His weakness was that, while usually he could appear impassive, especially when he was joking, if he really didn't like somebody, he couldn't hide it.

'It has been so long, I don't even remember.'

'You have children together?'

'The brats? They are away at public school.'

'And when they're home, which is their home?' Gilchrist persisted.

'Well, his, obviously.' She grimaced. 'These are boys brought up to think they are better than anyone else. They wouldn't want to be living in a poky flat above a café when they can imagine what it will be like to own all they survey. When will the will be read?'

'You don't want to know how he died?' Heap said mildly.

'Swallowed his dentures? Choked on a fur ball from his wig? I don't really care, except I hope he died how he lived. Badly.'

'His throat was cut,' Heap said.

Liesl Rabbitt shrugged. 'It should have been worse.'

'When was the last time you went to Beard's Pond?' Heap said.

'I've never been there. It's private. That *cray cray* bitch my husband had the hots for owns it. And, as for him, the last time I saw him I told him he could *xoshanha* himself. And he has. Now I have to get ready to close up, so if there isn't anything else . . .?'

'Well, she's quite something,' Gilchrist said to Heap as they walked back to the car. 'What's *cray, cray*, Bellamy?'

'I'm assuming it just means *crazy* but I don't know where it comes from. And, before you ask, ma'am, I haven't the faintest idea what *xoshanha* means – but it doesn't sound good.'

They got back in the car.

'Home, James,' Gilchrist said. 'You've got a lot of homework to do tonight while I'm out with your woman. So let me hit you with another one: a red herring. Is Mrs Rabbitt one?'

'Why do I get the distinct feeling you regard me as a resource like Google or Yahoo?'

'All men need to have some purpose, don't you think?'

'If you say so, ma'am.'

'I do.'

'William Cobbett. Herrings get kippered by smoking and salting until they turn reddish brown. They have a strong smell. Back in the early 1800s William Cobbett used one to lay a false trail while training hunting dogs. So they say.'

'Most of that was clear but, as usual, you got me on one part. Who is William Cobbett?'

'A radical. A polemicist. He rode about most of England to report on the plight of the working class during the Industrial Revolution. His *Rural Rides* is a classic, ma'am.'

Gilchrist shook her head.

'You continually amaze me, Bellamy.'

'Is that a good thing, if I might ask?'

'You might ask but I might not answer. So is Mrs Rabbitt one? A smoked kipper?'

'Too early to say, ma'am. But, before you ask, those carp in Ms Grace's lake are not the origin of the verb to carp.'

Gilchrist laughed.

'So neither these nor any other carp are bad-tempered and narrow? OK, now I am officially exhausted. Bellamy, you told Liesl that Mr Rabbitt had died from having his throat cut. Wasn't that jumping the gun? Bilson hasn't come up with anything yet. Remember last time – that guy who was stabbed to death *and* drowned?'

'I remember it well, ma'am. And, I'm sorry. You're right. I was trying to shock her but it was partly because I assumed the same confusion couldn't happen twice. Although we are in water again.'

'Murky rather than deep this time,' Gilchrist said. She dialled Bilson's mobile number.

'You still in muddy water, Frank?' she said when he answered.

'Definition of my work, Sarah, until my magnificent brain clicks into gear.'

'And magnificent it is,' Gilchrist said. 'So what have you got so far?'

'Dead man. Throat cut.'

'That's the cause of death?'

'I don't believe I said that, Sarah.'

Gilchrist groaned. 'Not again,' she muttered.

'You are referring back to the last one,' Bilson said. 'I understand that. But, no, not in this instance. Not water anyway. He was badly beaten before his throat was cut. Couple of broken ribs. Bruising.'

'All there at the lake?'

'Well, SOCO is looking around the entire lake. They're going to have to call in a dredger, of course.'

'And those white containers – could they somehow be involved?'

'White containers?' There was silence on the other end of the line.

'Are you still there?' Gilchrist said.

'Sure – covered in carp slime. I can see something white on the other side of the lake. You want me to send SOCO over? Oh, wait. I can see one of them has just arrived there.'

'See if the containers are linked somehow to the death,' Gilchrist said.

The silence was so long, Gilchrist thought the signal had gone. 'Bilson? Frank? Are you still there?'

'I'm here but I'm trying to figure out how on earth I'm supposed to make that link within my narrow parameters. Isn't that your job?'

Gilchrist sighed.

'You're right, Frank. I'm sorry. It's been a long day.'

There was another silence then Bilson said: 'Let's talk this evening. I'll bring you up to date with what I've figured out.'

Gilchrist looked at Heap. 'I keep thinking about those white containers and whether they are significant or not. How do you feel about going back to talk to Ms Grace about them.'

'I feel fine about it, ma'am.'

Francis let them in on the buzzer and as they drove up the drive they saw Nimue Grace plucking apples from one of the trees in her orchard. Gilchrist was surprised she wasn't wearing something wafty and diaphanous with a big brimmed hat – she'd seen the movies – but Grace was still in jeans and a work shirt and what looked like biker boots.

'Pull up here, Bellamy,' Gilchrist said and Heap drew in at a shallow lay-by beside a half completed wall.

Grace noticed them as they got out of the car and called out:

'Be careful there – the ground is very uneven.' She started towards them as they picked their way up a small mound with broken bricks sticking out of it. Gilchrist saw Grace brush her upraised hand against a low hanging branch of one of the trees. Several apples fell and, without even looking at them, she caught two, one in each hand.

They met beside what looked like a pear tree.

'Good catch,' Gilchrist said as Grace handed her and Heap the apples she'd caught.

'Did a juggling course at drama school,' Grace said. 'These are the best eaters I've got. It's been a good year. Go on – take a bite.'

Gilchrist and Heap both did. The apples were sweet and fragrant. A mobile phone rang back in the car. Heap patted his pockets then excused himself and went back to the car.

'Nice – thank you,' Gilchrist said.

'Take some, if you have time to pick some – I can give you trays.'

'I don't think we'll have time,' Gilchrist said.

'Lunch was very nice, by the way,' Grace said. 'Interesting, decent man, that Bob Watts. Therefore, not my type. Why would I want anyone like that when I can get a shit who will treat me like shit?' She raised an eyebrow. 'Pathetic, eh?'

'I couldn't claim to have any insight into relationships, Ms Grace,' Gilchrist said, feeling awkward. Then, not believing she was being so revealing: 'Mine have all been disasters.'

'Including the one with Bob Watts?' Grace saw the look on Gilchrist's face. 'You think he told me? Are you kidding? A man with that much probity? I guessed it. If you don't mind me saying, Sarah, I'm sure you're a good copper but I can't imagine you're any good at interrogation because you can't keep stuff off your face. You might as well be the one writing the confession.'

Jesus, how had Gilchrist got herself having a relatively intimate conversation with someone who may prove central to a murder investigation? She glanced back at Heap, who was talking into his phone in the car. Well, maybe because she didn't think Nimue Grace was a suspect. So, in for a penny . . . 'I wrecked Bob's career,' Gilchrist said quietly.

'Bullshit. He wrecked his own career. Don't take that on yourself, whatever happened – and I've no idea what happened. He doesn't seem like the kind of man who can be easily led.'

Gilchrist didn't say anything, just kind of nodded. Grace pointed at the pear tree. 'These look beautiful but they're as hard as rocks. They need cooking for about an hour then . . . *deliciosa* . . .'

'We wondered about the lake,' Gilchrist said abruptly, trying to get the conversation back on track. 'Those white containers on the opposite side to the island.'

Grace frowned. 'I don't know about any white containers. Probably somebody dumping stuff. They do it all the time. I don't understand people. They go to such a beautiful place and despoil it.'

'They were tied in place. We wondered if they contained some kind of chemicals for your lake.'

Grace shook her head. 'I have it tested every so often to ensure

I'm not swimming in sewage but there's no regular treatment. Tied together, do you say?'

'When you drained the lake they weren't tied to rotting wooden struts on the far side of the lake?'

'That was once a small boathouse, I understand. No, they definitely were not.'

'And nobody working for you would have put them there to do with upkeep of the lake or anything?'

'I told you – I do hardly any upkeep of the lake. Why, what was in these containers? How many were there?'

'We're not exactly sure of the number,' Gilchrist said. 'And we're still investigating what might have been in them.'

'What is in the ones that are still there?' Grace said.

'Nothing as far as we can tell,' Heap said as he joined them.

'But they didn't float? I don't understand.'

'Neither do we at the moment,' Gilchrist said. 'With your permission we'd like to get them moved and analysed.'

Gilchrist was still puzzling over how unusually frank she was being. Was this what star power was or some kind of movie star effect? Or was it just that she was repaying Grace's frankness with her own?

Grace frowned again. 'You think they are somehow connected to the death at my lake?'

Gilchrist showed her palms. 'In a murder investigation we have to spread the net wide.'

'Really? I thought most murders were committed by people very close to the victim.'

'Except those that aren't,' Heap said.

Grace looked at him with her big clear eyes and raised one of her famous eyebrows. 'I can't decide if that is quite profound or stating the obvious, DS Heap.'

He flushed. 'I often have the same problem, Ms Grace,' Heap said. 'It seems as if several of the containers have been removed. Not by you though, from what you say.'

'That's right. I'm not guilty.'

'Mr Kermode, perhaps?'

'You'd have to ask him.'

'Indeed, Ms Grace. You said you didn't like Major Rabbitt. Was that just because he was bothering you or was there more?'

'*Bothering* me. Haven't heard that expression for a long time. Well, men have been *bothering* me and pestering me for sex from the age of about twelve. And then in Hollywood, of course, I was immediately chased by all those infamous creeps and womanizers.

'There were these two major male movie stars. Top of the pile. Known as much for their womanizing as their acting. Great friends. They wanted to do a film together. A Howard Hughes project – it never happened. It bore no relation to the Marty/Leo collaboration that came out about Howard Hughes many years later. So I go to the house of one of them on Mulholland for a meeting/audition for one of the female leads and I'm directed by the butler down to the tennis court. The two men are in their whites playing in the heat of a Los Angeles afternoon. And that's hot.

'"Take a seat," one of them yells when he sees me coming. "We won't be long."

'Except they are long because these are two competitive men. And it's really hot and there's no shade and I don't have a hat. They finish after about half an hour and come off the court towelling the sweat off them. The one whose house I'm at points to these cabin changing rooms. "We're going to shower this sweat off," he says. He looks me up and down and that glint comes into his eye and he gives me his famous shit-eating grin. "You're hot," he drawls, the double meaning hanging in the air. "Why don't you join us?"

'I smile nervously, as if he's my granddad – which he's old enough to be. "I'm fine right here."' She shrugged. 'I didn't get the part. I've never gone for threesomes. I disagree with Woody Allen on that. Oh, not in the way everyone is disagreeing with him about something else these days. I mean his gag: "Sex between two people is great; sex between three is fantastic." And, actually, despite what the press used to say, when I was young and a bit of a blabbermouth, I've been very choosy about simple twosomes too. In that I've only ever chosen badly.'

Her Woody Allen impersonation wasn't half bad.

'So, no. I've been *bothered* by professionals, so to speak, therefore the Major's unwelcome advances just needed a fly swat. It was the fact he had delusions of grandeur about being the lord of the manor that was the problem.'

'To you personally or generally?'

'Well, certainly to me because I have the jewel in the crown of his estate – the lake. I bought the lake fifteen years before he got here but when he got here and bought the estate he decided it could never be complete without the lake, the watercress beds and the woods right in its centre. But I have never had any intention of selling. It's for me and my children and their children and so on.'

'And this peeved him?' Gilchrist asked.

'I should say,' Grace said. 'Especially as I have no children and am unlikely to have them now unless I adopt. I've got an email from him saying that as long as I own the lake and wood there will always be antagonism between us. So he tried to put the kibosh on everything I tried to do. He would threaten to go to the redtops with stories about how this famous movie star and supposed environmentalist was wrecking an area of outstanding beauty. Which was bollocks, of course.'

'Do you know Liesl Rabbitt?'

'The harpy? Yes, I have that misfortune. A hard-faced, nasty piece of work. I wouldn't want to get on the wrong side of her – though I probably already have.'

Gilchrist responded only by saying: 'Do you know if there's anyone in Rabbitt's life now?'

'I would imagine so. He's rich. It's surprising what character flaws women will overlook for money. Have you not been up to the Big House yet?'

'Yes, but his sister was not very forthcoming.'

'Tallulah? I always think of her as Mrs Danvers. Seething passions underneath a cold exterior.'

Gilchrist didn't respond except to give a little nod. 'Thanks again for the offer of the apples,' she said, getting back into the car. Grace watched them go, then walked back into her orchard.

Gilchrist looked at Heap as they drove carefully along the winding lane. 'Home, James.'

TWO

B ob Watts, Brighton Police Commissioner, had enjoyed his encounter with the movie star. Lovely woman, in every sense. He'd won morning coffee with her at a raffle for some charity at a dinner at the Royal Pavilion. He'd had no idea who she was – he wasn't a film-goer and she wasn't actually at the dinner – but he wanted to support the cause. The meeting had been sorted out by email through the charity.

He'd googled her before their appointment – he thought of it as an appointment – but at the end of his reading he was not much wiser. She'd made a lot of big and small films but he hadn't seen any of them. More recently she'd done theatre, often in Chichester. She was anti-fracking in Sussex. She supported a number of charities, some eminently worthwhile, some, he thought, a little cranky. The link between liberal actors and half-baked movements usually had a certain mathematical correlation but not in her case.

He could see that she had been stupidly frank in interviews. She was now stuck with her openness and indiscreet words for ever on the web. The one thing she'd kept shtum about was her reason for leaving Hollywood so abruptly at the height of her fame to go into seclusion.

When they'd parted she'd repeated her offer for him to swim at the lake whenever he wanted, as long as he alerted her to the fact in case there were other things going on there. She had given him her phone number.

He was attracted to her, there was no doubt about that – but then who wouldn't be? He'd pulled the plug on his last romantic entanglement before there was, in fact, any entanglement. Nice enough woman but too young for him and a coldness to her. Nimue Grace was more his age. And totally out of his class, of course. Yet a part of him wondered if she'd really given him her phone number only so that he could visit the lake. He'd have to phone and find out.

Watts was bored. He liked to think he was a man of action, although the last action he'd done hadn't worked out so well. Swimming alongside his niece, Kate Simpson, to support her in her Channel swim attempt had seemed doable. And indeed it would have been had an unfortunate coalescence of bad things not prevented the swim's completion. For one, the scars from the jellyfish stings would probably never disappear.

Mostly it was the weather – it had been terrible once they started. Even then he felt she could have made it but it was the pilot who was in control because he was in touch with the coast-guard services of both England and France. It had been tough going for her anyway but she was a tough-minded young woman and, all else being equal, would never have given up until she stepped onto the beach at Cap Gris.

But the pilot had decided to stop them three miles off France. The tide was changing, the current would be running counter to their progress for the next eight hours; the weather was already scooping up the water into huge, rebellious waves.

So – she didn't achieve her ambition. Kate, he knew, had been planning to try again. Then her mother committed suicide.

Watts hadn't seen her mother, Lizzy Simpson, for years but when he was close to her husband, William Simpson, he saw her a lot. He found her frosty, aloof and ambitious. He had no idea why she had left Simpson, aside from the obvious fact he was a total shit. But, with hindsight, Watts recognized that she would know Simpson had always been a total shit and she had accepted that from the start of their marriage.

Watts had not really expected Lizzy to be on board the Channel swim support boat – he would have been astonished if she had been – but nor did he expect her to kill herself. She had never struck him as the suicidal type. But it was some years since he'd seen her and she had changed dramatically around the time of the Milldean Massacre. She had always put up a front but around that time she added fortifications and a drawbridge.

Leaving her husband, Watts's erstwhile friend, William Simpson, was a positive act, he'd thought, as indeed was divorcing that corrupt man. But it hadn't seemed to make her any happier; it had just given her an excuse to withdraw even more.

He thought about his own wife, Molly, living in Canada with

another man. He'd treated her badly but it still seemed extreme that she wouldn't have anything more to do with him, but there it was. His relationship with his two children was equally disastrous. Not so much the elder of them, his son. It was just that, like most young men with anything about them, he was on his own trajectory. And that involved living on the other side of the world and rarely keeping in touch.

It was his daughter he felt he had lost. She was married to a fundamentalist Christian and was following a path he couldn't approve of but couldn't do anything about. She seemed happy but in that false smile, false cheerfulness, Polly-Anna way cults gave all their followers. She too lived in Canada now but on the opposite side of the country to her mother in some religious camp that sounded horribly like a cult.

Watts sighed and poured himself a glass of wine. He walked to the window and called over his shoulder: 'Alexa? Madeleine Peyroux, please.'

Sarah Gilchrist's phone rang just as she was hurrying through the Lanes to the Hotel du Vin to meet Kate Simpson.

'Those white containers, Sarah,' Bilson said.

'Yes, what have you got for me, Mr Bilson?'

'Nothing to report, I'm afraid. Nothing in them. I can only assume they were used as some kind of ballast.'

'Well, except Ms Grace says she didn't put them there. And I thought ballast was supposed to make things float not sink.'

'Good point,' Bilson said. 'But another one: you believe the delectable Ms Grace? Is she delectable in person, by the way?'

'Down, Frank. For the moment I do.'

'OK, then – they were there before she bought the lake maybe?' Bilson said.

'She had it dredged when she first bought it. They weren't there. Somebody has anchored them there since. Secured them pretty efficiently. But why?'

'If I were to hazard a guess I'd say drugs. Or drug money.'

'We've just been discussing county line drug trafficking with Haywards Heath district and I thought it might be linked with that.'

'But the containers were sealed so this is not a regular drop.

But this actually is outside my area of expertise, Sarah. You think
Ms Grace might be involved?'

'I don't know. Perhaps it was Major Rabbitt. But it could be
anybody. It's early days, yet.'

'How *is* the delectable Nimue Grace, by the way?'

'Will you please stop using that adjective, Mr Bilson? She
seems to be a very nice, accomplished woman.'

'She swims naked in that lake, I hear.'

'Frank, behave for goodness sake.'

'I merely meant that I admire that. I have done my share of
cold-water swimming and I must say swimming with no clothes
on is very liberating. You should try it.'

'I doubt it,' Gilchrist said.

'Are you sure I can't entice you to join me?'

'Goodbye, Frank.'

'At least make it *au revoir*, Sarah.'

Gilchrist hung up.

Kate Simpson arrived first at the Hotel du Vin. She settled herself
on one of the sofas that ran along the wall to the left of the bar.
She sipped her wine and gazed up at the rafters far above.

Sarah Gilchrist came in soon after, dressed in her regulation
uniform of jeans, T-shirt and leather jacket.

They hugged and Gilchrist ordered a large glass of wine.

'How are you feeling?' Gilchrist said. 'Daft question though
that is.'

'It's odd,' Kate said. 'Mum and I never really got on. She was
a cold bitch, frankly. But her suicide has really got to me.'

'Suicides do that,' Gilchrist said. 'They leave a lot of questions
and few answers.'

Gilchrist's wine arrived. They chinked glasses.

'The main question is why did she do it?' Kate said. 'I mean,
I would never have imagined in a million years that my mum
was the suicidal type. But then again she never gave anything
away. Especially after she left dad. Then she closed up even
more.'

Gilchrist thought about Kate's father, William Simpson.
Gilchrist had been badly affected by her own part as a firearms
officer in the so-called Milldean Massacre – a police raid that

had gone badly wrong some years earlier. Simpson, a government spin doctor at a time when the term was fashionable, had been somehow involved in it. Quite how was never satisfactorily explained and he had got away with whatever he had done while his then friend, Bob Watts, had lost his job as chief constable of Brighton thanks to Simpson's machinations. Those machinations had involved exposing the one-night stand Gilchrist and Watts had shared at a police conference. In consequence, Gilchrist had no time for Simpson.

'How is your father being?' Gilchrist said.

'Himself,' Kate said. 'With all that implies.'

'Is he interfering much with whatever you're planning for the service?'

'He's not interfering at all – far too busy. But, to be honest, I'm not sure what I'm planning for the service. I just want it over with. And that crematorium has bad memories for me so that doesn't help.'

Some months earlier, Gilchrist knew, Kate had been assaulted by a gang of teenage hoodlums in the cemetery beside the crematorium.

'Is he paying for the burial?'

'He is. At least he said so and nobody has asked me for money.'

'Will there be many people coming?'

'Hardly anybody. Mum really kept to herself.'

'If you want to swell the numbers I'll come and I'll bring a date.'

Kate laughed. 'If you had a date.'

'Ouch.'

'What's happening on that front?' Kate said, clearly eager to change the subject.

'Well, a strong woman in a relatively senior position who works all the hours God – or somebody – sends finds it ain't exactly easy to find a suitable date.'

'I'm sure Bob still carries a torch for you.'

'Bob Watts?' Gilchrist shook her head. 'That ship sailed long ago. There was a time but that was then. Besides, he prefers young dolly birds these days.'

'You mean that swimmer who is a business colleague of dad's? He never pursued that.'

'How do you know?' Gilchrist said.

'He tells me stuff. He's like my uncle.'

'You mean Bob's your uncle?' Gilchrist said, laughing uneasily. Uneasily because she knew Bob Watts actually *was* Kate's uncle though Kate didn't know it. Watts had confided it to Gilchrist once and she had urged him to tell Kate but she didn't think he had. Bob's father, a charismatic but nasty piece of work, had had an affair with Kate's grandmother. The dread William Simpson and Bob Watts were half-brothers.

'Bob said that woman was too young, plus he has a thing about integrity. And he didn't think that as a hedge fund manager she could have any.'

'He told you those things?' Gilchrist said. 'He's probably right but I have enough trouble figuring out my overdraft – hedge funds are way beyond me.' She shifted in her seat. 'Listen, your father's name has come up again in a new investigation we've just started.'

'Again? Oh, you mean after the Milldean thing.'

'Well, there was that too but, no, his name came up a few months ago in the course of our investigation into those swimming murders. His business links seemed a bit dodgy but we didn't have time to follow it up.'

'You didn't tell me.'

'You were a bit busy at the time, as I recall.'

'True – for what good that did me.'

'The attempt on the Channel did you a lot of good – you were so near reaching France!'

Kate shrugged. 'But now you do have time to follow it up.'

'Well, something else has come up that we might need to move on. This is just a heads up to you really. I thought it would be easier if I told you rather than Bellamy.'

'Can you say what you're working on?'

'Death of a businessman over Plumpton racecourse way. Richard Rabbitt. Excuse me: Major Richard Rabbitt. Did you ever meet him?'

Kate shook her head.

'No bells going off. And the death was suspicious?'

'The businessman was found in Nimue Grace's lake with his throat cut.'

'Jesus. That sounds pretty suspicious. But it also sounds like the start of a movie. You mean Nimue Grace, the movie star, right? Did you meet her?' Gilchrist nodded. 'How did she look?'

'Sickeningly beautiful, even dressed down and without any make-up.'

'Bitch.'

'Exactly. Interesting though.'

'Really? I always assumed she was one of those women who define themselves by their breasts. You know: *I have great tits, therefore I am.*'

'Me too, but she's not like that.'

'Does she still act in films?'

'Apparently not. I read she turned her back on all that but nobody knows why.'

They sat in silence for a moment but Kate clearly couldn't settle.

'So what has my dad done this time?'

'Not sure yet but he's in business with the murder victim.'

Kate sighed and leaned forward over her drink. 'The funeral's Thursday. Do bring a date.'

THREE

'What about paying a visit to Rhoda Knowles in Plumpton Green?' 'My thoughts exactly,' Gilchrist said. Just then her phone rang.

'Ms Grace? Good morning.'

'Good morning,' Grace said. 'Listen, why don't you two come over for lunch. There is other stuff I need to tell you that may or may not be relevant but you said you have to cast your net wide, right?'

'Perhaps a more formal interview – lunch isn't necessary.'

'But you've got to eat, surely? Or is it sandwiches in the car usually?'

'Usually.'

'All the more reason to have a proper meal when it's offered. You can caution me or whatever you do, if that makes it feel more normal.'

Gilchrist laughed. 'That won't be necessary. OK, then. Around 12.30?'

'Perfect.'

'Ms Grace – do you know Richard Rabbitt's secretary, Rhoda Knowles?'

'Met her a couple of times. Nice enough woman but not much to say for herself. I always assumed he was shtupping her.'

Plumpton Green was a long straggly village on the east side of the Lewes–London railway track. Plumpton racecourse lay on the west side and the gentle slopes of the Downs were vividly etched against the blue sky in the south.

'You a race-goer, Bellamy?'

'Not me, ma'am. Though I came to a huge car boot fair on the racetrack here once.'

'Get anything good?'

'Couple of cockney spivs selling bootleg DVDs.'

'Ah, those days before streaming and Netflix.'

'Ma'am.'

Rhoda Knowles lived across the road from the village shop and sub-post office in a small, 1950s cottage behind a high, neatly tended privet hedge. It was hard to tell if the bell worked as they couldn't hear it ring in the house. Even so, a bright-faced woman in her early thirties answered the door in jeans and a fleece. Bright-faced but with puffy eyes and downturned mouth.

'Rhoda Knowles?' Gilchrist said then introduced herself and Bellamy Heap. 'It's about Richard Rabbitt. May we come in?'

'Major Rabbitt,' Knowles said, stepping aside. She ushered them into her small cluttered living room. Cluttered mostly with soft toys of all kinds and sizes. Knowles shifted three cats and a teddy bear off the sofa for them. As they sat she stood before them, hugging the soft toys.

'I can't have cats,' she said. 'I'm allergic.'

Gilchrist nodded.

'Major Rabbitt's death has hit you hard, I can see,' Gilchrist said. 'Was he a good employer?'

'He was good to me,' Knowles almost whispered. She was still standing over them, hugging the soft toys.

'Please – sit, Ms Knowles,' Heap said gently.

Knowles kind of backed into an armchair, still holding onto the soft toys.

'When was the last time you saw him?'

'The day before his body was found,' Knowles said. 'At the end of my working day.'

'What exactly did you do for Major Rabbitt?' Gilchrist said.

'What do you mean by that?' Knowles said, suddenly indignant.

Gilchrist frowned. 'Exactly what I asked. What were your duties?'

'I was his secretary. I performed secretarial and clerical duties. Arranging appointments, typing up his correspondence – all the usual stuff.'

'Was he a very busy man?' Heap said.

'Very,' Knowles said. 'But he always found time for a kind word.'

Gilchrist tried not to raise an eyebrow. If Rabbitt wasn't *shtupping* Knowles, Knowles certainly wanted him to.

'Fingers in a lot of pies?' Heap said.

'For sure.'

'Does that mean he could make enemies?' Gilchrist said.

Knowles thought for a moment. 'He might have had enemies but they weren't necessarily of his own making.'

'Did he have enemies?' Heap said.

'As I said, he might have,' Knowles said carefully.

'Would you know if he had?' Gilchrist said.

'Not necessarily,' Knowles said.

'You can see why we're asking the question?' Heap said.

Knowles nodded. 'I just don't know the answer.'

'You're sounding a little evasive, if I may say,' Gilchrist said.

'You're the police, you *may say* anything you like with impunity.'

Gilchrist frowned. 'You've had a bad experience with the police?'

'No more than most people,' Knowles said.

'We're sorry you have that view of us,' Heap said. 'We're just trying to find out who murdered your boss.'

Gilchrist nodded. 'But you can't think of anyone who might wish him harm? He hadn't had a recent falling out with anybody?'

Knowles sighed. 'There were people he didn't get on with, naturally. That's normal. But usually it was because they were trying to destroy the environment he cared so much about.'

'He was an environmentalist?' Gilchrist said.

'No – I mean, yes, he was, of course. But I was referring to his immediate environment. He had a vision for the estate, for restoring it to its original beauty, but he was constantly frustrated by the plans of his neighbours.'

'They had their own ideas?' Gilchrist said.

'Telephone masts for mobile phones,' Knowles muttered. 'Ostriches . . .'

'There is an ostrich farm nearby?' Heap said.

'You mean you haven't seen the stupid creatures wandering around?' She snorted then seemed to address the teddy bear in her arms. 'A flightless bird – what *is* the point of that, eh?'

'So no enemies you can think of,' Gilchrist said. 'No one who might wish him harm?'

Knowles was still looking at the teddy bear.

'Not that I can think of.'

'Do you have his diary?' Gilchrist said. 'It didn't seem to be in his office when we went there earlier today. We need to see his appointments for the day before his death – and, indeed, the day of his death.'

'I haven't got it. It should be in the desk in the office. But there would be nothing in there for the day before – that was a Sunday and he only did social things on a Sunday.'

'His computer isn't there either.'

'I don't know why that would be. It was on his desk when I left work yesterday.'

'Do you know where Tallulah Granger is?' Heap said.

'I have very little to do with her.'

'What about the Airbnb she administers for the major? Does that not overlap with your work?'

'Completely separate. The major just lets her get on with it. He disapproves of it actually but recognizes it is a valuable revenue stream.'

'He makes a tidy profit, I would imagine,' Heap said.

'Well, it is his house,' Knowles said tartly.

'Did you see Tallulah Granger yesterday?' Heap said.

'Briefly. Passing in the hall kind of thing.'

'Can you think where she might be?' Heap persisted.

'Perhaps at her flat in Oxford? She rents it out but I think she's between tenants.'

'Do you think she might have removed the computer?' Gilchrist said.

'I'm not sure how I'm supposed to answer that,' Knowles said, 'except to say that I have no idea. She has full access to the left wing if she needs it.'

'You have the address of her Oxford flat?'

'No, but I'm sure you'll be able to find it in the office.'

'Ms Knowles, can you think of a reason Major Rabbitt might have been down at Nimue Grace's lake.'

'Where is his car?' Knowles said.

'I'm sorry?'

'Was his car parked by the lake?'

'As far as I'm aware there was no car parked by the lake,' Gilchrist said.

'Then I don't know why he was by the lake. I thought he might have been driving by and seen something that made him get out of the car.'

'Are you also suggesting his car isn't parked at the house?' Heap said.

'Exactly right,' Knowles said. 'So where is it?'

'Give us the details of it before we leave and we will follow that up,' Heap said. 'Thank you for that information.'

'Are there particular business partners we should be talking to?' Gilchrist said.

'Not that I can think of,' Knowles said.

'Ms Granger mentioned a Said Farzi?' Gilchrist said.

'A charming man, though I've only met him a couple of times. Moroccan, I believe. Speaks perfect French – better than his English, actually. I think they were going to invest in property in Brighton together. I wouldn't be involved in that kind of business. Major Rabbitt kept some things to himself.'

'And William Simpson?'

Knowles thought for a moment. 'I'm not familiar with that name.'

Gilchrist and Heap left shortly afterwards. At the door Knowles gave them Rabbitt's car details.

'Have you had a chance to do any research on Said Farzi, Bellamy?' Gilchrist said.

'I put Sylvia Wade onto it, ma'am. You think he might be involved – or you hope he might be involved?'

'Well, yes, I don't think this is coincidence.'

'I'm willing to believe he's not above board,' Heap said. 'You know how it works, ma'am, with any newly arrived immigrant community. Criminals arrive too and they feed off the other immigrants – protection rackets and so on – before they expand into making everyone else's lives a misery after they've got into conflict with home-grown villains who've done their share of feeding off their neighbours. And Said Farzi may well be one of these. First he will have started exploiting his fellow Moroccans, then he would work out from there.'

'So we need to talk to Rabbitt's sister – if we can track her down – about that business arrangement with her brother. And Nimue Grace about her neighbour. What do you think about Nimue Grace?'

'I've never met anyone like her,' Heap said.

'I don't think any of us have. She got to you?'

'Not in that obvious way. But yes. Didn't she get to you?'

Gilchrist looked out of the window. 'Yes,' she finally said. 'As discussed. I found myself telling her all kinds of private things.'

'Well, I want to do right by her if she is innocent of any crime but this somehow washes up at her door. I hate the way the tabloids work. And they are going to be onto this story any time now.'

'Don't we all, Bellamy? But can we be certain yet that she is innocent of any crime?'

'As discussed, ma'am.' Heap tilted his head. 'Did you notice that bit of puckering by her left ear?'

'I did but I thought not plastic surgery?'

'I agree, ma'am. Scarring though, for sure.'

'Let's go back to the lake. The dredger is supposed to have arrived by now.'

*   *   *

DC Sylvia Wade phoned with Tallulah Granger's Oxford address as Gilchrist and Heap were watching the small dredger being winched off the back of a lorry. 'It's just behind Oxford station, ma'am, so you might want to let the train take the strain.'

'Park at Gatwick,' Heap said. 'Train to Reading, change there for Oxford.'

'We'd better see if she's there first,' Gilchrist said.

'I took the liberty of asking the Oxford police to pop round and see,' Sylvia Wade said. 'She's there.'

'Well done, DC Wade. Please phone them back and say that, with their permission, we'd like to call on her. And can we organize some divers down here. This dredger is great but it's going to need help in a lake this size.'

'Already on their way ma'am.'

As they drove up to Gatwick, Gilchrist phoned Frank Bilson.

'Frank. It's Sarah. Anything on the Major Rabbitt killing?'

'You think you need to tell me it's you? As if I didn't know that voice. There's this new Orson Welles film showing at the Duke of York's, if you'd like to come along.'

'I've vaguely heard of Orson Welles – didn't he die years ago?'

'All the more reason to see his new film, I would say.'

'Ha! It's a tempting offer – sort of – but I'm more interested in your absolute silence about our murder victim.'

'What's to say? The throat was cut by a curved blade, probably of Tibetan origin, from right to left, so the killer was probably left-handed and, judging by the angle of the cut, was some inches taller than the victim – let's say six foot six. He walked with a limp – the indentations in the soft soil near the corpse – possibly made by an artificial limb. He had spent some time in India. He has a beard, a pockmarked face and answers to the name of Juggles.'

Gilchrist had started making notes but stopped. She glanced over at Heap. 'Very funny, Frank. Are you all right?'

'Never better. Why do you ask?'

'Are you, by any chance, drunk?'

'Not exactly. Next question.'

This was a first.

'Not exactly?'

'You've never been drunk, Sarah?'

'More times than I can count.'

'Well, then, you will recognize the difference between someone who is drunk and someone whose mood is merely elevated.'

'Fair enough,' Gilchrist said. 'I won't ask why your mood is elevated.'

'I will answer your unasked question nevertheless. It is because of the absurdity of existence. But I am clinging to Camus's remark that the realization that life is absurd cannot be an end, but only a beginning.'

Gilchrist couldn't think of anything to say. She'd never known Bilson to be in such a weird mood. 'I'll let you get on. I'm sorry to disturb you.'

'You've been disturbing me for as long as I've known you, Divine Sarah.'

Gawd.

'But there's something else SOCO asked me to pass on if I spoke to you,' Bilson said.

'About the white containers?'

'No. Nor about the victim's dentures – they're still looking for them for me, but then they'll be dredging the whole lake so who knows what else they'll turn up. The carp are very unhappy, I imagine.'

'The dredger has just arrived. We've just left the lake. What else?'

'A fixed camera hidden in a hide on the other side of the lake up near the cattle grid.'

'A Peeping Tom thing?'

'Well, I'm not sure. It's a pretty sophisticated one and it's filming digitally and sending the images somewhere – finding out where is your area, I think. Motion sensitive I would imagine so it sleeps most of the time.'

'You say it's fixed – what is it pointing at?'

'Well, it's hard to say what the lens is – how wide angle, I mean – but in the general direction of the island.'

'You're saying it might have filmed Rabbitt's murder?'

'Who knows how lucky you might be? But perhaps you can check with Ms Grace to see if she knows anything about it?'

'Frank, I could k— hug you.'

'Well, I'd welcome that but I can't take the credit alas. Still, you might be less keen to hug those hairy SOCO men and women – funny lot, as you know – so I'll accept it on their behalf. When next I see you.' Bilson hung up.

'Did you get that?' Gilchrist said to Heap. He nodded. Gilchrist called Grace and put her on speakerphone. 'Ms Grace, we're not going to be able to make lunch. I'm very sorry but we have to go to Oxford for a couple of hours.'

'No problem. Listen. I'm having a little party this evening. Not to celebrate Rabbitt's death, I hasten to add. Bad timing I know but it's been in the local winemakers' calendar for ages. Nothing fancy and certainly not showbizzy. It's more of a wine-tasting thing. Mostly neighbours who you'll probably want to speak to more formally at some point anyway. Bring your significant others – or your insignificant others, if you prefer.'

'Er, sure,' Gilchrist said. 'Thank you. Perhaps I could bring Bob Watts?'

'Who? Oh, him. As long as you two don't get up to anything on top of everybody's coats in the designated bedroom-cum-coat dump.'

Gilchrist glanced at Heap but couldn't think of a witty retort so said nothing.

'Just kidding. This won't be a student party. As I said, local winegrowers showing off their wines. Sussex sparkling always does very well in competitions even though, like the whites, it's overpriced. Sparkling and white are both good though. Not much in the way of reds yet, so if they are your tipple, bring your own.'

'My significant other is busy this evening, I'm afraid,' Heap said.

'But perhaps you can pop by anyway?'

'Sure – but, Ms Grace? We called about another matter. We found something by your lake. A camera.'

'Not again. I thought they'd moved on to drones by now.'

'We're not sure this is paparazzi or a Peeping Tom. It's fixed focus, possibly wide angle. It's hidden in a hide at lake level. Pretty much opposite your island.'

'Oh, shit – I forgot about that.'

'You know about it?'

'It's not exactly CCTV but they use it for recording nightlife in the wood and duck breeding patterns, day and night. There were two. One in a hide and one up a tree on the island but that tree one got vandalized a while ago. I get sent footage every month but it's mostly shots of not much happening on a placid pond.'

'You forgot?'

'Yes. You find that hard to understand? I don't go to that particular part of the pond very often, as I explained. Plus I've got a lot on my plate.'

'You said "they"?'

'Waterfowl fanatics. I never look at the footage. It's one of those webcam things so goes straight to someone's computer. Somewhere in Bristol, I think. I get sent particularly interesting stuff once a month or so.'

'So you have a contact?'

'Of course. Hang on, I'll get the case for one of the DVDs.' She came back on the line after a moment. 'Not Bristol. Oxford. The Wetlands Centre. Maybe you can call in when you're there.' She read out the phone number. 'You think perhaps they filmed Rabbitt's murder? I was in a Tony Scott film once where that happened. If it's anything like that film, Angelina Jolie's dad is your killer.'

'I'll bear that in mind,' Gilchrist said.

'That would be a great break, wouldn't it? Not Jon Voight – I'm sure he's got an alibi – but a film of the murderer.'

'It certainly would.'

Gilchrist looked at Heap when the call ended. 'She doesn't seem overly concerned about a death at her lake.'

'Maybe she's the life-goes-on type,' Heap said. 'And she was upfront about not liking the major.'

'Camus?' Gilchrist said, harking back to Bilson's odd behaviour.

'I think we'd be here all day if I even began to answer that seemingly straightforward question. I can see one question begetting another and that one begetting another.'

'You're sounding quite biblical, Bellamy. But point taken.'

FOUR

The trip to Oxford took under an hour. Tallulah Granger's house was on Abbey Road, two streets behind the station. Gilchrist and Heap walked down a slip road from the station, past a YHA on one side and a café in a wooden hut on the other and did a little zigzag onto Abbey Road. It was a road of tall terraced houses, all with bay windows. From the map on Heap's iPad they had seen that her house was on the side of the road that backed onto the river and canal complex at the bottom of Botley Road. It was on a flood plain and Heap mentioned that Osney Island, on the other side of Botley Road, regularly flooded.

Coincidentally, the Wetlands Centre was just a few hundred yards up the Botley Road on marshland on the right beside the River Cherwell.

Tallulah Granger opened the door and led them down a narrow corridor past a closed door and into a high-ceilinged room. The floor was stripped wood and a fireplace, in which a coal fire burned, had been stripped back to the brick. There was a long wooden table in the centre of the room with four chairs around. A laptop was open on the table.

'You disappeared on us, Ms Granger,' Gilchrist said.

'I do apologize,' she said. 'I didn't think you had any further use of me. I assume you were able to get what you needed from Richard's office without me.'

'There seem to be one or two things missing,' Gilchrist said as she wandered over to a set of French windows and looked out into a paved yard. There was a garden brazier there. It looked like papers had been recently burned in it. There were a couple of sandbags placed against the base of a back gate. Over the back wall, Gilchrist glimpsed the river and, on the other bank, allotments.

'His computer for one thing,' Heap said, looking pointedly at the laptop on the table.

'I've just made some vervain – would you like some?' Granger said, walking into a narrow kitchen that was obviously a later extension to the house. It ran along one side of the yard.

Gilchrist followed her in. 'His diary is missing too.'

'The river is just on the other side of my back gate – well, the towpath and then the river,' Granger said. 'Did you see?'

'Ms Granger? The missing items?'

'Yes, I know,' Granger said, dropping a tea cosy over an ornate metal teapot she'd put on a tray with three mugs. 'I'm afraid I don't do biscuits.'

'Do you get flooded often?' Heap called from the other room.

'Never. Although the insurance companies don't believe us, since we're designated as a flood risk. The premiums are sky-high.'

'I heard this whole area flooded regularly,' Heap said.

'You're mistaken. There is something about the confluence of the canal and the river – which occurs just a hundred yards up the river there – that means the current takes the water over the other side. Those allotments are under water regularly. I'm surprised somebody isn't growing rice.

'The water surges down under the bridge on Botley Road and floods Osney Island and the bottom end of Botley Road. But here, on this side of the river, we've never got more than a little spillage. I have sandbags by the back gate but they are hardly ever needed.'

She carried the tray into the other room and set it on the table. 'Help yourself but use the tea cosy to lift the pot – that metal handle gets very hot. I bought the teapot in Marrakesh – where indeed I bought the loose leaf vervain. For some reason it's impossible to get over here – even in fashionable Oxford covered market – and vervain tea bags just aren't the same.'

As Heap poured the herb tea into three mugs, Granger continued. 'This is my laptop, not Richard's. When I left on Monday evening his desktop computer was on his desk. He didn't use a laptop. Very old-fashioned was Richard. He couldn't type, except with one finger, which is why he needed a secretary. Well, that and for other comforts. If he could have used a quill pen for all his correspondence he probably would have.'

'You're saying he and Rhoda Knowles had a relationship?' Gilchrist said.

'I have no idea whether they had a relationship or not but he certainly would have tried it on. He had quite a high turnover of secretaries. The Me Too movement hadn't penetrated as far as Plumpton Down House.'

'The diary?' Heap said.

'I didn't notice his diary but I wasn't looking. I didn't take it. But do bear in mind the house is constantly full of strangers because of the wretched Airbnb business he insists on, because it's more profitable than simply letting out the rooms longer term. He used to insist on, should I say.'

Gilchrist frowned. 'I understood he wasn't keen on the Airbnb – he just let you get on with it.'

'Who told you that? Rhoda? That was his Squire Rabbitt pose – you know, letting rooms was below him – but in private he told me otherwise. He was an avaricious man, as interested in the pennies as the pounds. Then again, everybody in the area seems to do Airbnb these days – I think they even have a couple of rooms they rent in Danny House over at Hurstpierpoint. And when you say he let me get on with it that just means I did all the work.'

'It looks like you've been burning papers,' Heap said, gesturing to the brazier in the yard.

'Does it? You're mistaken. Not papers – pornographic magazines. I had tenants here until the weekend and when they left my cleaner discovered they had left them behind. I only rent this out to visiting academics so that's a sorry state of affairs, is it not?'

'Why did you leave Plumpton Down House so abruptly?'

'As I have said, I did not realize that I had. You may look at my calendar on my laptop to see that I always intended to come here on Monday. I had intended to come earlier in the day but then the police called. Evening was the earliest I could get away.

'I always visit when there is a changeover of tenant to ensure everything is shipshape and also to spend a few days in this house and city I love so much before the next tenants move in. I studied here – Christchurch. In fact, I bought this house from Christchurch – they own the freehold on the entire street.' She looked out of the window. 'There are lovely walks along both river and canal that end up at the Meadows and nearby Jericho.

And there's nothing quite like having breakfast amid the bustle of the covered market.'

'Did you drive here?'

'I did.'

'In Major Rabbitt's car?'

'In my own car.'

'Do you know where Major Rabbitt's car is?'

'Somewhere around the perimeter of the house, I imagine.' She looked from one to the other. 'Isn't it?'

Gilchrist shook her head. 'It's missing.'

'I can't think where it could be.'

'We spoke to Rhoda Knowles earlier today,' Heap said. 'She suggested there was some hostility between your brother and an ostrich farmer?'

'You think Mark Harrison stole my husband's car?'

'No,' Gilchrist said. 'Sorry, that was an awkward segue.'

'It was. Yes, my brother hated the idea of such alien creatures on land that he regarded as properly his – you know his ambition was to put the Plumpton Down Estate back together after it had been sold off in parcels back in the nineties? A common ambition, I understand, of people who have rather grand ideas about their own importance.'

'Did he have the same objection to the llamas?'

'Oddly not. Indeed, that herd belongs to him. He'd taken a trip to Machu Picchu and became very taken with the llama while in Peru, so he decided to import a few.'

'They don't seem in keeping with his general ethos about the estate.'

'I know – made no sense to me, except as a rich man's hobby. They are not economically viable, especially when you factor in the salary of Reg Dwight, the full time shepherd or herdsman or whatever a llama keeper is called. They only cost £500 each but they don't breed quickly enough to be any good as meat and you can't get enough fibre off them – they don't call it wool – to turn a profit. But my brother got fixed ideas and he wasn't exactly consistent.'

'Can you think where his computer and diary might have gone?' Gilchrist said.

Granger shook her head. 'Rhoda has no idea? Well, as I said, we have a lot of strangers wandering about the right wing of the house and the public rooms. I vet them as best I can but I'm sure a criminal element could slip through. Perhaps it was opportunist theft. Though why the diary too, I have no idea. Perhaps that has just been misplaced. This visit to Oxford is a short one, alas. I'm coming back this evening – you could have saved yourself the journey – so I'll have a root around, with Rhoda's permission.'

'Are you in charge of the whole thing now?'

'I suppose I am,' Granger said. 'I hadn't thought. I mean, the boys will inherit it but until they are of age . . .'

'What about Mrs Rabbitt?'

'I think she's pretty firmly excluded from the will though I fully expect her to contest that.'

Gilchrist rose and Heap followed. 'Thank you for the tea,' Gilchrist said. 'Vervain did you say? Very refreshing and a nice scent. I've not had it before.' At the door Gilchrist turned and said: 'Did you burn the pornographic magazines before or after the Oxford police called round today to tell you we were coming?'

Granger smiled: 'Do you know, I can't remember. So much on my mind that everything is a bit of a blur at the moment.'

As they walked down the street Gilchrist said to Heap: 'She sounded quite plausible. And certainly assured.'

'That's Oxbridge for you,' Heap said. 'And probably means she's hiding something.'

'Indeed – you old cynic you. Let's hope the Wetlands Centre has something for us.'

The Wetlands Centre did indeed have something for them, though it took a while to find it on the film footage of Grace's lake. They had the help of a Barry Fitzgerald, an earnest young man in a suit and horn-rimmed glasses.

'Can we look at the footage from Beard's Pond in Plumpton Down over the past week?'

'All of it? It would take you a week to watch it.'

'The camera doesn't operate on some motion sensor thing?'

'It does but that particular sensor often has a mind of its own. We can fast forward and reduce the watching time. What are you looking for?'

'A man or men coming into the frame on the footpath behind the lake.'

'Hardly ever happens there – it's a private lake.'

'Hardly ever? That suggests that sometimes it does.'

'There's one guy who crops up from time to time, swimming naked. And once . . .' He tailed off.

'Once . . .?' Gilchrist said.

'I think Ms Grace forgot about the camera and she swam into shot.' He saw their looks. 'You couldn't see anything! And even if you could it was private.'

Gilchrist gave him a severe look. 'No keeping it for yourself for those cold lonely nights or putting it out there for good, dirty money?'

'Excuse me! If she had feathers and a beak I might be interested but from the little I could see of her, swimming breaststroke, she had neither of those attributes. And, therefore, as far as I'm concerned, no attributes.'

'You were doing fine until the last sentence but now you're worrying me,' Gilchrist said. Fitzgerald's eyes widened. He started to stutter a protest. 'Just joking,' Gilchrist said. 'OK, can we do a speed-through backwards, starting Monday morning?'

The footage was mostly water with the occasional duck or flotilla of ducks getting in and out from the island. Then Gilchrist spotted something behind the island.

'Can you pause it there for a moment,' she said quickly. There was somebody on the towpath. 'And move it forward slowly.' She looked at the time code. Early Sunday evening. 'Go on.' She was trying to remember what colour trousers Rabbitt had been wearing since all she could really make out now was a pair of red trousers. She was sure he hadn't been wearing those.

'Those trousers are the colour that, for some reason, ex-officers in the armed forces favour,' Gilchrist said. 'Or maybe ex-public schoolboys. Usually matched – or rather mismatched – with a chequered sports jacket and a brightly coloured shirt.' She'd sometimes wondered why that garish colour was their trouser of choice. Perhaps because their uniforms were so drab these days compared to a hundred and fifty years ago? She had no idea.

She watched this pair of legs walk along the path she and

Bellamy had followed, disappearing and reappearing between bushes. The camera had a narrow range so it only covered about twenty yards. It was also pitched low, which is why she could only see the legs.

'OK, red legs is gone so speed it up again, please.'

Seconds later on the speed up another pair of legs appeared.

'Slow again,' Gilchrist said.

'That's Rabbitt,' Heap said.

'You're sure?' Gilchrist said.

'As sure as dammit,' Heap said. 'I recognize the trousers.'

'OK then. So he's about to meet red legs. But we can't be accurate about timings can we, if this camera stops and starts?'

'You're wrong,' Fitzgerald said. 'We can do the maths on how much time has passed between active filming from the digital clock set in it. So it's just a couple of minutes.'

'OK. Let's keep it moving.'

Fitzgerald was watching it as closely as they were. He stopped the video and said: 'Look at that.'

Gilchrist and Heap looked and could only see blank lake. Then Gilchrist pointed to bottom left. 'The ripples?' Gilchrist said. Fitzgerald nodded. 'Red Legs is putting the body in the water,' Heap murmured.

'Body?' Fitzgerald said. 'What body? I thought we were looking at ducks.'

'Did you really think the police would be interested in investigating ducks, lovely as they are?' Gilchrist said, not taking her eyes off the screen as she watched the ripples widen then slowly dissipate. She looked at the time – about ten minutes later – and saw Heap note it down. 'We're investigating a murder, Mr Fitzgerald, and this footage is extremely helpful.'

Fitzgerald frowned. 'Well, would it help if you had earlier footage of other people coming and going along that path and in the pond? I mean we cut it out of what we use and what we send Ms Grace but it's still there in the raw footage.'

'Is there much traffic?' Gilchrist said.

Fitzgerald shrugged. 'As I said, not so much but from time to time.'

'You've got no audio, I suppose?'

'As I said.'

'Well, perhaps you'd better give us the raw footage for the previous month to see what we can come up with?'

'You wouldn't like me to look through it for you? I'm pretty proficient at sifting through this stuff.'

'You have time to do that?'

'Waterfowl and water creatures are my interest – my partner would say my obsession – but it's nice to refresh the palate with something different for a change. I'll get on it straight away and can send you what I've got tomorrow.'

'That would be great,' Gilchrist said, shaking Fitzgerald's hand. 'Anything at all that strikes you as not water creature related.'

Heap nodded to him. Outside Heap muttered something.

'What?' Gilchrist said. 'Enunciate for goodness sake. You know I'm stupidly tall for a woman so I can't hear you if you're talking into your chest.'

'Ma'am,' Heap said loudly. 'I said you were spot on about red and maroon trousers. Military, past or present. Officer class.'

'I suppose you're going to tell me why these men do that?'

Heap shook his head. 'That would come under the heading of social mores and my computer brain doesn't have an algorithm for that. Just the facts, ma'am.'

'That sounds like a quote but I don't want to hear where it's from. I repeat – I don't want to hear where from.'

'Ten four, ma'am.'

'You're doing a film reference there, I know you are, but I'm not going to be drawn.'

'Quite right, ma'am. Let's track down Red Legs.'

'Yes, we might have caught a break here. We don't have any other CCTV footage to go on – the local constables have checked and none of the houses down that way have cameras. Anything from Sylvia Wade about the car?'

'Negative, ma'am.'

'Well, let's get the train back for Grace's party. I must admit, I'd prefer just to go to bed but, who knows, Red Legs might be there. And it's good to *refresh the palate*.'

'Ten four.'

FIVE

B ob Watts was sorry but he had other commitments that evening – attendance at a city council meeting for his regular monthly briefing on police performance and activities. Gilchrist and Heap went to the party together, Heap carrying a couple of bottles of red wine. Gilchrist had slept on the train from Oxford to Reading – with very little drooling, Heap assured her – so was feeling a little livelier.

'I've never been to a wealthy person's party before,' Heap said as they drove along Beard's Lane. 'But obviously bringing a bottle still applies.'

'I don't think she's wealthy,' Gilchrist said. 'I think she's skint. Relatively speaking. Big house like that and she doesn't have any staff except Francis, who can't even bring a cup of coffee when asked. And who seems to have disappeared, incidentally.'

'But she must have made a fortune,' Heap said.

'And spent a fortune, probably. I bet she's mortgaged to the hilt.'

At the door they were let in by a tall, tanned man with an Antipodean accent. 'Mark Harrison, ostrich farmer,' he said, holding out his hand. 'And you're new to these parts, I surmise.'

'Sarah and Bellamy and we're not really from these parts at all.'

He led them to the kitchen and gestured to the booze. 'Nimue is down the other end of the house somewhere having her ear bent by various winemakers. Help yourself to whatever you want before they come and bore you about what you're drinking. The sparkling and the white are both damned good.'

While Heap was pouring drinks, Harrison said: 'Are you actors too?'

Gilchrist shook her head. 'Your accent – are you Australian?'

'New Zealand. And I've heard every joke that exists about a Kiwi raising ostriches.'

'They're related though, right?' Heap said. 'Kiwis and ostriches.'

'Darwin predicted *ratites* – that's the overall term for flightless birds – were related and they obviously are connected but actually ostriches, kiwis, emus, rheas, cassowaries and the like all developed absolutely separately across the world. But they share the fact that they have flat breastbones, which means they lack the keel that anchors the strong pectoral muscles birds need for flight. And their tiny wings can't possibly lift their heavy bodies off the ground. Hence flightless.'

'Do yours wonder where they are?' Gilchrist said.

Harrison smiled. 'They are perfectly well suited to this climate. Just give them grass to graze and they are happy. They only require small amounts of land although they do need shelter from wind and rain and a dry sleeping area. They also need six-feet-high fencing to keep them in because the buggers can really jump.'

'So do they do much more than put their heads in the sand and lay eggs?' Gilchrist said.

'That's a fallacy – the head in sand thing. They lay their heads down on the ground to keep an eye on something that might be threatening them. And they can run like billy-o. A stampeding ostrich can run at up to forty-five miles an hour.'

'But why keep them in this very English countryside?' Heap said.

'You forget that the first English colonists of New Zealand and Australia imported creatures that weren't indigenous. Foxes for fox hunting among the nobs? English birds, even.'

'Fair enough,' Heap said. 'But why farm them at all?'

'Very productive bird the ostrich,' Harrison said. 'I've got African Blacks – the most commonly domesticated though some try with the Red Neck and the Blue Neck. Ostriches are good breeders. An ostrich will probably live as long as we do and the female is fertile for thirty years.'

'That's a lot of eggs in a lifetime. If you have a breeding trio – a male and two females – as I have, you're going to get around thirty to fifty eggs a year. Each female produces that number but only about half hatch so then I sell the other half. The ones that do hatch reach slaughter weight – that's ninety-five to one hundred and ten kilograms – in a year to fourteen months. From each slaughtered ostrich you end up with about a quarter that weight in deboned meat.

'Despite their size they're classified as poultry, believe it or not, and under poultry regulations I'm allowed to slaughter on the farm if I only sell locally – which I do. I sell the meat and eggs at local farmers markets and through a couple of organic outlets. But I also have them processed in a specialist slaughter facility down the road to sell elsewhere. The leather and feathers I sell to craftspeople in Lewes and Brighton to turn into all kinds of things.'

'And this is your full-time business?' Heap said.

'Nah – it's a hobby. A pretty time-consuming hobby, mind. I work from home in my proper job, which is what makes it possible.' He looked from one to the other of them. 'Now lovely as it has been to bang on about my favourite subject, you didn't actually tell me what you two do.'

'We're in the police force,' Heap said. 'And we need to speak to you formally at some point.'

'That sounds ominous.'

'Not really. We met Ms Grace because you may have heard that your neighbour, Major Rabbitt, has been murdered. His body was recovered at her lake two days ago.'

Harrison snorted.

'That's an odd reaction,' Gilchrist said.

Harrison held up his hand, palm towards Gilchrist. 'I regret any person's death, of course I do. I was snorting at the *major* thing.'

'Explain,' Heap said.

'He was no more a major than I can lay ostrich eggs.'

'How do you know he wasn't a major?' Heap said.

'Because he was never in the regular army. He was in the Territorials back in the day when it was still called the Territorials – so back in the days when it was just fun and you weren't going to find yourself getting blown up in Afghanistan or Iraq by an IWD. And the highest rank you could make back then was second lieutenant.'

'How do you know this?' Heap said.

'I checked. It's pretty easy to do.'

'Why would you do that?' Gilchrist said.

'Because I don't like bullshitters – excuse my language. And I could see straight away that this guy was just a wealthy bag of wind. And one who liked to make trouble for his neighbours.'

'He made trouble for you?' Heap said.

'You bet. It was only a letter of support from Nimue that got me permission to start the ostrich farm. Rabbitt never forgave either of us.'

'So you're not disappointed to see him dead?' Gilchrist said.

'I wouldn't go that far – and I certainly wouldn't go as far as knocking him off, if that's what your next question is going to be related to.'

'Kind of related,' Gilchrist said. 'When did you last see him?'

'The day before his body was found, actually. In the pub at lunchtime slobbering over some woman in the back corner.'

'Which pub?' Gilchrist said.

'The Jolly Sportsman, over near the old church. My liver has been complaining that it's worryingly close to my place.'

'What woman?' Heap said.

'No idea. I looked by mistake and didn't make the same mistake twice.'

'When was that?' Heap said.

'Lunchtime, as I said. I don't know the exact o'clock.'

'Is he blahing on again about creating a dinosaur from ostrich DNA?' a burly red-faced man said loudly, putting his arm around Harrison's shoulders. 'How're you doing, you bleeding drongo?'

'I keep telling you, Reg, that's an Australian term. We Kiwis are much more refined.' He turned to Gilchrist and Heap. 'This here is Reg Dwight, llama farmer for the late *Major* Rabbitt.'

Reg, clearly drunk, grinned a red-lipped, red-toothed grin. Drunk on red wine, then. But he didn't bother to reply. 'You're those coppers who've been sniffing about, aren't you? I've seen you yesterday. Major Rabbitt kicking the bucket? Couldn't happen to a finer man.'

'You knew him well?'

'Well, I work for him – I don't know if that's the same thing. *Worked* for him, I mean. My current employment status is now uncertain, which is why I thought I'd get pissed.'

'You don't need an excuse to get pissed, Reg,' Mark said.

'True enough. Where's Nimue? She's wary of me – thinks I'm a hypocrite for saying rude things about the major behind his back while hobnobbing with him at his parties and his interminable slide shows. But I work for him, for God's sake, and I only go to his dos so I can piss in the punch, metaphorically speaking.'

'Not always just metaphorically, from what I've heard,' Harrison said.

'That was only the once. Anyway, keep your friends close and your enemies closer, I say.'

'Was Richard Rabbitt an enemy?' Heap said.

Dwight peered blearily down at him. 'Where's your truncheon and whistle?'

'Was he an enemy?' Heap repeated.

'Not particularly to me but he was a tricky bastard. He tried to make life difficult for everyone round here in his attempt to be lord of the manor. Let's leave it at that, shall we, as this is meant to be a party not a police interview?'

'Fair enough,' Gilchrist said. 'So why llamas? What's wrong with sheep and cattle with maybe a few goats thrown in?'

'Llamas are great for mowing.'

'So are sheep.'

'True but these are also excellent guards because they make a racket and can be threatening when they see someone they don't know. Llamas mark their territories with their dung. If a fox comes into their field the llama will scare him away by walking up and staring him out. They can use their back legs, and will spit, but that's a last resort.'

'Geese are excellent guards too – and they can break your leg or bite you. Llamas just spit?'

'They hardly ever spit at people. They're a herd animal with a pecking order – if any of them try to change that order they'll spit at that one. But they're usually gentle. In the mornings they sit down either in a circle or a line. And if they're in a line it will be in a size order. They like this climate – they are used to extremes of temperature in Peru. We have alpacas in our herd – smaller with silkier coats. They hum.'

'You mean they smell?'

'No, they literally hum when they're feeling good. They cluck too.'

'So get hens.'

'You wouldn't catch a hen happily carrying a third of its own body weight. They can pull a cart or trap with the right training. They're pretty cheap to buy – £500 for a male. The drawback is they don't breed very quickly. Ostriches, you know where you are – you can make a business plan based on how many eggs you'll have this year and how many the next, right, Mark?'

'Damned right.'

'Llamas only have one baby a year and it might not be every year. As a commercial proposition they are definitely long term but as pets they're great. Major Rabbitt occasionally did llama-trekking up on the Downs.'

'You're kidding.'

'I never kid about llamas. Llamas are very sure-footed and because they have small feet with a leathery pad, they don't cut up the paths like heavier animals.' He raised his glass and took a swig. 'Anyway: the major is dead; long live the major. Not. Who next, I wonder?'

'You mean who is going to be killed next?' Heap said. 'Why should there be someone else?'

'You think things happen in isolation round here? This is a rural community.'

'That's a bit of a stretch, isn't it?' Heap said.

'I don't see why. Everyone is interlinked here, whether they like it or not.'

'I think that, on the contrary, people who aren't born in rural communities but choose to move to one do so because they enjoy isolation,' Harrison said. 'They don't actually want to be part of a community except on their own terms. So they buy somewhere isolated enough from other houses to be able to do their own damned thing.'

'Interesting point of view,' Heap said.

'A correct one too.'

Grace came proffering a bottle of wine to fill up glasses. She grinned that killer grin when she saw Gilchrist and Heap. 'You made it! Great!' She looked from Dwight to Harrison. 'But let me take you away from these reprobates and introduce you to people who can string more than a single sentence together.' As she pulled them away, filling Gilchrist's glass as she did so, she murmured: 'Did Reg make a pass at you?' Gilchrist shook her head. Grace grinned. 'The night is young.'

'Your friend seems quite a character.'

'A drunk, you mean?' She leaned in close and lowered her voice. 'Reg is not my friend. Nobody here is. They are either acquaintances or people round here I need to keep on side so they don't block whatever little plans I have for my orchard or my lake.'

'You have plans?'

'Nothing out of keeping – I'm not going to start breeding kangaroos or anything – though I was tempted to get a giraffe so Reg and Mark could see what a real long-necked creature looks like. Have you noticed, by the way, how long Reg's neck is? I think with llama owners it works the same way as with dog owners – you know, looking like their dogs.'

'Let's hope for Mark's sake the same doesn't apply to ostrich owners,' Heap murmured.

Grace looked at him and burst out laughing. 'I do like you, Sir Galahad. A protector with a sense of humour.'

Gilchrist expected Heap to blush but, oddly, he didn't. 'What are your plans?'

'Oh, I'd like bees at the bottom of the orchard and a telephone mast for mobile phones in the watercress beds part of my wood because the signal round here is crap and everyone would benefit. A gypsy caravan in the wood, with a wood-burning stove so I can use it in the winter.

'But you've got to jump through hoops round here since the South Downs became a National Park. I mean, I think National Parks are a very, very good thing, but it can be hard for individuals to get permission for minor things, while the local football club, for example, can carve out a football stadium from prime Downs land.'

She put her hand to her mouth. 'Better not talk too loudly – I've invited a couple of case officers from the Parks Authority.' She gave a little jerk of her head. 'Over there behind me talking to Cruella de Vil.'

Gilchrist and Hope looked over and saw two tall men, both bearded, flanking a tall woman with long black hair and a lot of make-up and bright red lipstick. She was wearing a figure-hugging black dress that she didn't quite have the figure for, except for her big breasts spilling out of the top.

Grace grinned. 'I know – she didn't get the memo. Never knowingly underdressed, our Kip.'

'She's a neighbour?'

'She's my American agent here on a visit. Staying at Pelham House over in Lewes.'

'I'm going to be staying there,' Gilchrist said, blushing slightly. 'Just for the duration of this investigation.'

'Great – that makes us almost neighbours.'

'Your gypsy caravan in the wood sounds great too,' Heap said. 'So you'd stay there in it?'

Grace turned her mouth down. 'It's a pipe dream. If I had a partner to share it with I'd spend a lot of time down there. But I don't. I can't really picture myself staying down there on my ownsome.' She grimaced. 'My life hasn't exactly turned out as I expected.'

'So far,' Heap said quietly. 'But there's a lot more to go and many more wonderful things to happen to you, I'm sure.'

Grace leaned over and kissed him on the forehead. 'My Galahad,' she murmured.

'Hey, kid,' Kip said, suddenly appearing beside Grace. 'Who knew National Park policies on sheep management could be so interesting.' Then she vigorously shook her head.

She looked Gilchrist and Heap up and down. 'You're not gamekeepers as well, are you?'

'I'm not sure what those men over there do qualifies as game-keeping, Kip,' Grace said. 'But, actually, these two kind of are. They are the police.'

Kip looked from one to the other.

'Cops? You're shitting me.' She leaned towards them. 'It's only for recreational use.' She brayed a laugh. Gilchrist and Heap smiled politely. Kip nudged Grace. 'So you're pals with cops now? Good, good – now you know who to call on the next time one of your creepy boyfriends beats the shit out of you.'

Grace lowered her eyes and flushed a little. 'I hope that's all in the past,' she said quietly.

'I hope so too, kid. But you and me, we're programmed to

pick the arrogant pricks not the stand-up guys.' She pointed at Heap. 'You a stand-up guy?'

'He's my Galahad,' Grace said.

'Alan Ladd?' Kip said puzzled. 'Because of his height?'

'Sir Galahad – my knight in shining armour.'

Kip couldn't help her double take. 'You and him?'

'Not like that.' She smiled mischievously at Heap. 'But only because he's taken.'

'That wouldn't stop me,' Kip said. She touched Grace's arm. 'But I know you got morals.' She looked at Gilchrist and Heap. 'Made her stand out like a sore thumb in Hollywood.'

'All right, enough indiscreet talk about me – you know I'm a very private person. And excuse me for a moment.' They all watched Grace go back into the kitchen then stood awkwardly together.

'So you know Nim through your work?' Kip said.

Gilchrist nodded. 'A neighbour of hers was murdered and dumped in her lake.'

'Ugh!'

Reg Dwight barged back in.

'And why have we never met?' he said to Kip, peering at her exposed breasts.

'My good fortune, I guess,' she said, peeling herself away with a little backward wave of her hand to Gilchrist and Heap.

Dwight looked from one to the other of them. 'Well, that was brief. Story of my life these days.' He *did* have a long thick neck, Gilchrist observed. 'It occurs to me you must want to question me as one of the last people to see Rabbitt alive.'

Heap gave him a sharp look. '*Are* you one of the last people to see him alive?'

'I would think so. Seven p.m. Sunday night. He was found a bit later by that plonker, Kermode, I believe.'

'You know Kermode?' Gilchrist said, trying quickly to process what Dwight was saying.

'Everybody knows him and his collection of Nimue Grace's underwear. He probably wears more of her underwear than she does.'

Gilchrist didn't feel like exploring that. 'Kermode told you he'd found Rabbitt? And the time he found him?'

'Kermode told pretty much everybody,' Dwight said.

'He's popular?' Gilchrist said.

'It's a small community,' Dwight said. 'Not the same thing.' He looked across at Grace in the other room deep in conversation with her agent. He leered. 'And who wouldn't want to get into Nimue Grace's knickers?'

'Where did you see him at seven?' Gilchrist said, determined to turn the conversation away from Dwight's Nimue Grace obsession.

'Not where I'd expect to find him,' Dwight said.

'Which is where?'

'Did I tell you I was trying to recreate a dinosaur from ostrich DNA?' Harrison said as he suddenly appeared and put his arm round Dwight.

'No, no, you didn't,' Gilchrist said. 'Would you excuse us for a moment?'

'Sure,' he said. 'Come on, Reggie, we're outstaying our welcome.'

He turned and pulled Dwight away from Gilchrist and Heap. Gilchrist sighed and looked at Heap. 'Reg,' she called after them as she followed them. 'Mark.'

Harrison turned, swivelling Dwight with him. 'Oh, you do want to hear about it. Good, because it's a great story, ostriches being the nearest thing to a T. Rex we have.'

Gilchrist sighed again. 'I just want Reg to say where, if you would, Reg.'

Dwight shrugged. 'Here.'

'This is all looking very serious,' Nimue Grace said as she swanned up to them with a full glass of sparkling wine held at an alarming angle. Heap reached out and corrected it. 'My Galahad,' she mouthed.

'Your attractive copper here is giving me the third degree,' Dwight said. 'I was just telling her I saw Dickhead Rabbitt here at seven p.m. Sunday night.'

'Here?' Grace said.

'Just leaving the place,' Dwight said with a leer.

'That's a lie,' Grace said indignantly. She looked at Gilchrist. 'He wasn't here.' She looked back at Dwight. 'More to the point now, if that's true, what were you doing here to be able to see him?'

Gilchrist looked from one to the other. 'Why were you here, Reg?'

Dwight shrugged. 'I'd been having a drink with your neighbour in the stables.'

'You had a drink with Said Farzi?' Grace said, looking astonished.

'He's a neighbour,' Dwight said.

'He's been making my life a bloody misery, as you well know.'

Dwight shrugged. 'He's a neighbour.'

'Rabbitt wasn't visiting me,' Grace said forcefully.

'Well, some bloke sure as buggery was,' Dwight mumbled.

'Nobody was,' Grace insisted fiercely, before taking a glug from her wine glass.

'You said Farzi makes your life a misery,' Gilchrist said to Grace.

Grace looked around. 'Look, this is meant to be a party. I'm not sure this is the right time to have this conversation.'

She was right, of course. Gilchrist looked at Heap, who had taken out his phone. 'Could we have your phone number, Reg, to follow this up tomorrow? Yours too, Mark.'

'Well,' Dwight said, 'I'd rather give it to the organ grinder than the monkey, but if you insist.'

Gilchrist saw Heap's jaw clench but he said nothing.

'I think, actually, they are both organ grinders,' Harrison said pleasantly before giving Heap his number. 'Someone else around here is the monkey.'

That passed Dwight by as he gave his number while Grace glowered at him. Gilchrist turned to her. 'I'm sorry. You're right. This is a party and we've probably outstayed our welcome.'

Grace was quick to respond. 'No, no – please stay – if you're willing – we haven't had a proper conversation yet.'

Gilchrist nodded. 'Sure.' She started towards a stripped wood door in the far wall. 'Is this the bathroom?'

'No,' Grace said, catching up with her and taking her arm to steer her away from the door. 'That's the door to the apple cellar. Even if you fancied an apple, navigating the lethal staircase on the other side of that door at this time of night is a very bad idea.' She pointed towards the foyer behind the front door. 'Through that door there.'

'This is turning into quite a party, Bellamy,' Gilchrist said when she rejoined him. 'Though no red trousers in evidence.'

'Indeed. But there is a lot for us to do in the morning.'

Gilchrist looked at Grace heading out into the garden. 'There may be a lot to do tonight.'

For the next twenty minutes or so, Gilchrist and Heap stayed in the kitchen observing the mix of people. Pretty much all local and comfortably off, they surmised. The exceptions were Cruella de Vil and a loud, theatrical-seeming couple who were throwing *darlings* around like confetti.

'I've *got* to find out who they are,' Gilchrist said. 'Back in a mo.'

Heap wandered over to the piano in the drawing room. The sheet music on the stand was for a song he vaguely knew called 'Two Sleepy People'. He examined a chess game in progress on a table beside it. He noticed a pamphlet with the card attached was still on the small table by the sofa. It was the Hassocks blockade pamphlet he'd seen yesterday. He had no idea what the Hassocks blockade was but assumed it was to do with smugglers and revenue men back when. He went through the French windows and out onto the terrace. He inhaled the fragrant smell of the honeysuckle.

'Heady, isn't it?' Nimue Grace was standing in the shadow of a broad-branched poplar, smoking a cigarette. Correction, not simply a cigarette, Heap realized, as he smelt something else, instantly recognisable and definitely heady. Grace put a 'got me' expression on her face. 'Oops,' she said.

'We don't make a fuss these days, Ms Grace, especially in your own home and even more particularly when it's used for medicinal purposes.'

'Am I using it for medicinal purposes?' Grace said.

'I imagine you're in shock at the discovery of your neighbour's murdered body in your lake. But I hope you get it from a reliable source – there's some skunk out there now that can lead to psychosis.'

'My Sir Galahad,' Grace said gently. She proffered the joint.

Heap shook his head. '*That* would be unacceptable,' he said. He looked around. 'You're out here alone at your own party? Am I disturbing you?'

'Not at all. I'm just not that big on parties,' Grace said.

'Then why . . .?'

Grace tipped back her head and blew a plume of smoke into the air. 'The winemakers. Plus it's my birthday and old habits die hard.'

'Your birthday?'

Grace put her finger to her lips and made a ssssh sound. 'Our secret, Sir Galahad.'

Heap nodded. 'It's a nice party, full of quite interesting people.'

'Who I hardly know – and *quite* interesting – how sad is that?'

'Not sad at all.'

'You're *quite* interesting yourself. Tell me about your Kate – is it Kate? Is she the *lurve* of your life?'

'Whatever that means,' Heap said, uncomfortable.

'Now don't go all Prince Charles on me, Bellamy.'

Heap smiled. 'She's having a tough time because her mother recently committed suicide. Her funeral is on Thursday.'

'I'm very sorry to hear that – but shouldn't you be with her tonight?'

'I wanted to be but she wanted some space for the evening.'

'I'm sorry to hear that too,' Grace said quietly. 'Did her mother leave a note?'

'No. But that is more often the case than people realize – we're misinformed by TV crime shows that assume that if there is no note a death is suspicious.'

'Did Kate and her mother get on?'

Heap shook his head. 'She was not a very motherly mother.'

'Hmm. I hear that. Mine wasn't either.'

'Is your mother still alive?'

'Not to me.'

'That's a great shame.'

'She is what used to be called a paranoid schizophrenic. I'm not sure what they call it now. Bipolar doesn't cover it. Besides, in Hollywood, bipolar has become the go-to word to excuse bad behaviour.' She took another drag on the joint, its embers growing bright at the tip. 'Most women I know have felt liberated when their mothers have died, however close they felt to them. A kind of unconscious oppression lifted. But I don't know how that would work with a suicide. Especially without any explanation.

'No closure. No relief. Just questions that can probably never be answered.' She shook her head. 'Suicide is the most selfish and the cruellest act anyone can inflict on people who love them, I think. You owe it to them to carry on. To yourself too.'

'You've never had those impulses?'

'Not even in my darkest moments. Have you?' Heap shook his head. 'I'm glad to hear it. I hope that, like me, it's because you love life too much.' She gestured around her. 'Even this pathetic half-life.'

'Doesn't seem at all pathetic to me.'

Grace smiled sadly. 'You would say that, Sir Galahad.'

'What's the Hassocks blockade?'

Grace frowned. 'I haven't the faintest idea. Why?'

'That pamphlet by your sofa.'

'Is that what it's called? There's a local historian who lives in the cottages at the bottom of the drive. He dropped it off. He's hoping for a quote from me, I suppose. I get that a lot. There's a poet – self-published – who sends me volume after volume of poetry. All of it not only dedicated to me but inspired by me and about me, he insists.'

'Is it any good?' Heap asked. Grace raised one eyebrow. Heap hurried on. 'I noticed you have a chess game in progress set out over by your piano. You play against yourself?'

'You're a chess player, Detective Sergeant?'

'I used to be.'

'Excellent. We must play some time. Not that game – that is me as Lasker, trying to beat Steinitz, the first World Champion. But I think I'm going to lose, as Lasker did in the actual match.'

'You've always played chess?' Gilchrist said.

'I was taught by a lovely Italian actress on some long, boring shoot and I really took to it.' She looked at Heap. 'You're surprised, aren't you? Airhead actress playing chess?'

'I try not to deal in stereotypes, Ms Grace,' Heap said. 'And, if I may say, I've never thought for one moment you are an airhead. One only had to see you in *The Dance of Death* at Chichester to see your intelligence shine through.'

She gave him a warm smile. 'You saw that?'

Heap nodded. 'I thought you were terrific.'

'I was too young for the part really.'

'You pulled off playing older very well, I thought.'

'Worryingly well – none of the critics even commented on the age disparity between me and a character who has been married twenty-five years.'

'You were brilliant.' He smiled slyly. 'But then remember I always thought Robert Duvall was a good actor too . . .'

Grace cackled, actually cackled. 'Sir Galahad – you sod! I can see I'm going to have to watch you – there's more to you than meets the eye.' She tilted her head and eyed him fondly. 'So – you really are a cultivated copper, eh?'

'I find most police people are pretty bright,' Heap said. 'And have a wide range of interests.'

'What are Detective Inspector Gilchrist's interests?'

'You'd have to ask her that, ma'am – I'm sorry, Ms Grace – I don't know her that well.'

Grace suddenly shifted subject. 'Did you always want to be a copper?'

'I did, Ms Grace. Yes.'

'Does it run in the family?'

'It does, Ms Grace. Yes. My mother's father and his father before him.'

'What rank did they achieve?'

'Chief superintendent and chief inspector respectively. In Somerset.'

'My grandfather was a chief constable in Gloucestershire.'

'I know, ma'am.' Heap saw her quizzical look. 'Wikipedia.'

'Of course. What else does it say about me?'

'You don't know?'

'I don't read anything about myself. I've never read reviews. I've never seen a finished film. I loathe how I look on screen.'

'That surprises me, Ms Grace. The loathing bit.'

'Why? Have you ever met a woman happy with how she looks?'

'No, Ms Grace, but you – well . . .' Heap flushed. 'You're luminous.'

'Why, thank you, kind sir. But my nose is too small, my ears too big, my breasts are different sizes, I have no waist to speak of, my knees are chubby and my ankles too thick. My feet you know about.' She lifted a hand palm outwards. 'And my fingers are stubby and podgy.'

Heap looked down then said, with the sly smile back on his
face: 'But aside from all that you're beautiful.'

She laughed a full-throated laugh now and Heap turned
crimson.

'There you are!' a woman called from the doorway of the
French windows. 'Nim, we have to go. It's been fab, as always.'
The female half of the theatrical couple.

'Am-drammers,' Grace murmured. 'Far worse than pro actors
in the *luvvie* stakes.' She put on a patently false smile and Heap
excused himself and went past the woman back into the house.
He glanced back to see Grace and the amateur actress air-kissing
goodbyes. *Darlings* filled the air.

Heap walked across to Gilchrist.

'I wondered where you'd got to,' she said. 'Been having an
interesting conversation?'

'Just chatting to Ms Grace,' he said.

'I wish I'd had an even mildly interesting conversation. Reg
Dwight and Mark Harrison grabbed me again – metaphorically
speaking. I now know even more about llamas and their husbandry
than I ever imagined I would want to. In fact, I'm not sure I do
want to but now it's all implanted in my brain. And did you
know you really can recreate a T. Rex from ostrich DNA?'

Heap smiled. 'I still haven't seen any men in red trousers –
have you?'

'I hope you're not talking shop,' Grace said as she joined
them. 'Cop shop, that is.'

'People have started to leave,' Gilchrist said, looking around.
'We probably should go too.'

Grace squeezed Gilchrist's arm. 'You know, as I said, I'd be
grateful if you two would stay on after the rest have gone.'

'I'm useless at washing up,' Gilchrist said.

Grace laughed. 'Not that, I promise. A bit of cop-shop talk
actually.'

'We can't talk about the case,' Gilchrist said quickly.

'But I can,' Grace said. 'I know you're off duty but there's
stuff you might need to know for context.'

'Sure then,' Gilchrist said. Grace looked at Heap. He nodded.

'Great,' Grace said. 'And, you know, I have guest bedrooms
if you want to stay over since I intend to ply myself with drink

and I hope you won't let me drink alone. Let me get rid of everyone else.'

They sat on the large sofa in the high-ceilinged sitting room with the French windows open.

'What did you want to talk about?' Gilchrist said. 'Oh, actually before you tell us that – do you know any men round here who habitually wear red trousers?'

'What . . . a military type you mean? Rabbitt probably. Why?'

'We found footage of someone in red trousers by your lake at the same time Rabbitt was there.'

'But it's not Rabbitt?'

'We don't think so.'

'That's a clue, right? I'll have a think and keep my eyes peeled.'

'What did you want to talk to us about?' Gilchrist said.

'Am I in any danger?'

'Because of what happened to Rabbitt?' Gilchrist said. 'Why would you think so?'

'I just feel very vulnerable. What Reg Dwight said about Rabbitt leaving here the other evening – well, Rabbitt didn't visit me. If he was here he was up to no good – spying on me or worse. It gives me the creeps to think he might have been lurking in my garden, peering through my window. But then when he said if it wasn't Rabbitt it was some other man that really freaked me out. You see I thought someone else was doing that last night.'

'Someone you recognized?'

'I thought I did. He did it once before so maybe that's why. But it couldn't have been him – he lives thousands of miles away.'

'Bellamy, call the local community copper. Get him to liaise with Lewes about a patrol car driving by every hour or so tonight.'

'Ma'am,' Heap said. He went out into the garden and talked quietly into his phone.

Grace sighed. 'Listen, the tabloids are going to pick up the story of the death at my lake soon, if they haven't already. They're going to be doorstepping me and sending drones over and that whole "Whatever happened to Naughty Nimue?" thing is going to start up again.' She wrapped her arms round her body. 'That's what creeps me out more than anything.'

Heap came back in and sat beside Gilchrist.

'I'll be news again,' Grace continued. 'And the questions will start again. Why did you leave Hollywood, Nimue? Why have you retired, Nimue? What happened, Nimue?' She suddenly shouted: 'None of your fucking business!'

Gilchrist and Heap exchanged glances. 'But are there any people who actually might wish to harm you physically?' Gilchrist said.

'Loads who might wish harm on me. You never read the comments underneath articles in the *Daily Pustule*? There are so many people in this country full of hate and bile, especially when it comes to what are perceived as beautiful women and/or luvvies. A beautiful luvvy? That really enrages them.'

'Loads?' Gilchrist said.

'Sure. Have you ever read the novel or seen the film *The Day of The Locust*? Nathanael West wrote it in the late 1930s. Fans of movie stars from the underclass – which is what we have again in this country – feel shortchanged by their favourites and go on the rampage in Hollywood.'

'You think that is what is going to happen to you?'

'Ha! That came out wrong didn't it? No, I went off at a tangent. I didn't mean quite that but there are oddball fans out there who can behave quite frighteningly. Donald Kermode is on the harmless end of the spectrum.

'When I was doing *Cleopatra* in Chichester I needed a bodyguard because of someone obsessed with me who suggested we meet in a café in town and when I didn't turn up – because I never said I would and had no intention of doing that – began to post very aggressive messages to the stage door. All because of my stupid looks.'

'Your career has never been all about your looks,' Heap said.

'Why, Sir Galahad,' Grace said, 'more gallantry.'

Heap flushed, a little smile on his face, but said nothing. Then he excused himself to use the bathroom. Gilchrist and Grace watched him go, then Grace said, almost sadly: 'They'd eat someone as kind and decent as him alive in Hollywood. It's not just that nice guys finish last; it's that they get trampled into dust.'

'Bellamy is a lot tougher and more resourceful than is immediately apparent. I don't think there would be anything he can't handle.'

Grace patted Gilchrist's hand.

'I believe you. You and he . . .?'

'No!' Gilchrist said.

'Oh, I know there's a height difference but that's the usual in Hollywood. That town is full of high-achieving midgets and the taller the woman they can cut down to their size the better they like it. The film business out there was founded on small man syndrome.'

Gilchrist laughed. 'I've met the type. But I've never seen Bellamy exhibit any of that. You know he lives with my best friend, Kate – around the same height.'

Grace nodded. 'I'd forgotten – I'm a bit tipsy. So what happened with you and the chief constable?' She saw Gilchrist stiffen. 'Oh, come on – I know you told me a bit but all the stuff I've told you? And I'm not a suspect, am I?'

'You're still part of an official investigation, Ms Grace,' Gilchrist said primly, though conscious there was a slight slur in her words.

'Of course I am. I respect that. Have another glass of wine and dish.'

Gilchrist barked a laugh just as Heap came back in. The two women both looked across at him. 'Saved by the Bell-amy,' Grace said and snorted. Gilchrist laughed again and a second or two later both were doubled over in fits of giggles, Heap looking on with a bemused smile on his face.

Grace looked up, her eyes watering. 'We weren't laughing at you, Bellamy,' she kind of hiccoughed. 'May I call you Bellamy?' He nodded. 'We were laughing at how daft we were being, right, Sarah?'

'Speak for yourself,' Gilchrist said, setting off a new round of giggles.

'I know about these contagions,' Heap said, grinning despite himself. 'Before you know it the whole village is infected.'

'I can't remember the last time I laughed like that with a girlfriend. Not that I have many girlfriends. Surprising how quickly friends melt away when you're not on the Hollywood radar anymore. Which means, of course, they weren't real friends anyway.'

Gilchrist smiled but Grace saw an awkwardness in it. 'Not that I'm saying we're girlfriends,' she said quickly, looking embarrassed. 'But I hope perhaps we might be.' Now it was Gilchrist's turn to look embarrassed.

'You don't want someone like me as a friend,' Gilchrist said. 'Not someone like you.'

Grace looked disappointed. 'Someone like me is more like someone like you than you might think. I was never like that Nimue Grace you see on the big screen. My entire career I've been waiting to be found out. I'm not this super-sexy movie goddess. I'm just little old frightened me.' She looked down, then up again, a bright smile on her face. 'What was it Rita Hayworth, that other redhead, said? Something like how disappointed men were when they went to bed with Gilda – her sexiest part, just the toss of her hair! – and woke up with Rita.'

'And Cary Grant,' Heap said, clearly wanting to help out. 'He said everybody wanted to be Cary Grant and, actually, so did he – because he was just plain old, tormented Archie Leach from Bristol.'

Grace pointed at Heap dramatically. 'Exactly! You know that other thing about him? The arc of an actor. Who's Cary Grant? Get me Cary Grant. Get me a Cary Grant type. Who's Cary Grant?' Grace suddenly seemed *very* drunk. Heap smiled and nodded. 'Here's one,' Grace continued. 'Knock, knock.'

'Who's there?' Heap asked politely.

'Nimue,' Grace said.

'Nimue who?' Heap said.

'That's show business!' Grace said, giggling again.

Gilchrist stood. 'We'd better leave you to get on. You'll be safe tonight. Well, and every night, actually.'

'I feel more secure,' Grace said. 'I'll see you out through the garden.'

'No need,' Gilchrist said, gathering her things.

'There is cos I have to lock up after you. Makes me feel even safer.'

Heap said: 'These are pretty high walls you've got around your garden. Somebody would have to be pretty determined – and agile – to get in here. You have security though?'

'Alarms on the doors and windows but no cameras.'

Heap glanced at Gilchrist. 'Maybe if something does kick off with the press we can justify the police putting some security cameras in.'

Gilchrist nodded. She was definitely feeling pretty tipsy herself as Grace led them through the French windows onto the terrace. 'Watch out for the uneven flagstones,' Grace called back. 'And don't trip over the trapdoor to the apple cellar. There's a chute underneath and a huge tub that the apples just roll into. I'll show you next time you're here. I'll need to move the skeleton of my mother out of her rocking chair first, of course.'

'Sorry?' Gilchrist said.

'*Psycho*,' Heap said.

'Clever copper. And watch out for the peacock shit. The sods crap everywhere and it stinks.'

'I didn't realize you had peacocks,' Gilchrist said.

'I don't. Horrible, noisy shitting things. The males prance around thinking they are God's gift because of their over-the-top tails. OK, I know that's like Hollywood men again. A neighbour has them but they don't exactly respect property boundaries. They seem to regard my terrace as their toilet for some reason. I wanted to hire a fox to eat them but that isn't feasible alas.'

She stopped at the solid, barred door set in the high Victorian wall. 'A local farmer who did some work for me when I first arrived told me how a fox killed his two peacocks. They nested in a really tall tree in his garden. The local fox could see them but he couldn't get at them. So he ran round the tree, his head cocked, staring at one of the peacocks. The peacock stared back and rolled his head to keep track of the fox as he ran round the tree. The peacock got dizzy and fell out of the tree and, voila, the fox had his dinner.'

Gilchrist laughed. 'I'm not sure I believe that. Sounds a bit like an Aesop's fable.'

'Good story though,' Grace said. 'Drive safely.' She watched them into Heap's car then she closed the big door and they heard the bolts sliding into place.

SIX

Heap was parked outside Gilchrist's flat when she emerged at 7.30 a.m., feeling like death warmed up, as one of her northern colleagues used to say. He jumped out and opened the boot for her suitcase.

'This makes sense, ma'am,' he said. 'You can't be coming back to Brighton every night the hours you're working on the other side of the Downs.'

'Yes, but Pelham House?' Pelham House had been for many years the County Council offices behind the High Street in Lewes until it had been converted into an upmarket hotel.

'If Lewes Police District has got a good arrangement with the hotel, no reason for you not to take advantage of it.'

'I guess. Do you feel as rough as me?'

'Probably worse. I didn't get much sleep last night as Kate wanted to talk. It's her mum's funeral tomorrow.'

'Did you get *any* sleep?'

'Not really.'

'Maybe I should be the one driving,' Gilchrist said. 'Or, better still, we get Sylvia driving and we can both kip in the back.'

'Maybe later in the day. Shall we drop your things off at the hotel then go and check on the dredging at the lake, see Said Farzi and also the ostrich guy?'

'Sounds like a plan. Has it broken in the papers yet?'

'Not a word but I get a sense of the vultures circling. We need to figure out a way to protect Ms Grace.'

'You *are* her Sir Galahad, aren't you?'

'Any woman's Sir Galahad, I hope, ma'am,' Heap said. 'If required. Isn't that what men are supposed to be?'

'Well, women can fend for themselves and maybe act as Dame Galahads for men, Bellamy.'

'I welcome both those things, ma'am. But on those occasions when they aren't able to be that, that is a man's job.'

'You're a good man, Bellamy. Who was Sir Galahad, by the way?'

'You don't want to go there, ma'am,' Heap said. 'Especially with a hangover. I studied the Arthurian legends and the Vulgate Cycle at university and this car journey is not long enough for me even to get in the foothills of what I know.'

'Useful for policing, that *Vulgate Cycle* learning, was it?'

'All these knights looking for the Holy Grail is a kind of investigation . . . It was a little side thing I did out of interest. And Ms Grace has misnamed me. She is thinking of chivalry and courtly love in Provence where a knight pledges to protect a lady. But Sir Galahad – who came late to the Arthurian legends – is essentially a celibate fighting monk who goes in search of and finds the Holy Grail. He's not interested in women – or men, in case you were wondering. In some versions he was actually Sir Lancelot's son by Eleanor, the one who drowned herself—'

'You're right, Bellamy – I don't want to go there.'

Pelham House was down one of the very narrow, steep lanes off the High Street in Lewes. Heap swung the car into the car park and opened the boot to get Gilchrist's bag.

'A quick in and out,' Gilchrist said. 'As somebody said to somebody else – oh, blimey – I must be tired.'

In the foyer they almost collided with Nimue Grace's agent, Kip, coming out of the breakfast room. She was dressed down compared to last night. Tight leather trousers, stilettos and bright pink cashmere roll-neck.

'Hey, Mr and Mrs Policeman – you looking for me?'

'No,' Heap said. 'Should we be?'

'Well, we didn't finish our conversation last night. You got time, come and join me for a coffee in this lounge place here.'

Once Gilchrist had left her bag with the concierge she and Heap joined Kip in the empty lounge.

'I ordered a big pot of coffee,' she said (pronouncing it *corfee*), 'I only take it black but I've ordered milk, hot and cold, for whatever you want.'

'Perfect,' Heap said. 'What was it you wanted to tell us?'

'You said last night that somebody had died. Did you mean the gangster next door got his comeuppance?'

Gilchrist frowned. 'By the gangster next door do you mean Richard Rabbitt at Plumpton Down House?'

'Who he? Nah – I mean the dodgy Moroccan guy who runs the farm next door to Nim and half of the slum properties in your Brighton.'

'No,' Gilchrist said. 'The murdered man was Richard Rabbitt from the Plumpton Down Estate house.'

'You got whoever did it?'

'We're working on it,' Gilchrist said.

'But you don't suspect Nim, do you?' Kip leaned in. 'Because if it's not the Moroccan guy that means she's still under threat from that gangster.'

'Why do you call him a gangster? And how do you know about the slum properties?'

'Cos he is a gangster – blood on his hands for sure – and Nim told me about his real-estate holdings. He's made threats. Made her life a misery. She's all alone there, you know. Doesn't have any man to protect her.'

'She's been receiving a lot of abuse?' Heap said.

'The least of it was a letter circulating around Plumpton saying she was broke and had put her old knickers and bras *and* her breast implants up for sale on eBay. There was another that the "porn star" was £25 million in debt and about to be bankrupt since when her tits sagged she lost her career. FYI – those tits have not sagged one iota and without any work on them either – certainly not implants. She'd still ace the pencil test. Miracles of nature they are.'

'You said death threats "not for the first time"?'

'She hasn't played you the voicemail tapes?'

Gilchrist shook her head and saw Heap frowning.

'Well, she picked very badly,' Kip said. 'You could see why – this guy had a big rep as a method actor – if you like that kind of thing: big hunk, lot of charm, lot of arrogance – like I said, that arrogance thing is something we're both drawn to. Macho – a punching bag was an essential part of his luggage when heading anywhere. All covering up the fact he was a real psycho killer.' She saw Gilchrist's look. 'Oh, not literally. At least I don't think so, but potentially, probably. A genuine socio-path. And certainly where Nim was concerned he became obsessed. And he frequently threatened her with the most disgusting forms of torture and death. That's the voicemails.

'But that's been her problem most of her life. She's *so* charismatic, *so* beautiful, *so* warm and lovely in every way men just get obsessed with her. Women too. I certainly am.'

'Did she do anything about these death threats from this man?' Heap asked.

'Could've but didn't. Lost a lawyer she went to for help because she wouldn't press charges for the sake of the kid. Didn't want her son growing up knowing his dad was a total douche. Well, not just a douche. A mental case.' Kip took a sip of her coffee. 'I'm telling you all this because I assume you guys are like priests and lawyers – all this is confidential, right?'

Gilchrist grunted non-committally. Thinking: *Kid? What kid? I'm sure Grace said she didn't have any children.*

'How long are you here?' Heap said.

'I'm in London for a couple of days then I'm back to LA.'

Gilchrist handed Kip her card. 'Please call me if you think of anything else you feel able to share.'

'Will do. But, hey, do me a favour, will you?'

'What's that?'

'Persuade her to start making movies again. And not just for my fifteen per cent.'

Gilchrist smiled. 'Goodbye, Kip.'

Heap was slow coming out of the hotel. As they drove down the rest of the steep, narrow lane, Gilchrist said: 'She has a kid?'

'She specifically said she didn't have kids,' Heap said.

'I heard that too. OK, let's park that for the moment. Get Sylvia to check out Donald Kermode's restraining order. In fact, we should go and see him to see if he knows anything about Red Pants.'

'Before we see the neighbour, Said Farzi?'

'No, let's make Farzi our priority after we've called by the lake.'

The dredger had two men aboard and two men in waders working beside it in the middle of the lake when Gilchrist and Heap arrived at Beard's Pond. They parked behind an empty police car and put on their wellingtons to walk along the path towards the island and to where Rabbitt's body was found.

The dredger was doing a good job of disturbing the silt and releasing gases. 'What a stink,' Gilchrist said between clenched teeth.

Frank Bilson was standing on the island in waders. He gave a little wave but seemed subdued. Perhaps he was embarrassed by the previous morning.

'Ahoy, Mr Bilson,' Gilchrist called. 'Can we come aboard?'

Bilson gestured towards a thick tree trunk laid as a bridge between the island and the main bank. There was a rope tied between a tree on the bank and a tree on the island. Grabbing hold of the rope to balance himself, Bellamy Heap crossed over nimbly to the island. Gilchrist crossed not-quite-so-nimbly.

'Found his teeth yet, Frank?' Gilchrist said as they approached him. He shook his head. 'Don't suppose they've found his car in there?'

'They haven't found anything,' Bilson said. 'It's proving to be a remarkably uninteresting lake.'

Heap was standing beneath the rickety-looking tree house. 'Have SOCO been up here, Mr Bilson?'

'I'm sure they have but I'm not entirely sure.'

Hanging down from the tree house was a rope knotted at regular intervals. Heap grabbed it and shinned up it, hand over fist.

'Bellamy – you Boy Scout,' Gilchrist called. Bilson looked at her. 'But I guess I already knew that. Are you OK, Frank?'

'Busy. Tired. Otherwise fine.'

'You don't seem your normal ebullient self.'

Bilson just shrugged and turned away to look through a pile of sludge spread in front of him. Gilchrist looked up at the tree house just as Heap was coming back down the rope. 'Anything up there, Tarzan?' she said.

'Interesting perspective on this wood and lake. And you can see the drive up to the big house.' He pointed in the general direction of Plumpton Down House. 'There's a gap in the trees that gives a very clear view pretty much all the way down.'

'So someone up here would be able to see Rabbitt heading down, whether he were on foot or in his car.' Heap nodded.

Gilchrist glanced over at Bilson, who still had his back to her, then said to Heap: 'Nothing more for us here. Shall we get on?'

Once they were in the car, she said: 'Something is eating Bilson and he won't admit it or say what it is.'

'When you phoned him the other morning and he was in that odd mood, he didn't say anything then?'

'Not a thing. But he was out of character during that whole conversation.'

Heap thought for a moment. 'Sometimes when someone is acting apparently out of character they are revealing their true character.'

'To misquote a famous movie star, Bellamy: I can't decide if that is very perceptive or stating the bleedin' obvious.'

Heap smiled. 'And, to misquote my answer to her: I haven't a clue either.'

As they came round the bend at the edge of Grace's wood and orchard below her house they saw a makeshift sign indicating the route to Said Farzi's farm was along a newly carved out temporary road surface. They started along it but realized it petered out pretty soon.

'Work in progress,' Heap said as he reversed out. Gilchrist looked around but couldn't see any signs of mechanical diggers or piles of road material.

'Or work abandoned,' she said.

They went up Grace's drive and drove into the farmyard. Half a dozen men of colour were busily moving around. A strutting, slender man of uncertain ethnicity, wearing jodhpurs and riding boots and carrying a riding whip appeared before them. He introduced himself as the farm manager, Abbas. When they asked him where Said Farzi was, he replied with an affected English accent. 'Away in Morocco tending to his business interests there and seeing family.'

'Do you know when he'll be back?'

'I'm afraid not. Mr Farzi keeps his own hours.'

'Do you know when he went?'

'Three days ago.'

'The day Richard Rabbitt was discovered dead.'

'Who?'

'Your neighbour, Richard Rabbitt. The proprietor of Plumpton Down House.'

'I don't know him. He's dead, you say?'

'He died the night before Mr Farzi went to Morocco. Mr Farzi knew Richard Rabbitt.'

'Mr Farzi may well know him. I don't. I keep myself to myself. I have enough work to do managing the farm.'

'I'm sure you do.' Gilchrist indicated his riding outfit. 'You have horses here too?'

'Just half a dozen.'

'So you're twiddling your thumbs most of the time,' Gilchrist said.

'I beg your pardon?' The farm manager adjusted his cravat. 'I don't understand what you mean.'

'Well, you seem to have quite a few staff here and with only six horses to look after I would think you're struggling to fill up your time.'

'I never struggle to fill my time up. These are Arabian polo horses. They require a lot of attention.'

'I believe Mr Farzi has vineyards. Do you get involved with them?'

'I do not. He has people for that.'

Gilchrist pointed to the whitewashed roofs of two greenhouses sticking out above a crest in a rough trackway between two big barns.

'And the greenhouses?'

'He has plans I'm sure but at the moment they are unused.'

'Mr Farzi doesn't take you into his confidence about his plans?'

'Not until they have come to fruition.'

'How long have you worked for him?' Heap said.

'Ten years more or less.'

'If I may say, you seem a fastidious dresser. Does Mr Farzi share your fastidiousness?'

'In what way?'

'Does he dress the part of a farm owner?' Heap said.

'You'd rather he wore a *djellaba* and a fez?'

'Not at all.'

'He dresses like an English gentleman with a certain station in life.'

'Do you think we might speak to the vineyard manager?' Gilchrist said. 'To see if he knows any more than you?'

'He's not here today. He doesn't live on site. I can give you his phone number if you wish.'

Heap handed Abbas his card. 'When you have a moment email his details through to me.' The farm manager nodded. 'Just out of interest,' Heap continued, 'how many people do you have working here?'

'That depends on the time of year. When it's grape picking time there are dozens.'

'They are day workers from the area?'

'No, no. Students mostly. We put them up in the big barns on bunk beds. It's quite an adventure for them.'

'I'm sure it is. So no foreign workers provided by gang masters?'

The farm manager looked at him for a moment.

'No, no,' he said softly. 'Nothing like that.'

'One final thing,' Gilchrist said. 'I'm sorry to be rude but what is your full name again?'

The farm manager narrowed his eyes. 'My name is Abbas.'

'Excuse my ignorance but is that your first or last name?'

'The only name I use,' he said with a quick nod before turning away from them and strutting back across the yard.

Gilchrist and Heap drove slowly back out.

'What do you think, Bellamy?'

'I think he's a gang master if ever there was one. And I bet he likes to use that whip. And I'd love to take a look in those barns. If there are bunk beds in there I'll eat Katie's swimming cap.'

'What do you mean?'

'I think people are kept like cattle in there. There will be stacks of mattresses.'

'Now?'

'At some time.'

'Workers from the EU?'

Heap shook his head. 'I'm guessing smuggled migrants from the Middle East plus Moroccan and North African and sub-Saharan African people. That man probably has a stack of passports locked away somewhere.'

'We should contact customs and immigration then.' They were driving past Nimue Grace's property. 'Hang on – pull over a minute. Are we going to see Ms Grace?'

Heap nodded. 'We need to find out about this guy who threatened her years before and in what way Said Farzi has been harassing her.'

'Let me just check with Sylvia Wade first.' Gilchrist called her in the office. 'Sylvia – any news on Said Farzi's property portfolio? And did you find out from the drug squad if he has any form or is a person of interest to them?'

'Nothing back from the drug squad. Three hundred properties. Judging by the addresses, all pretty run down.'

'Who lives in them?'

'That I don't know. Yet. I'm in touch with Housing in the Council to get them to do pretend random checks with us. Looking for overcrowding, out-of-date gas safety certificates, that kind of thing. I thought we should concentrate on the apartment buildings he owns – there are about ten of those.'

'I don't suppose you've actually looked up how many properties Richard Rabbitt has in Brighton?'

'No, ma'am. Sorry.'

'No need to apologize. Find out – and throw William Simpson into the mix while you're at it.'

'Ma'am.'

SEVEN

Gilchrist phoned Nimue Grace. 'So sorry to bother you, but we have a couple more questions related to your personal safety. And about Said Farzi. Are you free this morning?'

'Sure – come for coffee.'

'Well, actually, we're just outside – we paid a visit to Said Farzi's place just now.'

'Did you meet the creep?'

'He's in Morocco according to his farm manager.'

'Abbas? He's more than a creep. He's a viper.'

'Shall we come right in?'

'I think you should. The kettle is on.'

Grace was in what seemed to be her uniform of work shirt

and jeans. She was barefoot and without make-up, her vibrant hair tied up and tangled in a red scarf. She looked radiant, which made Gilchrist feel even lumpier and haggard than before.

'I'll make a cafetière.' She glanced across at Gilchrist. 'Unless you'd like hair of the dog?'

'Coffee is fine. Welcome, in fact.'

'Bellamy – can I trust you with the tray if I carry the mugs?'

'You can, Ms Grace.'

'I thought, as it's such a lovely day, we could sit under the California poplar – it's older than any of the buildings round here – over 500 years. It's got an incredibly thick bark.'

'Who would have planted it then?' Heap said.

'The oldest surviving place around here is Danny House, over Hurstpierpoint way, on the Danny Estate – impeccably maintained by the private owner and kind of a bookend in the west to Plumpton Down House here in the east.

'Danny House is much older than Plumpton Down House though. Elizabethan, so the age fits for this poplar. It probably came from a tree over there. I'm guessing some bird coming over from Danny House, dropped a seed over here and – voila. And it got here from California because the Elizabethan age was the age of exploration. Somehow, someone – probably Spanish since they ruled the New World – brought a seed or a cutting of a California poplar over to Europe and it ended up in Sussex.'

'There are roses growing out of it,' Gilchrist declared when they sat at a round table beneath the branches.

'Yes, they're growing out of stumps of sawn-off branches. There are crimson ramblers round the other side. Someone told me the California poplar – they call it a black cottonwood over there – was the first tree genome to be sequenced.' Grace turned her mouth down. 'I know how to say those words but I haven't a clue what they mean.'

Heap was looking round the garden appreciatively and up at Plumpton Hill beyond. 'You have a gardener?'

'That's a sore point. I did. I do it myself now, that's why it's looking so ragged.'

'It's not looking ragged,' Heap said. 'Big garden for one person to look after though.'

'You a gardener, Bellamy?' Grace said, a mischievous look in her eyes.

'Oh, I wasn't volunteering,' he said quickly. 'I was just admiring the fruit beds and those fruit trees against those outbuildings. And these alpine strawberries.'

'You *are* a gardener! Is Kate too? Next time you have a day off bring your trugs and your wellies and we're off!'

'I'm sure we'd like that,' Heap said, suddenly shy.

Grace looked Gilchrist up and down. 'And don't think you're going to be let off lightly, leather chick city girl.'

Gilchrist grinned. 'I always liked the idea of being a land girl actually.'

'In Lycra,' Heap murmured. Grace didn't hear but Gilchrist shot him a grin.

'Great – we're set, then.' Grace pointed at the beds. 'All this stuff has been growing here for 150 years. The gardener back then died falling off a ladder. He lived here and ran the market garden next door – that creep Farzi's place – for the big house. All those disused greenhouses and now what were fields of vegetables are planted with vines.' She looked around. 'I was thinking of following my neighbours into wine production but I don't think I can be bothered. You know one of my neighbours only planted his vines three years ago and he's going to be producing five thousand bottles this year?'

'I hadn't realized how many vineyards there were round here,' Gilchrist said, unintentionally slurping at her coffee. It flustered her. 'Do you mean Said Farzi producing all those bottles?'

'No, not that creep. A neighbour beyond him.'

'We are investigating him but are there other people who are now or have in the past threatened you?' Heap said.

'Are you asking that because of something Kip said at the party last night about violent, aggressive boyfriends?'

Gilchrist nodded. 'And we also bumped into her this morning at Pelham House.'

'*Bumped into her?*' Grace said suspiciously, her face hardening.

'Genuinely,' Gilchrist said. 'I told you last night I was checking in there for the duration of this investigation. She was coming out of breakfast as I was dumping my bags.'

'Loose lips sink Kip,' Grace murmured. 'OK – what did she say?'

'That you've got voice tapes of vile threats including death threats. And she repeated the thing she said last night about you both having fallen for violent, arrogant men.'

Grace's face relaxed. 'Only a couple such men, but two is more than enough.' She sighed. 'It's more that they're controlling men.' She took a sip of her coffee, eyes closed.

When she opened them, Gilchrist was surprised that Heap abruptly said: 'May I ask about that scar by your ear?'

Grace gave him what Gilchrist could only describe as *a look*. 'You're asking if I've had plastic surgery? What possible relevance can that have to your murder inquiries?'

Heap flushed, though not so much as Gilchrist expected he would. 'I'm certain you've not had plastic surgery, Ms Grace, and that wasn't why I was asking. I think you've had a relatively recent injury.'

Grace looked at Gilchrist. 'This one's a keeper, isn't he?' Grace gave them both a searching look then raised her arms above her head and took an extravagant breath. Gilchrist couldn't help but observe that she did still have great breasts.

'It's a few years ago, actually. A man turned up at the door not long after I moved in here. I was wary of everyone because this monster had been leaving vile death threats on my phone and ranting on about sending hitmen for me who would film my slow death on their phones for him to enjoy for ever. My eyes bugging out of my head as I was strangled, that kind of thing.' Grace looked off into the distance.

'And this unknown man turned up. I tried shouting through the door to him to ask him what he wanted and when he didn't reply I didn't open up. But he kept hammering on the door. He just wouldn't go away.'

'Was he the man who had been making the death threats?'

'No – as I said, this one was unknown. A ferrety man.'

'You mean you knew the man making death threats?'

'Unfortunately, yes. But please let me tell this my way. At right angles to the door there are a couple of old, leaded windows. I could see him standing at the front door, his hands in his coat pockets. I opened a window a bit and shouted to him that I wanted him to go away, that I wouldn't open the door for him. He was startled as it took a moment for him to locate where my voice was coming from but then he dashed towards the window, taking something from his pocket as he got nearer.

'It was a small glass bottle. I started to close the window and then he threw something from the bottle at me. Pretty much all of it hit the window but a drop or two caught me near my ear and on my shoulder and arm. The pain was worse than any pain I'd ever felt and I knew immediately what it was. You've got to realize this was years before the spate of acid attacks perpetrated by pathetic, cowardly men happened.

'But as a child actor I'd done one of those Jeremy Brett *Sherlock Holmes* things very early in my career before I hit the movies and in that the villain used acid to ruin the features of the women he used then discarded. Apparently acid attacks were all the rage in Victorian times, although, I'm sorry to say, it was, in those days, usually a woman's weapon of revenge.

'Anyway I knew what to do to try to limit the damage. I managed to call for an ambulance but by the time it arrived what damage there was to be done had been done. They took me to hospital and dressed my wounds and kept me in overnight. I agreed to stay, more to handle the shock of what had happened than the happening itself. It took a while to heal but I wasn't going out of the house much so nobody knew what had happened.'

'You didn't report it?'

'What was the point? I knew who was behind it but they'd never get him for it. I was just relieved nobody in the hospital tipped off the press. But I use Vivien Grace as my name on everything and people don't always twig.'

'The police could have warned him off if you'd reported it.'

'Who? The perpetrator or the man behind the attack? There was no way of tracing the perpetrator. He disappeared. And the other guy? Yeah, right – like he's scared of the police. He's rich and untouchable.'

'Nobody is untouchable,' Gilchrist said.

'I really wish that were true,' Grace said. 'Especially in Hollywood. The money-men there aren't just in it for the money you know. You know from this whole Me Too thing, money-men can be in it more for the beautiful women, whether the beautiful women like it or not. And most of the women endure it unless it gets really degrading. And, even then, some of them endure it in return for seeing their name in lights . . .'

'Is this man one of the money-men?'

Grace shook her head.

'But I'm not going to tell you who he is, so you can stop asking.'

'That could be interpreted as obstructing the police in the performance of their duties – not to mention hindering a murder investigation,' Gilchrist said, but without much strength in her voice.

'Oh, please. I don't for a moment think he had anything to do with Richard Rabbitt's death.'

'That's for us to decide. Is he the man you thought you had seen at your window?'

Grace nodded.

'Have you met William Simpson?' Heap said.

'Name rings a bell but I meet a lot of people and remember hardly anyone. The nature of the social side of my business. When I was in the business. And had a social side to me.'

'You still work though?' Heap said.

'But as out of the spotlight as possible if that doesn't sound paradoxical coming from an actor.'

'But you need to act to be, I don't know, complete?' Heap said.

Grace laughed a full-throated laugh. 'I need to act to pay the mortgage on this place. I'm determined not to lose it but it costs me a bloomin' arm and a leg. The outgoings are relentless. If I had enough money I'd never act again.'

'What would you do?' Gilchrist said.

'I wouldn't mind having a go at being a potter. Or painting in acrylics.'

'No offence, Ms Grace,' Heap said shyly, 'but the world is full of potters and painters. I'm sure you'd be very good at both but you have a rare talent for acting and, if I may, you still have a lot to give.'

Grace looked at him for a long moment without speaking. He blushed. Naturally. She smiled softly. 'Why, Detective Sergeant Heap, I feel quite overcome.' She reached out and touched his hand. Gilchrist saw him try hard not to flinch. He didn't much like being touched. Grace didn't notice. 'That's the nicest thing anyone has said to me for quite some time.' She looked round the room. 'I'm out of the habit of receiving kindnesses.'

'It wasn't kindness, Ms Grace. It was the truth.'

'I believe you. But I've lost the enthusiasm for acting, truth be told. Had it beaten out of me.'

'Who did the beating?' Gilchrist said.

'The man who issued the death threats. Before then it had been a long-sustained low-key attack that increased in tempo from someone who should have been my support. OK, he was a fellow actor. So, listen to this. My first night as Cleopatra on Broadway. Wanting to be taken seriously as an actress because I've always felt I am a serious actress but the *Daily Pustule* and the other tabloids had other ideas.

'I was a wreck through most of the rehearsals but the director was marvellous, the rest of the cast were impossibly patient with me. They were proper actors and I was Naughty Nimue, better known for being the sexual predator in the film that got me that nickname than for her acting.

'We'd been having our ups and downs, me and this anonymous man, which wasn't helping. But he turned up in New York for the first night. I was so thrilled. We hadn't seen each other for a month. I didn't see him before the show but he sent flowers to the dressing room, the whole thing.

'I remember that I was sick before I went on stage. The first and only time but I was so nervous. I had a lot to prove. But once I was on stage I flew. I could feel it. You know that phrase we use now: "being in the zone"? Well, I was definitely in the zone. I stayed in it during the interval and I really enjoyed the second half. Now New Yorkers are a tough audience but when the curtain went down and then back up for our call, the place erupted.'

'I remember reading the reviews,' Heap said.

'But this was before the reviews. This wasn't the critics. This was the audience response. Although the critics in New York have the power to close a show I only care about what the audience thinks. So there was this standing ovation that went on and on. So many bows. When I finally went backstage I thought he'd be in the dressing room but he wasn't.

'Didn't matter. There was a party afterwards at a nearby restaurant and I knew he'd be there. So the cast popped a couple of bottles backstage and we told each other how wonderful we'd been and how we'd nearly fluffed this and thought we had messed up that and hugged and kissed and all loved each other. And we did love each other – a company of actors working together forge such strong bonds – at least for the length of the run and, with luck, long after.

'So I go to the party and we have to pass through the downstairs restaurant and I hear chairs scraping back and when I look every person at every table is standing and I get a standing ovation from the customers in there too. So I get upstairs quite breathless. And I'm getting hugs and kisses and more congratulations as I edge slowly into the room and all the time I'm looking for him. He's tall, I'll tell you that much, so he's easy to spot.

'And finally as I reach the middle of this crowd of people I see him at the back of the room. He's looking at me with a big smile on his face. He raises his hands beside his head and gives me a little clap and a nod. I beckon him over but he shakes his head, gestures to all the people trying to get at me to say how wonderful I was and taps his watch, which I take to mean we'll have time later. All night, in fact.

'So I let myself be congratulated and there are brief speeches saying how wonderful I am and how long that lasts I have no idea. And if you're wondering how much acclaim one actor can take I can tell you – a limitless amount. It's never enough. But there's plenty more to come for me. Except that he suddenly appears in front of me and lifts me up at the waist – he's strong as well as tall – and throws me over his shoulder in a fireman's lift and says to those around us: "she'll wave goodbye as she leaves".

'And to me: "I can't wait any longer." And I find this a mixture of exciting and romantic and I-don't-know-what so as a way parts through the crowd, with everyone laughing and smiling, I'm waving at people from halfway down his back and saying "I have to go" and all sorts of inanities and then we're out in the street and he deposits me in the back of a waiting taxi.

'As we set off I start to say that was unexpected and fun but I hadn't actually finished thanking people but he puts his finger against my lips and says a line from the play: "Other women cloy the appetites they feed but she makes hungry where most she satisfies." Then he kisses me and, of course, everything goes from my head until after we've reached my room and had sex together for the first time in a month.'

She pauses in her headlong story.

'And then, after, we're lying side by side – he was never a cuddler, which I didn't notice at the time but is a signifier, I believe – and I said again that I hadn't finished at the party when he so romantically carried me away. "Couldn't you have curbed your lust a little longer," I clearly remember I said in a half-teasing, half-serious way. "It was nothing to do with lust," he growled, "I just couldn't stand any more people crawling up your ass complimenting you on a performance that was so false and contrived and so utterly crap in every way."'

Grace looked down.

'The reviews said otherwise,' Heap said after a silence. Grace smiled.

'*Everybody* said otherwise. But whose voice am I going to listen to? The voice of a man I think I'm in love with – because I'm confusing lust with love – who I think is a tremendously talented actor. Largely because he has told me that he is, I realize with hindsight, since all he can actually play is the psychopath that he is.

'But his is a voice that chimes in with my own secret fear that I've only got the parts and the acclaim because of my looks. Well, and, in one case, because my pubic hair proved I am a genuine redhead when I did the infamous bottomless rather than topless scene in one movie. Though on that occasion I was wearing a merkin as well so I wasn't actually doing a Sharon Stone.'

'What happened in the rest of the run,' Heap asked gently.

'The reviews came out the next morning and were uniformly glowing for me. But for the rest of that week I kept chopping and changing how I did it, much to the confusion of my fellow cast members. But each performance I was imagining he was in the audience judging me – and his approval of me was the only thing that mattered. By the Friday he'd given grudging approval for a flabby performance that scarcely earned me a curtain call. On the Saturday we had a row – or rather he rowed with me – and he left New York for Los Angeles. On the Sunday I quit the production citing ill health.'

Grace sat quietly, clasping and unclasping her hands.

'If you don't mind my asking,' Heap said, 'was he a less successful actor than you?'

Grace smiled at him.

'You *are* a clever copper! Only later did I realize he was seething with jealousy at my success. Always had done but I hadn't realized it because his putdowns were so subtle. He was a talented actor within a narrow range. But he had no genuine warmth on camera. The camera saw that – it really doesn't lie. He has made his living playing sociopaths really well, except, of course, I realized later, as I said, that he wasn't actually acting – that was him. He couldn't convincingly manufacture genuine emotions and he couldn't summon them from within himself using the Method he wanked on about all the time because his only true emotion was – is – narcissism.' She sighed. 'Is that even an emotion? He used to travel everywhere with a punching bag. Took it with him to wherever he was filming. He said it was the best way to keep fit but it was just to push this macho image.'

'So to pump himself up he needed to pull you down,' Gilchrist said. 'And did he destroy your career?'

'Pretty much, I'm angry to say. I was traumatized by him and associated him with Hollywood and couldn't go back. But that's what he set out to do.' She sat back and spread her hands. 'I may as well tell you. His name is George Bosanquet.'

'The South African actor?' Heap says. 'He *does* always play psychopaths.'

'The very same – except, as I said, he isn't playing. He *is* a psychopath.' Grace leaned back. 'I've just shared my biggest secret with you. And now you have the story the tabloids would pay a fortune for.'

'Your story is safe with us,' Gilchrist said.

'Tell that to Cliff Richard,' Grace said.

'We are not those police,' Gilchrist said.

Grace smiled. 'I believe you. I hope I don't live to regret that, as I have so often.'

'You won't,' Heap said. 'You have our word.'

'You don't strike me as the kind of woman who'd let that happen without fighting back,' Gilchrist said.

'You can fight back or you can go round,' Grace said.

'So do you mean you did that and now you don't feel beaten?'

'I mean I've learned better how to be the self I want to be.'

'Perhaps you could teach the rest of us,' Gilchrist said with a grin.

'Ha. I think it would only work for me. Not that it's made me a better judge of men, which is why I keep away from them. I can't afford to lose my heart again.' She looked down.

'You say you've never had children . . .' Gilchrist started cautiously.

Grace looked up and scanned her face. 'In Hollywood having children is complicated. There are those women who won't have children at all because their bodies are their livelihood and they don't want to mess up their perfect breasts or put on weight they won't be able to lose or, and this is remarkably prevalent, mess up their vaginas with the birth. On that latter point, as one actress said to me – who, I admit is one of those who takes her own casting couch to auditions: "Which of those guys want to put their little Johnsons in the Grand Canyon?"'

'And in your case?'

Grace wrinkled her nose. It was very distracting. 'I thought I was pregnant by Bosanquet. It went something like this. I tell him that and he says: "I don't want a fucking kid with you." I say: "Then why did you have unprotected sex?" He says: "It's not my job to protect you. That's your problem. Real men don't wear condoms. And anyway you didn't seem to mind me riding you bareback." I say: "I thought we were making a baby." He says: "I have no memory of that conversation."

'We did have that conversation. He was desperate to have a child with me and my hormones were raging and I was in lust with him. He was the chosen one because the time was right. But I realized why he was so keen for me to have a baby when I took refuge here and he got my number. He didn't know if I'd had a baby or not. But he left me vile messages saying my career was over now because I only got work because of my body and now everything would be bloated then saggy and who would want to fuck me?'

'Bastard,' Gilchrist muttered.

'As I said, a sociopath and a narcissist,' Grace said. 'Hollywood attracts the most charming ones. But he didn't just say vile things when I told him about the pregnancy. He beat me up and kicked me in the stomach.'

'So he didn't want kids?'

'*Au contraire*. As I said, he liked the idea of me being pregnant because he thought it would fuck up my career and my figure and it would take me off the table, so to speak. He was a jealous guy. He raged: "I'm supposed to believe it's mine. A whore like you putting out for every actor in Hollywood and I'm supposed to think it's mine?" Well, I wasn't exactly a nun but I wasn't that either.'

'What happened next?'

'He beat me up in a kind of a public place. The police were called and he was arrested. The police really wanted me to press charges but I wouldn't.'

'Why?'

'Because if I was pregnant with his child, I didn't want our child growing up knowing his or her father was a douche.'

'What did you do about the pregnancy?'

'Actually, I wasn't pregnant. My periods had stopped because of some stupid diet I was on.'

Gilchrist tried not to frown. She was still wondering why Kip had casually mentioned a child as if it were a fact. 'Tell us about the trouble you've been having with Said Farzi.'

'He owns the farm. And various properties in Brighton. He could probably give that legendarily nasty piece of work – what was he called, Rachman? – a run for his money on intimidating slum dwellers. Not to mention single female neighbours.'

'He's tried to intimidate you?' Gilchrist said.

'At first it was seduction – if you can call it that. When he first moved in several years ago he invited me round and offered to buy this place. Stroked my face – yech – and said I could still live here rent free. We both knew what that meant. He assumed a single woman living next door would let him fuck her. When I wasn't interested he took against me.'

'Enough to want to kill you?' Heap said.

'Well, not just for that – I have an ego but I don't fall for my own sex siren image. But there has been a constant bombardment.'

Gilchrist looked at the white knuckles of Grace's clasped hands. Her mellifluous voice had gone up half an octave.

'That's horrible – but exactly what kind of intimidation?'

'Bullying ever since. That drive you came up belongs to me but he has access rights to the farm. He's supposed to contribute to maintenance costs but when I politely asked he went ballistic.'

Grace's face had changed so remarkably as she spoke that she might have been a different person. Her mouth was set in an almost agonized downward grimace, her chin jutting out. It was an astounding transformation from someone who had looked so effortlessly beautiful a moment ago.

Gilchrist stood. 'I'm sorry to hear this. We're going to leave you now – we have a lot of work to do today, including investigating this.'

'We're going to follow up on these things,' Heap said. 'We're making rapid progress on all fronts. Be of good cheer, Ms Grace. Nobody is going to harm you.'

Grace stood and took Gilchrist's hand. 'Bless you both.'

Back in the car Gilchrist looked at Heap. 'That was a bit of a confident statement, wasn't it, Bellamy?'

'We have to believe in ourselves more than in the system, don't we ma'am?'

'You *are* a good man. Now, you know what I'm going to ask you, Bellamy.'

'It's a pubic wig, ma'am.'

'There are such things?'

'More things in heaven and earth ma'am, than we can dream on.'

'I don't think I'd ever dream on – or even of – a pubic wig. Or, what did she call it? A *merkin*?'

'Then you're not a true modern Brightonian, ma'am, if I may say.'

'I'm worried about Bilson. He's unusually subdued. I'm going to call him.' Just then her phone rang. 'I swear that man is telepathic. Hello, Bilson. Your ears must have been burning.'

There was a silence on the other end of the phone then:

'Not as much as yours, DI Gilchrist,' barked Chief Constable Karen Hewitt. 'What the hell do you think you're doing?'

'I'm not sure I understand, ma'am,' Gilchrist said, cursing herself for not checking who had called her.

'Well, you know jurisdictional issues are sensitive between the districts in this division. Yet, according to reports, here you and DS Heap go tromping in your wellies and Barbours over the districts of Haywards Heath and Lewes as if they were your private fiefdoms. So, I repeat my question, what the hell do you think you're doing?'

'Investigating a murder, ma'am. As I understood it, at Lewes's invitation. We have been seconded to Lewes district, if you recall, ma'am.'

'But the investigator from Haywards Heath district is back from leave and is eager to get his teeth into this murder. It seems this crime occurred at a cross-section of jurisdictional something or other. Which puts you in the crosshairs.'

'We are making good and rapid progress, ma'am.'

'Well, back in your actual district, in this sleepy little town called Brighton, there is the torture and murder of a young student called Joe Jackson in a block of flats on the seafront. Do you think you can drag yourself out of the cow pats and get back to uncivilized civilization?'

'Of course, ma'am. Who should I liaise with in Haywards Heath?'

'An experienced detective sergeant called Donald Donaldson.'

'Don-Don?' Gilchrist was worried her voice had become a screech.

'Oh, yes, your paths have probably crossed since he used to be stationed in Brighton, didn't he?'

'He did,' Gilchrist said flatly. 'I thought he was at Gatwick failing to sort out drone attacks?'

'They were sorted out and he is on secondment, I imagine. Is there a problem between you two I should know about? Anything personal?'

'No, ma'am. Certainly not. Nothing.' Except the guy was a total, steroid-using, body-building nutjob.

'OK then. I'd like you to drop whatever you're doing there right away and get down lickety-split to the crime scene here. I'd like you to come and see me at 8 a.m. tomorrow to hand over your files and notes to DS Donaldson.

'This Brighton killing was uncovered because of some kind of Council Housing department raid. We don't know yet when Jackson was killed. Frank Bilson has been summoned. There's a worry it's some kind of gang thing. Most of the other occupants of the apartment block are Moroccan and Sudanese. These communities have integrated really well in Brighton in the past twenty years but there is a rogue element, as there is in every community.'

'Ma'am,' Gilchrist said, then realized she was talking into an empty phone. She sighed. 'Shit.' Her phone rang again.

'It's Sylvia Wade, ma'am. In the course of checking Said Farzi's properties – and we have found enough irregularities to get him into court pronto – we found a young man who appeared to have been beaten to death. Some indication of torture. Name of Joe Jackson. I think you may be about to get a call from the chief constable about it.'

'We already did.'

'I'm sorry I didn't give you the heads up in time.'

'Not your fault. Where was this?'

'Nobby Court. One of those rundown apartment blocks on the seafront towards Hove. Most of the flats in the block were stuffed with mattresses piled up against walls. This flat was halfway decent. It looked like a student place judging by the posters on the wall, the dirty washing on the floor and the sink full of washing up.'

'Do you know anything about this Joe Jackson?'

'Not yet but his laptop and phone were there. Both cheap – he's not an Apple kid.'

'OK – thanks, Sylvia. Probably see you in a while.'

Gilchrist looked at Heap. 'I'm not sure how much of that you caught.'

'We've got to go back to Brighton. But there's a connection with Said Farzi.'

'Both those things are true. But – and remember you're driving precious cargo here when I tell you this – we have to debrief

Don-Don. He's our liaison in Haywards Heath. The chief constable wants him to take over the investigation round here for the moment.'

'Sod that,' Heap said.

'Bellamy! I've never known you curse before – I thought only I was allowed to do that.'

'Sorry, ma'am. But Donaldson? We can't let him loose on Ms Grace.'

'I'm not sure you've got your policing priorities in order there, Detective Sergeant, but I will let that pass since I know where you are coming from. However, Ms Grace has told us all she knows – she says – so he shouldn't need to bother her, unless it turns out she's lying.'

'With respect, ma'am, the minute Donaldson sees her name he is going to find an excuse to question her and probably gloat over her.'

'Why don't we see how much we can get done before we need to hand over to Donaldson? Who knows, maybe we can wrap it all up before he needs to be involved at all.'

'I like the thought but, with respect, I believe it unlikely,' Heap said.

'Well, me too, Bellamy, but no need to rain on my parade.'

'Ma'am.'

'You're a good man, Bellamy. If it's of any interest, I too want to protect Ms Grace from Donaldson or, actually, anybody who wishes her harm. I like her and I think she's a decent person. However, I don't know where we go from here.'

'We ignore Donaldson, I'd say,' Heap said.

'No offence, Bellamy, but that's easy for you to say since I take it in the neck, not you. And incidentally, partner, never use the phrase "with respect" as you did earlier because we both know it indicates there is a total absence of respect in what you are about to say. I deserve better.'

Heap slowed down and looked across at her.

'You're right. I'm very sorry. I was a bit discombobulated.'

'Well, that would be a first.'

'Not at all, ma'am. Believe me.'

'Before we head to Brighton, let's call by Plumpton Down House and see if Ms Knowles and Ms Granger have located Rabbitt's diary. And his car.'

EIGHT

As they parked outside the main door of the house, Heap said: 'DC Wade told me everybody who had been staying at the house on Sunday night has been interviewed. Nobody admits to seeing Rabbitt later than mid-afternoon, when a couple of long weekenders from Rawtenstall, wherever that is, saw him tinkering with the Lego.'

'He wasn't putting a Lego dead body in the Lego lake was he, in an act of clairvoyance?' Gilchrist said.

They went into the house and stopped to survey the scene in the reception hall. 'It looks like someone else has been tinkering with the Lego,' Gilchrist said.

'I'd say so, ma'am.'

The model village Rabbitt had constructed was scattered in big and small pieces all over the floor. They looked up. Rhoda Knowles was standing at the top of a flight of stairs, in front of a portrait of Richard Rabbitt. Gilchrist raised a questioning eyebrow. Rhoda Knowles shrugged and started down the stairs.

'Mrs Rabbitt is back in residence,' she said by way of explanation as she joined them. 'She felt her place was here to comfort the children, who have been taken out of school.' She gestured at the plastic debris. 'She suggested to them it would be helpful for them and her to express their sorrow by destroying Rabbitt's pride and joy, which they were never allowed to touch.'

'She hasn't had a go at his magic lantern stuff as well, has she?'

'I think she has other plans for that.'

'Is she in the left wing now?'

Knowles shook her head. 'The boys are, with a private tutor the major employs now and again. Mrs Rabbitt is in Ditchling. Doing a yoga class, I believe. Or possibly having a coffee with a friend in the museum there.'

'She doesn't strike me as the museum type,' Heap said.

'They do excellent coffee there,' Knowles said. 'And I think she's hoping the museum might want to buy the magic lantern and slides.'

'Is that hers to sell at this stage?'

'A moot point but Tallulah is saying nothing.'

'She's back then?'

Knowles nodded.

'Any joy with the diary or the computer?' Gilchrist said.

Knowles shook her head. 'Ms Granger told me of her theory that someone staying in the right wing was an opportunist thief but I'm not sure I agree. I always keep the left wing locked and Major Rabbitt was even more security aware.'

'I don't suppose he had CCTV fitted inside the house?' Heap said.

'Although he was considering it, Major Rabbitt was reluctant to enter the twenty-first century. Actually, he had not long moved into the twentieth.'

'No CCTV cameras on the outside of the house?' Gilchrist said.

'Actually there are but they are never switched on.'

'Can you remember if Major Rabbitt had any appointments in his diary for Sunday?' Gilchrist said. 'For lunch perhaps? Or in the evening with Ms Grace, for instance?'

Rhoda Knowles pursed her lips. 'As I believe I've already told you, he kept his weekends free from appointments. Especially Sundays. If he had an appointment with Ms Grace – which would surprise me – that would come under the heading of his social life. I'm not privy to his social life.'

'You didn't have lunch with him in the Jolly Sportsman on Sunday?' Heap said.

Knowles frowned. 'No. Was he there?'

'We have a report he was seen there with a woman.'

'I don't know anything about that. It wasn't me. Do you have a description of the woman?'

'Nothing except to say they were on very intimate terms.'

Knowles moved her mouth and jaw as if she were trying to swallow something. 'Were they?' she said flatly.

'They were,' Gilchrist said.

'Any thought about where his mobile phone might be?' Heap said.

'He didn't have one,' Knowles said in a monotone. 'That's why he needed a secretary.'

Gilchrist nodded and looked at Heap. He gave a little shake of his head. 'Very well then,' Gilchrist said. 'That'll be all for now.'

'You don't want to speak to Ms Granger?'

'Not just now.'

As they turned to leave, Knowles called: 'At least we have one mystery solved.'

Gilchrist half turned. 'We do?'

'The major's car. Mrs Rabbitt drove up in it. Though how she got it I have no idea.'

Ditchling Museum was by the duck pond in the centre of the medieval village. It was in an L-shape, comprising a refurbished barn with an in-keeping modern extension.

'What Knowles said about the coffee reminded me of an ad from way back for the V&A I read about,' Heap said. 'It made good coffee the litmus test of a good museum. The strap line for the ads was something like: "An ace caff with quite a nice museum attached."'

'I'm not big on museums,' Gilchrist said. 'Don't see the point really. What's past is past.'

'I'm *very* sorry to hear you say that, ma'am,' Heap said. 'I think that both personally and generally history is crucial to our existence. Not so much that you can learn from the past but that it should be part of your present and future living.'

'That's over my head, I'm afraid, Bellamy. And, frankly, a bit New Age. I'd rather talk about the fact that, judging by her reaction to the news of Rabbitt's rendezvous with some woman in the Jolly Sportsman, he was definitely getting his leg over Rhoda Knowles. I don't mean to sound cynical but we should be able to take advantage of that to prise open Rabbitt's business dealings.'

'If she knows what they are,' Heap said.

'Oh, I think she knows far more than she's letting on – or that Rabbitt realized she knew.'

'Should we go to the Jolly Sportsman too?'

'For sure.'

They parked by the duck pond and walked up to the glass-fronted entrance.

'It's mostly Eric Gill stuff in here,' Heap said, 'but they have exhibitions of forgotten local artists from time to time.' He paused at a poster attached to the glass door. 'Bill Parrett at the moment.'

'Who is Eric Gill?' Gilchrist said.

'He gave his name to one of the most famous – and elegant – typefaces but he was also a sculptor. He lived here back in the twenties and thirties. This museum is dedicated to him and his colleagues. He was a bit of a bastard. Obsessed with sex, including sex with his daughters, his sisters and even with the family dog. He lived at Sopers here in Ditchling and then over on Ditchling Common.'

'I don't think the Me Too movement would approve.'

'I don't think anyone should.'

On the other side of the door there was a long foyer with books and museum gift shop stuff down either side and tables and chairs down the middle. The ticket office at the far end served as the barista counter too. Liesl Rabbitt was sitting with another woman deep in conversation at a table near the counter, coffee cups in front of them. Rabbitt looked up and saw them but continued her conversation. Her eyes never left them, however.

Gilchrist stopped in front of her while Heap went to the counter. A smiling young woman said to him: 'Are you here for the book signing? Just go on through to your left there.'

'Book signing?'

'Well, pamphlet really. About the Hassocks blockade?' She pointed at a low pile of pamphlets beside the till. 'The author is in the Eric Gill room signing copies. You've missed the talk I'm afraid – but the signing means you do get into the museum free. There's a lovely lot of paintings to see by the late Bill Parrett too. Very English, very Sussex.' She gestured at a postcard in front of Heap. 'Children flying kites on Wolstonbury Hill with their mum; blustery white clouds in a pale blue sky; green, green grass. I love it.'

'I love it too,' Heap said, 'but I'll have to come back another time to see the exhibition.' Heap ordered two coffees and bought the postcard and the pamphlet. By now, Gilchrist was sitting beside Mrs Rabbitt. Heap glanced at Rabbitt's friend. Perhaps another Albanian-Greek since she had the same broad face. She too had blonde hair that looked like straw because of all the chemicals used to dye it. Her expression was hard.

'We'd like to ask you a few more questions,' Gilchrist was saying to Liesl Rabbitt. 'I don't know if your friend could excuse us or if you're happy to talk in front of her.'

'She can stay if she wants. She knows my situation only too well.'

The woman looked at her watch.

'No – I have to go. Let's have lunch in the Bull in an hour.'

She got up and sauntered out just as the coffee arrived for Heap and Gilchrist. 'Do you want more?' Heap asked Mrs Rabbitt. She shook her head.

'I see you've moved back into Plumpton Down House,' Gilchrist said.

'How else can I give my children the attention they deserve?'

'What happened with the Lego?'

Rabbitt shrugged. 'The boys needed to let off steam. Do you know how frustrating it was for them to have this giant Lego thing and not be allowed to play with it? Well, now they can.'

'What are you doing about your café?' Heap asked.

'Closing it for the time being. It is impossible to get the staff anyway in this *cray cray* country. Where else in the world would the government give a huge contract to a ferry company that has no ferries, no money and whose terms and conditions on its website are cut and pasted from a pizza takeaway shop? That's what your government has done, I see from the newspapers. Anyway, now my sole focus must be on my children and sorting out my late husband's estate.'

'Are you the executor of his will?'

'I am his wife.'

'Estranged wife,' Gilchrist said. 'Where are your children now?'

'At home, I presume. With their tutor.'

'Mrs Rabbitt, what are you doing with your husband's car?' Heap asked.

'Driving it.'

'I mean – how did you get it?'

'My husband allows me to use it whenever I want to. Allowed me.'

'Really?' Heap said. 'He gave you the keys when?'

'I have the spare set.'

'When exactly did you borrow the car on this occasion?' Heap said patiently.

'Well, I didn't *exactly* borrow it. Major Rabbitt left it with me when he was too drunk to drive.'

'OK,' Heap said. 'But when?'

'Sunday afternoon. He turned up out of the blue at the café, which was closed. I keep my Sundays sacred.'

'You're religious?'

Rabbitt laughed a harsh laugh. 'Religious about having a good time on Sundays, yes.'

'You told us you hadn't seen him for a while,' Heap said.

'Did I? I must have forgotten.'

'Were you with him at the Jolly Sportsman at Sunday lunch-time?' Gilchrist said.

'No. He was there with some floozy? That would explain why he arrived drunk.'

'What did he want?' Gilchrist said.

'To pay me off.' Rabbitt looked into the dregs of her coffee. 'He wouldn't divorce me because he knew I could take him to the cleaners so he hoped to get me to agree not to go after the big money by offering me a different deal.'

'What kind of different deal?'

'Shares in a new business opening he was discussing with that Moroccan guy.'

'Properties in Brighton?'

Rabbitt wrinkled her nose. It looked grotesque on such a hard face but maybe it was the only part of her Botoxed face she could move.

'Something else.'

'Can you say what?'

'He didn't go into specifics.'

'Legal?' Heap asked.

Rabbitt gave him a long look. 'He didn't go into specifics,' she repeated.

'We're going to need to impound the car,' Gilchrist said as

Heap pulled out his phone to call Sylvia Wade. 'There might be evidence in there.'

'How are me and the boys supposed to get around?'

'You don't have your own car?'

Rabbitt grunted.

'Where is his car now?'

'The car park of the Bull.'

'We can give you a lift back to Plumpton Down or into Lewes if you want to pick up your own car.'

'Now? Only I'm supposed to be having lunch with my friend in an hour.'

'Now,' Gilchrist said, as Heap finished his call.

The local community policeman took the car keys from Rabbitt as they all gathered in the pub car park on the other side of the High Street. He said he would drive Mrs Rabbitt into Lewes to get her car. Gilchrist and Heap left them there and drove over to the Jolly Sportsman.

They'd phoned ahead and the manager, a Sarah Loudon, was waiting. She was a striking brunette in a blouse and slacks.

'Major Rabbitt was sitting over in the corner there with a younger woman. Sunday lunch is probably our busiest time – our busiest family time too. I didn't approve at all of the way he was behaving. I asked him politely to refrain.'

'They were kissing?' Gilchrist said.

'Well, he had his tongue down her throat for certain but he was pretty much groping her.'

'Did they stop?'

'Not immediately. I had to ask him again more firmly.'

'Did they settle down then?'

'They left. Without paying for the bottle of wine he'd ordered and half drunk but I was just glad to get them out of here.'

'Did they arrive drunk?' Gilchrist said.

'I didn't see but my waitress said they were.'

'Is he a regular here?'

'Not to drink but to bring people to eat, yes.'

'And has he behaved like that before?'

Loudon shook her head. 'He's usually busy making not-so-subtle suggestions to me. He's a creep.'

'Was a creep. He was murdered that evening.'

Loudon put her hand to her mouth, her eyes widening. 'Well, I'm sorry for anyone who is murdered,' she finally said. 'But I can't actually say I'm *sorry* sorry. I don't think he was a very nice man at all.'

'Did you know the woman he was with?'

'To be honest I thought it was his wife – ex-wife? – the hard-faced blonde. But it was some other woman. Similar though.'

'Really? Gilchrist said. 'I don't suppose we could borrow you for twenty minutes to see if you recognize this woman.'

'You know who she is?'

'Possibly. With luck she's sitting in the Bull in Ditchling.'

'You want me to confront her?'

'No, no, nothing like that. To be honest, I want you to sneak a peek at her and tell me if it's her.'

'Sounds a bit cloak-and-dagger,' Loudon said cautiously.

'Doesn't it? But you'd be doing us a great favour.'

Loudon ran her fingers through her hair. 'Then sure.'

Heap left Gilchrist and Loudon in the car and hurried into the Bull.

'Was Mark Harrison in your place on Sunday?' Gilchrist said.

'Ostrich Man? Sure, just briefly.'

'He's a regular?'

'Well, for a drink. He doesn't often eat with us, even though we occasionally buy ostrich meat off him. Occasionally because people are cautious about it.'

'Have you tried it?'

Loudon shook her head. 'I'm vegetarian.'

Heap came back. 'She's in the back room sitting on her own – Mrs Rabbitt hasn't joined her yet – looking at her phone. If you're willing, Ms Loudon, we can do a walk through without her even noticing.'

'OK,' Loudon said.

'I'll stay here,' Gilchrist said. 'Going in mob-handed will only draw attention.'

While she waited she phoned Sylvia Wade. 'What's happened with Joe Jackson?'

'His body has been moved to the path lab and SOCO are still

at the crime scene, of course. I'm not sure there is much you can do here today, ma'am, if it's more important you stay there.'

Heap and Loudon came out of the pub. As they approached the car, Heap nodded. Gilchrist got out. 'OK – you've been very helpful, Ms Loudon. Thank you so much. We may need to take a statement from you but I assume you can be reached at the Sportsman?'

Loudon nodded. 'I have a flat there.'

'Which I'm sure you're keen to get back to.' She looked at Heap. 'DS Heap here will take you back. Thanks again.'

Heap opened the passenger door for Loudon. As he came back round the car Gilchrist said: 'I'm going to make a start on our woman in there before Liesl gets here. You get back as quickly as you can.'

'Of course, ma'am.'

The bleached blonde Gilchrist and Heap had seen with Liesl Rabbitt in the Ditchling Museum was still focused on her phone when Gilchrist went in. Gilchrist quietly asked at the bar what was in the glass of wine the woman was drinking and ordered another and a Chardonnay for herself. Well, why not?

She took over the Merlot and Chardonnay and sat down opposite the woman. The woman looked up expectantly and frowned when she saw Gilchrist. Gilchrist pushed the Merlot across and raised her own glass. 'Cheers,' she said. The woman just looked at her but Gilchrist took a sip of her own wine anyway.

'I wanted to talk to you before your friend arrived, to ask you about Sunday lunchtime in the Jolly Sportsman. Where did you go when you and Richard Rabbitt were asked to leave?'

The woman looked at Gilchrist and down at the glass Gilchrist had put in front of her.

'You're wondering who I am,' Gilchrist said. 'Sorry, it was rude of me not to introduce myself. I'm DI Gilchrist and I'm investigating the murder of Richard Rabbitt. And you've been identified as one of the last people to see him alive.'

The woman continued to stare at Gilchrist. 'Is your English not very good?' Gilchrist said. 'I was just hoping to talk to you before your friend joins you for lunch because I didn't want it to be awkward for you to explain what you were doing snogging her ex-husband in a public place on the day he died. Oh, sorry, snogging is probably too English a term for you if your English is not very good.'

'Her English is very good,' Liesl Rabbitt said, sitting down beside Gilchrist. 'She's just trying to decide if you are *cray cray* woman.' Rabbitt pulled the glass of wine Gilchrist had bought for the mystery woman towards her and took a large sip.

'Why would she think I was *cray cray*?' Gilchrist said.

'Well, maybe just square, then. You think I don't know about Sophia and my husband screwing? I've been in the same bed with them while they're doing it. You don't do threesomes, police lady? You don't know what you're missing.'

'But you didn't seem to know they were together on Sunday.'

'I care what my friend does for money with the weakling?'

'What did she do after she left the Jolly Sportsman, both of them drunk?'

'She drove him to me.'

Gilchrist gave her a stern look. 'You know there are severe penalties for withholding evidence from the police, Mrs Rabbitt?'

'Who is withholding what evidence?'

'You told us you hadn't seen your husband for ages, then it turns out you saw him the day he died. You told me you got the car when he arrived drunk. You didn't say he arrived with someone else.' Gilchrist addressed both of them: 'What happened when it was time for him to leave your café?' Someone touched Gilchrist's shoulder. She looked up. Bellamy Heap stood behind her.

'You drove him back towards his house,' Heap said to Rabbitt. 'I've just been informed on the way back here that CCTV footage from Lewes High Street has you leaving with Sophia here and Richard Rabbitt. Where did you go?'

'We went to the casino in Brighton Marina,' Mrs Rabbitt said.

'Richard Rabbitt went gambling with you?' Gilchrist said.

'No, just me and Sophia.'

'What happened to your husband?'

'We dropped him just by the cattle grid at the start of the lake. He wanted to walk the rest of the way up the drive to his house. He liked to survey all that he owned. Plonker.'

'What time was that?' Gilchrist said.

'Around six?'

'That would fit with the CCTV in Lewes, ma'am.'

'How drunk was he?' Gilchrist said.

'Pretty drunk. He'd carried on drinking.'

'What did you talk about with him that afternoon?'

Mrs Rabbitt smirked at Sophia. 'We didn't do too much talking.'

Gilchrist digested that. 'I thought you despised the man.'

'Money is money.'

'OK,' Gilchrist said. 'We're going to leave you to have your meal but immediately after that you are going down to the community policeman's house just down the High Street here so he can take your statements. He will be expecting you. If you don't, you'll be arrested. Your full name and address, Sophia? You don't say much, do you?'

'Not unless it's something worth saying,' the woman said, her voice throaty and smoke-damaged.

Back out in the car, Gilchrist said: 'We'd better get down to the crime scene in Brighton.'

Heap nodded. 'When DC Wade phoned about the CCTV she also mentioned that Mr Fitzgerald from the Wetlands Centre has sent footage from last week along to us. A whole bunch of people together on the other side of the lake. Including Donald Kermode.'

'Really? Well, we do need to talk to Kermode but I think we have to go to Brighton first.'

'Agreed, ma'am. DC Wade is going to download the film to my iPad, once I can get a signal.'

They drove back to Brighton via the Ditchling Beacon. 'What's this?' Gilchrist said, picking up from the footwell of her seat the pamphlet Heap had bought at the museum. She looked at the black and white image of a burning car on the cover. 'The Hassocks blockade?'

'No idea, ma'am. Looked interesting though.'

Gilchrist dropped it back in the footwell. They glanced out of the car windows at the views either side of the car as they crested the Beacon and headed across the Downs to the sparkling sea of Brighton in the distance.

'Ma'am, I can't be late tonight. Kate is in a state
mum's funeral tomorrow, even though there will only
ten people there.'

'Understandable. Why don't you go off after we've visite
crime scene?'

'There's something else, though. The wake is kind of unusua
How's your vertigo?'

Gilchrist frowned. 'What do you mean? Are we going on the
i360? That's novel for a wake.'

Heap shook his head. 'Weather dependent, we're going over
the Downs in a balloon.'

'Why?'

'I'll let Kate explain.'

Gilchrist thought for a moment. 'Can you steer those things?'

'They more or less drift on air currents as I understand it,
ma'am. Why?'

'How could that guy guarantee to get round the world in
eighty days then?'

'I don't think that was entirely by balloon, ma'am.'

'I was wondering what our crime scene might look like from
the air?'

'What indeed, ma'am? Perhaps we could also send up a drone?'

'Have you forgotten that Don-Don is in charge of drones for
the county? It probably wouldn't get much beyond hovering over
Katie Price's house.'

'I haven't forgotten Don-Don. I wish I could. Perhaps we
could cause a crisis over Gatwick again to get him back where
he belongs.'

'I definitely think that's worth considering.'

When they got to the rundown Art Deco block of flats on the
seafront they weren't expecting to see much. Joe Jackson's
body had already been removed. Sylvia Wade was waiting for
them when they climbed up four flights of rubbish strewn stairs
to the flat.

'I'm told the lift never works,' Wade said as they put on their
paper onesies at the door to the flat.

'Good exercise,' Gilchrist said, trying not to wheeze too loudly.
Bellamy Heap had, of course, scampered up like a mountain goat.

as been and gone?' Gilchrist said, mildly disappointed
e him.
asn't him actually, ma'am,' Wade said. 'He's not in work

A couple of SOCO officers were moving around the bedsit
.fting things. Gilchrist saw the splashes of blood on the rumpled
bed. 'It all happened there?'

'It seems like it. He was badly beaten and there were cigarette
burns on his face and chest. Something had been done to his
testicles too in that they were swollen to twice the normal size.'

'Has Bilson's colleague established cause of death yet?'

'Not yet, ma'am. In fact, it's not immediately obvious.'

Gilchrist looked at the film posters Sellotaped to the wall.
Horror films mostly, some vintage, some recent.

'Movie buff,' Gilchrist observed.

'Media studies student at Brighton University, ma'am.' Wade
pointed at a pile of cheap business cards on the table in the centre
of the room. 'Fancied himself as a Steven Spielberg though.' The
card said *Joe Jackson, Auteur*.

Heap was standing by Gilchrist. 'Just a fancy name for a film
director, ma'am,' he said.

Gilchrist turned to him. 'I knew that – even without being a
member of the Lewes Film Club.'

'Ma'am.'

'So what's happening in the rest of the building, Sylvia?'
Gilchrist said.

'Well, Customs and Immigration are all over it. Hundreds of
people of a range of ethnic origins on every floor but this
one. Crammed in, forty to a flat, though only twenty at any one
time since there's a night shift and day shift who take turns
on the same mattresses. Deplorable bathroom conditions,
dodgy kitchen appliances, boilers uncertified. No fire exits
in place. The lifts don't work. The four flats on this floor are
the exception – they seem to be legitimately rented by people
like Mr Jackson.'

'So it's reasonable to think that Farzi wanted to get the
people on this floor out to maximize his profits here,' Gilchrist
said. 'Is there a caretaker or building manager on site?'

'Theoretically, but he's nowhere to be seen,' Wade said. 'The whole building is being emptied and the "tenants" taken to a holding centre near Gatwick for processing.'

'What about the other flats on this floor?'

'Nobody home in the other three. Looks like they are students too. We are trying to reach them.'

'No sign of violence to them?'

'No, ma'am. But, ma'am, if this building is typical of Said Farzi's scores of other properties, we have a major scandal on our hands – and a major lawbreaker.'

Gilchrist nodded. 'We need to find out from Abbas exactly where in Morocco Farzi is. We need to get him back here. Do our governments get on, do you know?'

'I believe so, ma'am,' Heap said. 'It's a kingship, I believe, and the king is our ally in the war against terror. He runs a pretty authoritarian set-up – major repression of dissident voices.'

Gilchrist turned back to Sylvia. 'You have the footage from the lake, I believe?'

'I forwarded it to you and DS Heap. Bunch of young people, on the whole, as best you can see.'

'I'll look at it on my laptop this evening. Bellamy, you should go to Kate now.'

'You should come with me, ma'am. You're booked into Pelham House, remember? And I think your laptop is there.'

'Ha – I'd forgotten. I can do a bit more digging up there this evening then.' She turned to Sylvia Wade. 'Good work, Sylvia. I'll see you tomorrow.'

'By then we should have been able to access the phone and laptop of Joe Jackson.'

'Excellent.'

NINE

Heap dropped Gilchrist off at Pelham House and set off home. They had scarcely spoken on the way up from Brighton. Gilchrist felt bad she didn't offer to go home with him to comfort Kate but that kind of thing wasn't her strong point. Actually, this was one of those days when she struggled to think what her strong point was.

As she was registering at reception, the receptionist said: 'Will you be seeing the American lady you were having coffee with this morning again before she leaves the country?'

'I wasn't expecting to – why?' Gilchrist said, writing in her home address on the card in front of her.

'She left the cable for her laptop in her room. I thought she might need it before she gets back home.'

'I don't think I can help you but I can check with her friend.'

'Only if it's no bother.'

'It's no bother.'

'Is she an actress?'

'An agent for actors and actresses.'

'Oh, that explains it,' the receptionist said, taking the card back from her. 'I just need to take a swipe of your credit card for any extras and we're done. I'm afraid there's no lift – listed building – so you have to walk up those stairs to your room, but it is only one flight up. Your bags are in your room.'

'Explains what?'

'We had an actor staying in here for a few days before she arrived. He didn't have much to say for himself but I recognized him. Anyway, the two of them were having a conflab the other night.'

'Who was he?'

'Well, I shouldn't say, as we take our clients privacy very seriously, but my boyfriend is a bit of a fan of horror movies and that dark stuff. Give me *Mary Poppins Returns* anytime. Anyway, he's quite hunky in real life.' She giggled. 'Don't tell my boyfriend I said that! But I wouldn't have minded. Definitely don't tell him I said that either! In another life, of course.'

'Who was it? I'm a police officer – you can trust me.'

'Oh – you do know who he is!'

'What makes you say that?'

'You just quoted him in that film where he's an insane policeman who gets into women's apartments then strangles them with their own stockings during kinky sex. I must say, I wouldn't have minded going all *Fifty Shades of Grey* with him.' She put her hand to her mouth. 'Look at me, getting all flustered.'

'Did he have a boxer's punching bag with him by any chance?'

'I couldn't possibly say,' the receptionist said, making a gesture to zip her mouth while nodding at the same time.

Gilchrist nodded too, took her pass key and went up the ornate stairs. When she was in her room she immediately phoned Sylvia Wade. She wanted to phone Heap but knew she needed to leave him to have time with Kate.

'Sylvia – George Bosanquet was here in Lewes around the time Richard Rabbitt was murdered.'

'Who?'

'Sorry – you're not up-to-date on our investigation, are you? He's a sociopathic actor who in the past has made death threats to Nimue Grace. Can you find out how long he was here and where he is now? He must have an agent in Los Angeles – check with her or him.'

'It's still early in Los Angeles, ma'am.'

'So it is. Do you mind trying in a couple of hours?'

Gilchrist paced the room. She looked in the minibar but there was a card stating that if she wanted it stocked she should call reception. She grabbed her laptop and phone and went down to the bar. It was pretty empty. She ordered a large Chardonnay, sat in a corner and flipped open her laptop.

She would really have valued Bellamy's counsel but knew it would be outrageous to disturb him tonight of all nights. She half hoped he and Kate would walk in. She got the next best thing when her phone rang. Kate.

'My mum didn't talk to me much but one thing she did say a few times was that she'd always wanted to go ballooning but was scared to. I actually bought her a ride that she never used. I found the voucher among her things. It's still valid. So I thought I'd like to do it to remember her. I thought I should probably ask Dad but I need moral support. The basket can hold six. I wondered if, in addition to Dad and Bellamy, you and Bob would like to come. I can't think of anyone else but that doesn't matter.'

'Bellamy mentioned it. I'd love to.'

'Great – see you tomorrow then.'

Gilchrist finished her first glass of wine pretty quickly. When she'd made her way through most of the second she decided to call Nimue Grace.

'I don't want to freak you out, Ms Grace, but George Bosanquet has been staying at Pelham House in Lewes for the past few days. He left the day Rabbitt's body was discovered. Did you know?'

'I didn't know but it gives me a chill to think of it. And something else makes sense now. I thought I was going nuts because – I told you, didn't I? – I thought I saw his face at the window one night. You know, pressed against the pane, trying to look in. Scared the shit out of me.'

'Can you remember what night?'

'Please. I can't even remember what I had for breakfast this morning. Or even if I had breakfast. That's what I used to have a secretary for – to keep track of all that stuff. And two people to read my scripts.'

'To read your scripts?'

'Yeah. There was a time when I was big enough for the "Get Me Cary Grant" part of that joke. I was inundated with them. It's not the done thing to say which roles you turned down that made stars of other actors but let's just say there was a period when I got offered everything first and turned down pretty much everything.

'But when you keep turning stuff down, eventually, of course, they stop sending you scripts and you're forgotten. What was that phrase coined by some labour politician back in the sixties? "Ten minutes is a long time in politics"? Well, you get a nanosecond in Hollywood. Your star glimmers, shines bright then is extinguished – *phttt*. Just like that. You're past history. Forgotten.'

Grace seemed to have a rare talent for going off at a tangent. Was it a drug-related thing? Or just an actor thing?

'You're not forgotten, Ms Grace,' Gilchrist said, trying to get it back on track. 'Did you say Bosanquet was violent?'

'Only to women. Oh, and his punching bag. When he had a bit of money – in the time we were together that would be my money – he never travelled anywhere without the punching bag. I told you, didn't I? He was obsessed with his body and had decided punching this thing was the best way of keeping fit. But he was too cowardly to try punching men. He was frightened of being hit and couldn't take a punch anyway.'

'Would he have any other reason to be here in this area? Other than you, I mean?'

'Not that I can think of – unless it was some woman he'd come to fuck. But he'd probably just go to the nearest brothel. Is there a brothel round here? He's big on hookers because he doesn't have to make an effort.'

'No business interests here?'

'I don't think so. In the States he does invest in shopping malls and vineyards.'

'Shopping malls?' Gilchrist said.

'Yes – he owns three or four. And vineyards. He doesn't grow his own wine, like Sam Neill or Gerard Depardieu, but he invests in them in Napa Valley.'

'How are you doing, Ms Grace?'

'Fine and dandy. Why? Do you want to drop by for a drink?'

'I would be happy to say yes – I'm down at Pelham House – but I have a lot of work to do.'

'Admin is so tedious,' Grace said.

Gilchrist finished her drink. 'Actually, it's another murder in Brighton that may or may not be linked to Said Farzi.'

'What?'

Gilchrist bit her lip. Why had she said that? To impress a movie star? Or was it because she wanted to shake something up, in case Grace knew more about Said Farzi than she was saying? She didn't know but she ploughed on.

'There's no need for alarm, Ms Grace. It was a young student renting from Farzi in Brighton.'

'What was his name?'

'Why do you ask?'

'If somebody has died I think it's only respectful to give him a name.'

'Well, we haven't released it yet but, OK, I'll tell you in confidence. His name is Joe Jackson.'

There was silence on the other end of the phone.

'Ms Grace?'

'Oh, for fuck's sake, will you call me Nimue or Nim or Grace or You – anything but this *Ms Grace* shit?'

Gilchrist was startled by Grace's vehemence. She thought for a moment, listening to Grace's breathing down the phone line. She held her own breath.

'Do you by any chance know the victim?' she said slowly.

'I'm going to send a taxi for you – one of the few guys who knows how to find my place.' Grace hung up.

Gilchrist and Grace were sitting on Grace's terrace either side of the long table. It was almost dark but there were solar lights popping into life all around them. There was a bottle of wine in an ice bucket and Grace and Gilchrist were both sipping from large glasses.

'I know Joe Jackson, although I've never met him.'

'That comes as something of a surprise. How come?'

'Drama students and film students write all the time to people like me – *stars* – asking for financial help for their studies or a film. I'm selective but I do help – not with vast amounts of money but a bit more than a token gesture. He was one of them.'

'Why did you select him?'

'I can't honestly remember. How did he die?'

'I can't say.'

'But you're treating it as murder?'

'We are. And I will say he died badly.'

'Poor Joe.'

'You say you never met him.'

'That's right. I've never met any of the youngsters I support.'

'About how many do you support?'

'Why? Do you think some weird serial killer is going to knock them off one by one? Although, of course, all serial killers are weird.'

'No, I don't think that. I was just curious.'

'About fifty over the years. Maybe a couple a year.' Grace took a deep breath. 'Look, I forgot to say Joe and some film students were making a short down at the lake last week.'

'A short?' Gilchrist said.

'A short film. They're usually fifteen minutes of not making any sense but film courses swear by them and I've made a few for friends over the years. There are short film festivals all over the place. Doesn't make the short films any better, of course.'

'How long were these filmmakers down at your lake?'

'Four days, I think.'

'You didn't go down there to keep an eye on things?'

'Er, not likely. Joe was the director so I let them use it as a favour. They still signed the usual waivers so I didn't have to worry about any injuries – or, rather, I didn't have to worry about being sued for any injuries. And while I am thought of as being retired that doesn't mean that I couldn't be exploited if I'd turned up. I find it hard to say no. In that regard at least.'

Gilchrist remembered the footage Sylvia Wade had sent on to her. Presumably that was the film people. Could Jackson's death have something to do with him being at the lake rather than him living in Said Farzi's slum property? Or could it all be connected? She excused herself and went inside to phone Donald Kermode. He didn't answer but she left a message on his voicemail asking him to call her as a matter of urgency. She wanted to know what he had to say about the filming as the footage showed him with the film students.

Gilchrist went back out and sat at the table again. 'If the wind is in the right direction I may be passing over your house tomorrow. If I do, do you want any photographs?'

Grace frowned then grinned. 'Are you the Snowman now? You're a bit early, aren't you?'

'The Snowman?'

'You know Raymond Briggs lived over in Westmeston and with his wife just down the road here in Plumpton. The Snowman actually flies over this house.'

'I didn't know any of that. But I'll be in a balloon.'

Grace giggled. 'Isn't ballooning a bit old school policing? There are these things called drones, you know – although I recognize by that Gatwick debacle nobody in Sussex police actually knows how to use them. I should put you in touch with some of my old stalkers and the paparazzi – they use them all the time over my lake and house. They seem to be pretty expert. And in the movies certain film cameramen specialize in using them. The old days of crane shots or breaking the budget to do a helicopter shot from above are long gone – a drone can do all that at a tenth of the cost.'

'It's not police work – it's a private thing.'

'Room for one more?'

'As I said, it's a private thing, in memory of a friend of mine's mother. Kate – Bellamy Heap's partner.'

'Oh, yes – Bellamy told me about Kate's mother's suicide. You're scattering ashes over my house?'

'No – there's a tree being planted somewhere. The ashes will be scattered there sometime in the near future.'

'Did she balloon over here a lot?'

'She had a vertigo problem. So she never ballooned anywhere.'

'OK,' Grace said slowly.

'It's to honour her wish to do it.'

'Fair enough. Balloons are beautiful things but for me, because of who I am, they can be a bit intrusive. I've seen balloons coming over, guys leaning out of the basket snapping me in the hope I'm sunbathing nude. I never sunbathe nude these days.'

'I'd like you to meet Kate. I think you'd like her.'

'I'm sure I would.'

'Although I'd be worried you'd call DS Heap your Sir Galahad in front of her. That might cause him complications at home.'

'Don't worry; it wouldn't be my first barbecue. I know how to behave with women, even if their men don't know how to behave with me.' Adding quickly: 'Not that I mean that about DS Heap for one single second.' She sighed theatrically. 'More's the pity.'

TEN

Chief Constable Karen Hewitt didn't raise her head when Gilchrist and Heap walked into the room at 8 a.m. on the dot. Donald Donaldson, however, peeled himself off the wall he'd been leaning against and walked over, sticking out a hand to Gilchrist.

'Sarah, it's been a long time.'

Gilchrist took his hand reluctantly, expecting a fierce handshake but Donaldson's grip was gentle, almost soft, even though he was as pumped up as ever. Over her shoulder, he grinned at Heap. 'How are you, Junior G-man?' he said.

Heap nodded but didn't speak.

'Good,' Karen Hewitt barked from behind her big desk. 'I'm glad you're all getting reacquainted. Detective Sergeant Donaldson is keen to be informed of all the fine work you have done so far on this case.'

Gilchrist looked at Chief Inspector Hewitt, still Botoxed to the hilt, still corseted in her latest tight-fitting power suit – and probably corseted beneath it, truth be told.

'I think there's more for us to do on the other side of the Downs,' she said.

'I'm sure DS Donaldson can do it for you,' Hewitt said shortly, with a tight smile on her face.

'I'm sure I can too,' Donaldson said, the big smile intact on *his* face.

'Share all your notes as a matter of urgency with DS Donaldson – DS Heap, you can see to that – and then I have this murder and illegal immigrants thing to talk to you about.'

Heap nodded. 'DS Donaldson, I'll get everything to you by the end of the day.'

'Call me Donny, Bellamy, or Don-Don. No need for formalities between old sparring partners, eh? Great stuff. It will be in safe hands.' He looked round the room. 'OK then, I'll make my departure with your permission, ma'am.'

'Keep me informed,' Hewitt said.

'That goes without saying, ma'am,' Donaldson said as he exited the room.

After the door had closed Hewitt looked from one to the other of them. 'Personally,' she said, 'I think he's a total dick but what can I do when you've been trampling over boundaries?'

'We have some delicate stuff given to us by Ms Grace because it was us and we were trusted,' Gilchrist said. 'That needs to be handled sensitively.'

'You mean the woman who is one of your suspects? Pass it along to Donaldson. It will be fine.'

'Ma'am—' Gilchrist started.

'It will be fine,' Hewitt said peremptorily. 'Now we have this illegal immigrant problem, which is entirely within your Brighton bailiwick so at least you won't need wellingtons.'

'Ma'am?' Gilchrist said. 'You think the savage murder of Joe Jackson is linked to where he was living?'

'Don't you?'

'Ma'am, there is potentially a link between this murder and that of Richard Rabbitt. The solution to Joe Jackson's death may be on the other side of the Downs. That's why we should be over there and not here. Ma'am.'

'I'm not taking you totally off that case; I'm just suggesting Donaldson does the heavy lifting over the Downs. So are you saying you have already made progress with the Joe Jackson murder?'

'Well, he's renting from Said Farzi, who lives over the Downs and has as yet unspecified links with Richard Rabbitt. Our initial thinking was that Jackson was being *persuaded* to move out of his flat so that twenty illegal immigrants could be stashed there and it got out of hand. But Jackson has a connection with the lake too in that he was making a short film there last week.'

'Well, your first proposal sounds like a reasonable hypothesis. Farzi sends his thugs in to persuade him to leave and they get carried away. I assume you've discounted robbery as a motive?'

'His phone and laptop were still in the room. The techies are working on breaking into them. But the connection with the lake—'

'Offers a more nebulous theory,' Hewitt said. She looked from one to the other of them. 'All right then. Get on with it and keep me informed.'

Gilchrist and Heap parted outside the station. Heap was going up to the crematorium in the official car and Gilchrist was making her own way there. She actually arrived before the hearse to find Bob Watts standing outside the crematorium with a couple of perfectly coiffured and turned-out older women Gilchrist didn't recognize, except as the type that lived in Brighton's Regency squares.

The hearse was preceded by a black limo carrying Kate, Bellamy and William Simpson. Kate clung to Heap and William Simpson walked up to Watts, holding out his hand.

'Bob, it's been a long time.'

Watts took the hand reluctantly.

'I'm glad you're here,' Simpson continued. 'Not just for Lizzy's sake, although she was always fond of you, but because there's something I need to talk to you about.'

'This isn't really the time and place.'

'I go off again later today,' Simpson said, 'I don't know when there'll be another chance.'

'You're not going in the balloon?'

'No time, I'm afraid.'

'All right then,' Watts said as Simpson moved on to introduce himself to the two women. Watts raised his eyes to Gilchrist.

It was a gloomy service. Nobody else came. Kate had decided not to speak and William Simpson chose not to, so the vicar rattled through a lacklustre eulogy, complete with the usual muddling up of name and details typical of such events. Kate had told Gilchrist the one thing her father had insisted on was the choice of music for when the coffin trundled behind the curtains at the end of the ceremony. God, Gilchrist hated the mawkish sentimentality of 'Candle in the Wind'.

There was not going to be any formal wake but Kate had suggested they all raise a glass in the pub beside the entrance to the cemetery. The two frosty women were invited but they politely declined. Watts said he'd be along shortly then hung back with William Simpson.

Watts looked Simpson up and down. He still had the lean and hungry look of Cassius, the man that Julius Caesar hadn't trusted. And, yes, when he was chief constable, Watts had seen his fall as similar to that of Caesar, though less lethal. Hubris was nothing new to him.

Watts hadn't seen Simpson for several years now, ever since the farrago of the Milldean Massacre that had wrecked the career of Watts as chief constable. Simpson's involvement was suspected – more than suspected – but unproven. But he had definitely played a major part in bringing Bob Watts down.

'How are you, brother?' Simpson said. His face was drawn and his expression solemn.

'Half-brother,' Watts said automatically. He towered over Simpson.

'I've heard about your penthouse in Brighton on the sea-front. Well, who wouldn't want a slice of that? I hadn't realized

clean coppers earned so much. Or did our father's money pay
for that?'

'What do you want to talk about, William? Surely not Lizzy?
I don't believe you've been in touch with her for years.'

'And you know that how?' Simpson said, his eyes alert.

'Because Kate has seen her regularly and she told me.'

'My Channel-swimming daughter. How is she?'

'Channel swum, more or less. But you don't think it odd that
you ask somebody else how your own daughter is when you've
just travelled here in a car with her?'

'Conversation didn't exactly flow,' Simpson said. 'So how is she?'

'In the circumstances she's doing fine.'

'And that midget?'

'Don't be childish. His name is Bellamy and your daughter
doesn't discuss her relationships with me.'

'What do you discuss exactly?' Simpson said.

'Lately? Swimming strokes, mostly. Now why are we here?'

'That's the big question for all of us, isn't it?'

Watts turned away.

'I'm not interested in playing silly games with you. If you
won't tell me why you're here I'm off down the pub to join the
others.'

'I'm here about your wife actually.'

'Your wife?'

'No – *your* wife.'

'My ex-wife, Molly?'

In his rush to the top, Bob Watts had ignored his wife,
Molly, and the anguish she went through when their children
left home. She had turned to drink. Then he had his one-night
stand with Sarah Gilchrist and the scummy tabloids found
out. And that was the end of his marriage and his children's
relationship with him.

'What have you to do with her?'

'Life works in mysterious ways, does it not? A business deal
I have going in Canada is going a bit tits-up because of a flaky
business partner. The other partners are getting impatient. The
other partners are not people you want to make impatient.'

'Dangerous business partners? There's a surprise. What has
this got to do with Molly?'

'Can't you guess? The flaky business partner is Molly's bloke.'

Watts exhaled quietly.

'What has this got to do with me?'

'He needs bailing out. Pronto. Which means your wife needs bailing out.'

'Ex-wife.'

Simpson laughed.

'Come on, Bob. You're not going to abandon the mother of your kids. I know you that well. You're a soft touch. Always have been. You still feel for her, even if it's only guilt.'

'The penny has dropped. You want money from me.'

'Your father left you a pretty penny I know. And by rights some of it should be mine as he was my father too.' Simpson clasped his hands. 'But this isn't about me. It's about helping your wife.' He scratched his nose. 'Maybe saving your wife.'

Watts came up close.

'Are you threatening my wife, you little shit?'

Simpson looked up at him.

'Please don't do the macho thing, Bob. I wasn't threatening.'

Simpson moved round him and walked over to his car.

'Think of it as a heads-up,' he called back. 'Her bloke has a month to come up with the money or bad things will happen.' He put his finger to his lips theatrically, considering something. 'I have this secret – my guilty secret. You see I live with guilt too. I wonder, should I share it with you so that you can decide whether to share it with my daughter.'

Watts didn't say anything.

'It's about Lizzy. It's her secret really that she didn't want anyone to know. She stupidly felt guilty, even though she had nothing to feel guilty about as she wasn't to blame. I was to blame, if anyone was, for putting her in that position.'

'What position?'

'Back when things were complicated after the Milldean Massacre a gangster was putting pressure on me and he tried to get a message to me through Lizzy. But it didn't work because she never passed the message on. In fact, she left me rather than tell me.'

'But at some point she told you.'

'Much later. In a rage. It wasn't a proper message, more of a warning that he could mess up my family and me. He came to the house and raped her. And she's never been the same since.' Simpson opened his car door. 'So that's my dirty secret and my guilt.'

ELEVEN

'**Y**ou OK, Bob?' Gilchrist said when he went in the pub. There was a pint of lager waiting for him on the table and four packets of crisps torn open.

'Just had an odd conversation with Kate's father.'

'Nothing new there then,' Kate said. 'You know he didn't say two words in the car coming here.'

'He has his mind on a business deal in Canada that there seems to be some urgency about.'

'Canada?' Kate said. 'What can there be in Canada that Dad would want to invest in?'

'I've been thinking about that on the way down and I think I know but I need to call my ex-wife to confirm my suspicion.'

'Your ex-wife,' Gilchrist said. 'Does she talk to you?'

'Rarely. But her chap has got himself caught up in something with your father, Kate, which he apparently can't handle.'

'Something illegal?' Kate said.

'Oddly, something utterly legal if my guess is right,' Watts said.

'Marijuana,' Heap said.

'Give that man a coconut.'

'I don't get it,' Kate said.

'Did you miss it in the papers?' Watts said. 'It was big news at the time. Canada is the first G7 nation to legalize cannabis for recreational use nationwide. The shops are open, business is already booming and money men are buying what are being called "pot stocks". What was earning criminals billions illegally is now earning a fortune legitimately.'

'It's always better to bring a product under control rather than let it flourish underground,' Heap said. 'It's been slow happening in the United States, although medical marijuana has been available in some states for some time now. Only nine states have made it legal for recreational use.'

'Bellamy,' Gilchrist said. 'I didn't expect you to be so liberal.'

'Then, with respect, you don't really know me as I thought you did.'

'Go on, Bellamy,' Watts said. 'You obviously know what you are talking about.'

'I was just going to say that aside from anything else it's a pragmatic thing. The stuff is tested for impurities so consumers know it is high quality. In the UK at the moment the money from drugs doesn't benefit anybody except the criminals it enriches. Enriching criminals is not exactly going to enrich society. The war on drugs costs a fortune and fails miserably. We all know the statistics. Crime caused by the drugs; dealers promoting high-strength, psychosis-inducing skunk. Drug-related deaths are rising not falling despite government clampdowns.' He shrugged. 'I'll get off my soap-box now.'

'But you're right, Bellamy,' Watts said. 'And legalising it is going to be a game-changer. When other countries follow Canada's lead marijuana is going to transform agriculture, pharmaceuticals, mental health and the drinks trade. Cannabis products are going to outsell beer. There's already a crossover into food and drink. You can already buy a sauvignon in LA infused with cannabis – and the wine producers in the Napa Valley and Sonoma County have set aside land for marijuana estates alongside their vineyards. There are sommelier classes training cannabis sommeliers.'

'But if it's all going to be legal and above board, why is your ex-wife's partner in deep shit?' Gilchrist said.

'I'd guess that the crime syndicates that currently control the illegal drug trade are not going to let their cash cow leave their greedy grasp,' Heap said. 'They'll be moving into the legitimate businesses, founding them or becoming partners in them. Every gangster film you ever saw the gangster dreams of getting out from under and going legit. With this they can. The new global industry is estimated at $200 billion a year.'

'I think you've hit the nail on the head, Bellamy,' Watts said. 'We know William Simpson – no offence, Kate – will get into bed with anybody if he can see profit in it. Molly's partner maybe just got into the wrong bed.'

'So what are you going to do?' Gilchrist said.

'Well, after our balloon ride I'm going to make some calls and then decide.'

'And on that note, we need to be going,' Kate said. 'We're going to set off from the Downs near Lewes prison and then the plan is to come down at Plumpton racecourse. There'll be a minibus there to bring us back to Lewes. All this is wind dependent, of course, but the minibus will come to wherever we do land.'

They went to the launch pad in Watts's car. Gilchrist sat in the front seat with him, Heap sat in the back with Kate. Gilchrist's phone rang almost the moment they got onto the Lewes Road. It was Sylvia Wade. Gilchrist twisted round and said to Kate: 'I'm so sorry but I have to take this.'

'Of course you do,' Kate said. 'You're in the middle of two murder investigations.'

'Sorry to disturb you on such a sad day, ma'am, but I finally heard back from Bosanquet's agent. He was here on a private visit. She said he was "on hiatus", whatever that means.'

'It means she's very American,' Gilchrist said, putting her phone on speakerphone. 'How long was he here?'

'Just those three days over the period Rabbitt was killed.'

'And now? Is he still *on hiatus*?'

'No, he's making a film in a place called *Wazzazat*. It's spelt Ouarzazate and it's in Morocco.'

Gilchrist disconnected the number. 'Did you get all that, Bellamy?'

'Most of it, ma'am.'

'Morocco, eh?' Watts said. 'That's where most of the cannabis in Europe and Britain comes from, through Spain and Gibraltar. Wow, look at that!'

The balloon was sitting about a hundred yards in front of them looking like a big, fat exclamation mark. Kate, Heap and Gilchrist all jumped out and headed over there while Watts parked. As they drew nearer, they could see the burning gas jet spurting into the balloon every few seconds with its distinctive sound, somewhere between a hiss and a roar.

'Crazy concept, isn't it?' Watts said cheerfully as he caught up with them, lugging a large wicker basket. 'You float by putting a fire inside a flammable object.'

'They provide the basket to sit in you know, Bob – you don't have to bring your own,' Gilchrist said.

'Ha – I thought a couple of bottles of champagne to toast this little adventure in honour of Lizzy wouldn't go amiss.'

'That's so thoughtful,' Kate said.

'Perfect timing,' the pilot said from inside the basket. There was another man standing a few yards away looking up at the balloon. The pilot introduced himself as John Benfield. 'Can you get into the gondola OK or do you need the rope ladder? You're OK – great.' They all got in easily enough. 'Now when we're in the air, try not to all move to one side. You'll be safe but you might be alarmed by the wobble.'

Gilchrist and Watts took one side, Heap and Kate the opposite side. Heap put his arm round Kate.

'Ready for lift off?' Benfield said. The other man was unhitching the ropes that were mooring the gondola. When the last one had been unhitched the balloon lifted up, surprisingly quickly.

'Whoa,' said Gilchrist as the gondola rocked. Then: 'Wow.'

The balloon was drifting in the direction of the Ditchling Beacon. It seemed only a matter of minutes before they reached Plumpton Hill. 'Look,' Watts said, 'there's the Half Moon. And beyond, can you see the racecourse?'

'What are those squares and rectangle shadows kind of underneath the grass in that field?' Gilchrist said.

'The outlines of a long-gone Roman villa and its outbuildings. That stuff never disappears from the landscape. You could see much more all around the country last summer when it was so dry.'

'I think we're going to go over Nimue Grace's house,' Gilchrist said. 'I'm going to phone her.'

'That's the lake and the wood there,' Heap said to Kate, 'and the house and gardens and the orchard just up there.'

'Ms Grace? Sarah Gilchrist. If you feel like coming out and waving that balloon heading your way is us. We're just at the bottom of your orchard.'

Far below, Grace appeared on her terrace a moment later, her phone in her hand. 'If you try to drop something on me I will be so pissed off.'

'Actually,' Gilchrist said, turning at the sound of a pop behind her, 'we're just about to have some champagne.'

'Where are you going to land?'

'Theoretically at Plumpton racecourse.'

'Why don't you all come up to the house after?'

'I'm not sure what our plans are. Wow, I didn't realize how many greenhouses Farzi had.'

'Well, his property was the market garden for Plumpton Down House in Victorian times,' Grace said. 'His fields were essentially a market garden and the greenhouses produced more exotic, weather-sensitive stuff.'

'What does he use them for now?' Gilchrist said as they passed over them.

'Nothing as far as I know. I don't think it's a producing farm.'

'There seem to be lights on,' Heap said. 'Or heaters.'

Gilchrist repeated that to Grace.

'I have no idea about greenhouses,' Grace said. 'Do they get damaged left to themselves? Do you need to keep them heated? Maybe it is something to do with his vines?'

'You know as much as me,' Gilchrist said, conscious the others were waiting to make a toast. 'I'd better go now. We'll maybe see you later.'

They toasted Lizzy Simpson and each other as they passed over the Jolly Sportsman but Gilchrist was thinking about Said Farzi and how they had enough on him from their raids in Brighton to justify a raid on his farm. Sipping her champagne she texted Sylvia Wade, instructing her to sort out a warrant.

When they were landing it looked at first as if they were going to land on the railway line but they settled in a field behind the race track. The minibus was there. Gilchrist elected to go back into Lewes with the others to see about raiding Farzi's stables the next morning. She was still staying at Pelham House as the room was paid for anyway. She called Grace to make her apologies and said she'd like to speak to her later in any case.

She told Bellamy her plan. They went their separate ways and

Gilchrist went back to Pelham House. In her room she called Sylvia Wade. 'All set?'

'All set, ma'am. Should I inform DS Donaldson?'

'I don't think we need worry him with this.'

'Quite, ma'am.'

'I'd like you with us though – it would be good for you to get some hands-on experience.'

'I'd like that, ma'am.'

'Is there anything of interest on the phone and laptop of Joe Jackson?'

'We're still trying to unlock it, I believe. Our techies are a bit overwhelmed at the moment.'

'OK, Sylvia, see you tomorrow bright and early. Put all the clobber on. Oh, and bring mine, would you?'

'Yes, ma'am.'

Gilchrist phoned Grace. 'Two things. The first is that I wanted to tell you that George Bosanquet has left the country, so you should feel a bit safer from him. He's filming in Morocco. Place called Ouarzazate, wherever that is.'

'It's in the east of the country. It's where people like Ridley Scott make their medieval and biblical-era films. Science fiction films too, I think. If I remember rightly, the Jerusalem Scott built for his film *Kingdom of Heaven* outside town is now a tourist attraction. Actually, the city is where my American agent, Kip, was en route to when she called by here . . . Perhaps best for me not to think about that coincidence with George too closely.'

'You've filmed there?'

'Just twice but I have loads of mates who are there all the time. And thanks for your reassurance. What was the second thing?'

'Now this is an unusual request. Could you leave your gate unlocked tonight?'

'Why?'

'I can't say – it's nothing to do with your property. So keep your windows and doors locked.'

'It's about access?'

'Very early in the morning but I can't say any more than that.'

There was silence on Grace's end of the phone. Then: 'You're going to raid Farzi's place, aren't you?'

'I can't say – and please don't repeat that kind of speculation to anybody.'

'I wouldn't dream of it,' Grace said. 'Guide's honour. Although I did get kicked out of them.'

'Why?'

'Best not go there, at least until I'm two shots of tequila in. But if you're doing something really early out this way – why don't you and Bellamy come and stay at the house tonight? You'll be right where you need to be first thing then. Come on – early supper and early to bed.'

'That would be very unorthodox . . .'

'But eminently sensible. Get here as soon as you can. I do a mean chicken tagine, if I do say so myself.'

Gilchrist relayed this to Heap. 'You should definitely be there but these bozos would never find the property in the dark on their own,' he said. 'I'll bring them up from Brighton. Why don't you take Sylvia if she's coming on the operation?'

At her front door, Grace looked from Gilchrist to Sylvia Wade, who flushed. 'Bellamy might be dressed as an attractive young woman but I'd recognize that blush anywhere,' Grace said. 'Boy, you really take your undercover work seriously, don't you?'

'This is DC Sylvia Wade. I hope it's OK if she stays here instead of Bellamy.'

'Sure.' She looked from one woman to the other, a glint in her eye. 'Will you still want two rooms?'

Now it was Gilchrist's turn to blush. 'Of course.'

'So what's Bellamy's excuse? Can't tear himself away from his lovely girlfriend? My powers are definitely waning.'

'For operational reasons he needs to stay with the men.'

'So they don't get lost, you mean?' Grace said, grinning. 'Or raid the wrong property.'

Gilchrist said nothing. Grace ushered them in. 'So, Sylvia – it's OK to call you Sylvia? – how long have you been a copper?'

'Five years, ma'am.'

'Don't you start with that "ma'am" shit, not when *mia casa è sua casa*. I'd prefer you call me Nimue but I'll settle for Ms Grace, or just Grace, which is the best I'm getting from your two colleagues.'

'Thank you, Ms Grace.'

'What would you say to a glass of Chardonnay, Sylvia?'

'I'd say thank you but no thank you, Ms Grace.'

'Are you doing that no-drinking-on-duty thing?'

Wade shook her head. She blushed and grinned. 'You just haven't offered me the right drink yet.'

Grace laughed and turned to Gilchrist. 'I like her.'

Gilchrist looked at Wade and smiled. 'I like her too. She has hidden depths.'

'So what is your tipple?'

'Vodka neat on ice.'

'Way to go,' Grace said. 'Are you going to be picky about the brand? I've got some cheap Polish vodka in the freezer.'

'That would be fine.'

'Shall we all have a shot before you and I move onto the Chardonnay, Sarah?'

'Sure.'

Grace rummaged in her freezer and brought out not just the long-necked bottle of vodka but three frosted shot glasses.

'This is going to taste better without ice,' she said.

'OK,' Wade said.

The vodka came out in slow, viscid gloops. 'Always keep your cheap vodka in the freezer. It thickens beautifully. Never freezes. But the good stuff – Grey Goose or something – freezing it takes away the subtle tastes.' They raised their glasses. 'To woman power,' Grace said.

Grace and Gilchrist each took a sip. Wade tilted her head back and downed hers in one. Gilchrist gave a little cough as it hit the back of her throat. Grace handed Wade a bigger glass and pushed over an ice bucket half full of ice and the bottle of vodka. 'Help yourself from now on.'

They ate in the kitchen. In the centre of the long table a much-used terracotta tagine, with its long-funnelled lid, was set on a terracotta brazier containing burning charcoal.

'I've never seen a tagine like this before,' Wade said.

'The brazier you mean?' Grace said. 'I picked it up with the tagine in a market in Essaouira when I was filming there once. That and about twenty beautiful scarves and half a dozen beautiful rugs.'

'That's in Morocco?' Gilchrist said.

'Yes – lovely little place on the Atlantic coast. Very peaceful. Hippies used to hang out there back in the day. Cat Stevens converted to Islam while staying there. Have you been to Morocco?'

'I went to Marrakesh for a long weekend once,' Wade said. 'A hen party.'

'I dread to think what you were all wearing as your party ricocheted around town,' Grace said.

'What, you mean silly hats and T-shirts with slogans on and ridiculously high-heeled shoes?' Wade said with a laugh. 'No, nothing like that – we were all quite sober – well, not sober in every sense but modestly dressed and pretty well-behaved. We'd splashed out and stayed at the Mamounia so we had to be a bit on our best behaviour.'

Gilchrist was listening but thinking about something else and Grace noticed. 'Which country are you in, Sarah?'

'Oh, I'm here but I was thinking about whether to mention that odd coincidence of Bosanquet and your agent overlapping at Pelham House and now in Morocco.'

'I can't speak for the first but it's not so odd they might coincide in Ouarzazate. As I said it's the film capital of Morocco. They make a load of Bible films there, often at the same time. And all the different film crews pretty much stay in the same hotel. You'll see three Jesuses wandering around the swimming pool. There was a scandal once when Mary Magdalene from one film was caught canoodling in the corner of the hotel's candlelit restaurant with a Jesus from another film. I once saw the guy from *Frasier* – Kelsey somebody – in full costume as King Herod having breakfast with Sir Ben in full costume as a pharaoh. I regret to say I'm not up on pharaohs so I don't know which one.'

'Sir Ben?' Gilchrist said.

'Kingsley. Gandhi as was? Except it's much publicized that nobody in the business is allowed to call him just Ben anymore. He's one of those who insist on use of the title they've deservedly received. It's Sir Ben, although if you're favoured you may just call him Sir. Wait until I get made a dame – there'll be no living with me.'

'What have you made in Morocco?' Wade asked shyly.

'Most recently I came out of seclusion to do some *Game of Thrones* rip-off. I ended up on the cutting room floor. My heart wasn't in it really but I desperately needed the money. I'm constantly broke trying to hang onto this place without working any more. I was so relieved I wasn't in it when I saw the final film because it was utter crap.' She turned to Gilchrist. 'I met Bosanquet on the only proper film I did in Morocco. A late Bertolucci. I was supposed to get the hots for him and, actually, I did. As he did for me. Declared undying love for me on about day two.'

'Love at first sight,' Wade said.

'Lust at first sight,' Grace said.

Wade helped herself to more vodka. Gilchrist noted how much she was making herself at home. 'Sounds like a toxic relationship,' Wade said. 'He gaslighted you?'

'Worse than that. Much worse than that.'

'Gaslighted her, Sylvia?'

'I know it's only just come back into vogue with the Me Too movement but I like it,' Wade said. 'Quite a neat description of emotional abuse. Oddly, Ms Grace did a well-received revival of it at Chichester.'

'You saw that?' Grace said.

'My kind of thing,' Wade said. 'You were brilliant.'

'Thank you,' Grace said, patting Wade's hand. 'It certainly had resonance for me.'

'I'm lost,' Gilchrist said. 'Revival of what?'

'The play *Gaslight*,' Wade said. 'There have been a couple of film versions too. Written by a Brighton icon, Patrick Hamilton. It's about a husband trying to drive a wife mad to get her money. He persuades her she's hearing things when she thinks she can hear footsteps in the attic. It's about dangerously controlling men.'

'Is it set in Brighton?' Gilchrist said.

'London, I think,' Wade said. 'Why?'

'You said he was a Brighton icon.'

Grace explained: 'Oh, his novel *Hangover Square* with its group of seedy characters is mostly set in Earls Court but ends up in Brighton and he has a trilogy about a con man and the first of them, *West Pier*, is set in Brighton. I think Graham Greene liked that one.'

They went to bed soon after. Grace led them up to the first floor. The house was actually smaller than Gilchrist expected. There were just two bedrooms here, both small, and a bathroom.

'I'm on the next floor up,' Grace said. 'If you need anything, holler. I won't get up in the morning so help yourself to any breakfast you want. I have an allergy of early mornings after years of having to look gorgeous on a film set after a 4 a.m. call. Good luck with whatever you're going to be getting up to.'

TWELVE

Next morning, over a strong coffee, Gilchrist suggested Wade – bright and breezy despite having downed about half a bottle of vodka – stay at Grace's house until she left two more policemen there to guard the actress. Gilchrist opened the front door quietly. It was a fresh morning but the smell of honeysuckle was everywhere. She walked quietly down the drive to the gate and waited for the vehicles. She heard them before she saw them. The lead vehicle was on low beam, the ones behind were driving by side lights. She joined Heap in the front vehicle and they stopped to let two policemen out at Grace's front garden.

'I'm expecting that if those two barns aren't stuffed with migrants, those greenhouses are – I think that's what the heating or lights or whatever we saw is about,' Gilchrist said.

'There are other cars down by the bridleway and police already in position there,' Heap said. 'A helicopter is on standby. Half a dozen buses are parked in the Half Moon car park to ferry whoever is here up to the Gatwick assessment centre.'

Gilchrist nodded. 'You decided not to tell Donaldson?' Heap continued.

'That's right.'

'He won't be best pleased,' Heap observed.

'When is he ever?'

Twenty men and women went into the yard, half a dozen fanning out to cover the barns, the others continuing on down to the greenhouses. Heap went with that group, Sylvia Wade tagging along by his side.

Gilchrist came to the first barn as two police vehicles drove up in front of its doors. It was padlocked on the outside. Two more vehicles blocked the farm entrance. A first-floor light went on in one of the stable's buildings. Abbas's flat. Gilchrist had stationed somebody outside his door with the search warrant. He was also going to be brought in for questioning in relation to Joe Jackson. She signalled for a constable with a bolt cutter to take the lock off the barn.

He did so; two more constables pulled the barn doors wide open and the lights on the vehicles came on with blinding power. Mattresses were packed one next to the other, covering the whole floor in rows with narrow alleys between. Humped shapes lay on each mattress. By the near wall were a row of buckets with the stench of urine and shit coming from them.

She could hear Abbas arguing with her constable as she moved on to the second barn, leaving three officers to sort out all the people in the first. She heard the buses make their slow progress up Grace's drive.

It was the same story in the second barn. She left the rest of her officers there and walked down the rough road to the greenhouses. If they too were full of refugees this place must have a couple of thousand people here, living in utter degradation with minimal facilities of any sort. She clenched her jaw. *Fucking people smugglers. Fucking Said Farzi.*

Sylvia Wade was standing about twenty yards along the path from the first greenhouse.

'How many have you found?' Gilchrist called.

'Just a handful in each greenhouse. Working.'

'Working? On what?'

Wade gestured behind her with a wave of the arm. Gilchrist saw through the brightly lit doorway a lot of green foliage.

'That's a lot of tomatoes,' she said as they walked nearer.

'That's a lot of marijuana, ma'am.'

'Marijuana? In every greenhouse?' Gilchrist said as she saw Heap hurrying up the rough track from the other greenhouses.

'This is a major bust,' he said, as he came up to them.

Gilchrist nodded. 'Thank goodness for Lizzy Simpson's fear

of ballooning. Sylvia, call the helicopter in. I want it hovering over this until daylight. Bellamy, any word of anyone making a break for it via the bridleway?'

'Negative, ma'am,' Heap said.

'OK, then leave a couple of vehicles and half a dozen officers over there and bring the rest round to help out here. We need to get the people in the barns out to Gatwick for processing. We're going to need some more medics up there to examine them and we need to make sure there's enough food for them. The pros at Gatwick can do the interviewing.

'Bellamy, DI Mountain in Lewes is back from leave. Take Abbas down to the nick there and brief Mountain and ask her politely to interview Abbas. We need to know about this operation; we need to know Farzi's exact whereabouts in Morocco; we want to know if there are any links with the death of Richard Rabbitt. Then there's Joe Jackson's torture and death. See if he knows anything about that.

'Sylvia – you're hoping the techies will crack Joe's laptop and phone today, right? Keep onto them. But first I want you to come with me to Plumpton Down House to talk to Mrs Rabbitt, Rhoda Knowles and Tallulah Granger again. I want to know exactly what the business Rabbitt was planning with Farzi was. And we need to talk to the other neighbours to find out how Farzi could run this operation for God knows how long undiscovered by any round him.' She took an exaggerated breath out. 'It's going to be a long day, boys and girls.'

'Ma'am, there's something else,' Heap said. 'Liesl's friend Sophia mixes in some very bad company. You remember a couple of months ago the chief constable gave us a heads-up after she'd been briefed by the National Drug Enforcement Agency that Albanian gangsters are now controlling pretty much all the hard drugs trade in the UK? They control the supply chain from beginning to end, from supplier to user. They import from South America into various ports around the country to supply. Well, Sophia is mixed up with them somehow.'

'How did you find that out about Sophia?' Gilchrist said.

'The NDEA has a file on her brother and so they've made her a person of interest.'

'You think Liesl and Sophia sicked these men onto Rabbitt?

That Albanians killed him? But he wasn't any kind of competition. They are hard drugs only.'

'For now. They are ruthless. Giving someone a beating like that then slitting his throat wouldn't even register as a hard day at the office.'

'But what would they want with him? I mean, if he was going into business with Farzi to produce marijuana, what would be the advantage in killing him?'

'Maybe to take over that business?'

'No – they'd want him to front it. Or someone. He'd be a perfect cover for them.'

Heap nodded. 'We need to talk to Farzi.'

Nimue Grace phoned as Gilchrist and Heap were walking past her cottage. 'Anything I need to know?' Grace said.

'You've been living next to a major cannabis farm worked by what appear to be slaves from the refugee community.'

'What? How? Have you time to come in and explain?'

Gilchrist stopped and said to Heap: 'You go ahead and come back up here when you're done.'

The door was open when Gilchrist and Wade got to it. Grace was in the kitchen boiling a kettle, barefoot, wearing her usual costume of baggy work shirt and jeans. Gilchrist looked down. The left foot had a big bunion and was a bit bashed up, as Grace had said earlier in the week. Dancer's feet indeed.

'All that would explain all those lorries and vans and cars coming in and out all day and all night that fucked up my drive and caused the spat that got totally out of control.'

'And you challenged him on this?'

'Damned right.'

'And how did he respond?'

'Sneeringly,' Grace said, pouring the water into a cafetière. The aroma of the coffee quickly filled the room.

'That's when he started to threaten me and he started spreading rumours about me. Although, actually, he did that last in collaboration with that snake, Richard Rabbitt, I think. I really just wanted to be left alone to live my life here quietly, but neither of them was going to let me do that.'

'But you'd no idea Farzi was growing cannabis in the greenhouses?'

'No idea. I never see the greenhouses. They're beyond that little rise. I thought that, covered in whitewash as they are, they'd just been left to fall down. I think a couple of them have.'

'And you never heard any ruckuses from the stables?'

'Never. I saw various workers from time to time. And at grape-picking time there were a lot of people there.'

'Locals?'

'Perhaps – they were all people of colour. You may have noticed there aren't many people of colour around here in general. For that matter, when I first moved to this area there weren't many people of colour in Brighton either.' She thought for a moment. 'What will you do with Abbas?'

'What do you mean?'

'Well, I assume he's up to his neck in it.'

She poured the coffee into three mugs and indicated the milk and sugar on the table.

'He's been arrested. Aside from this we need to talk to him about the death of Joe Jackson.'

'He's implicated? Bastard.'

'When was the last time you actually saw Said Farzi?'

'Couple of weeks, maybe. Why?'

'Just trying to establish timelines. Reg Dwight had a drink with him the night Rabbitt was killed?'

'So he said. But, thinking about it, Reg was probably seeing Abbas.'

'Why?' Gilchrist said.

Grace raised one of her famous eyebrows. 'They're both gay.'

'You think Dwight and Abbas are an item?'

'I didn't go that far. But might they have hit it off? Sure.'

Gilchrist drove up to Plumpton Down House probably more pumped up than she should have been. Rhoda Knowles was in the lobby. The debris from the Lego Plumpton had been swept up. Knowles gestured to a table beside the bottom of the stairs. A desktop computer sat on it.

'I thought you said you didn't know where it was?' Gilchrist said.

'Yes, well, I know now.'

'And you know what is on it?'

'I've had a look.'

'Why are you being so cooperative?'

'Liesl's friend Sophia might have something to do with it.'

Gilchrist nodded. 'Is Mrs Rabbitt here?'

Knowles shook her head. 'This is part of Richard I didn't like,' she blurted.

'Liesl and her friend?'

'No. That's just men and their weaknesses. I mean the marijuana thing.'

'What marijuana thing?'

'The arrangement he was trying to put together with Farzi for when cannabis was legalized in this country.'

'No deal before it was legalized?'

'What do you mean?'

'Never mind. And was William Simpson involved in this?'

'I told you before, I don't know who that is.'

'So that was it – they were going to go into business to grow marijuana on their land.'

'Well, it was a bit more than that. They were quietly buying up all the land round here. They were going to have a massive marijuana estate. Plumpton, Ditchling and Hurstpierpoint were going to become sales hubs with high street shops selling a range of products. It was a good business plan, actually.'

'But dependant on marijuana being legalized in the UK.'

'Yes.'

'And if it wasn't?'

'More bloody vines.'

Gilchrist nodded. 'Thanks for that – and the computer. Is Mrs Rabbitt in?'

'I believe so.'

'Can you get her, please?'

Knowles looked at Gilchrist. 'I don't work for her. There's a bell over there.'

Gilchrist nodded. 'What are you going to do after this?'

'Well, there may be still work for me here once all this has settled. If not – every time a door closes another one opens. Right?'

'Right,' Gilchrist said. She rang the intercom bell. Liesl Rabbitt's distinctive harsh voice answered. Why would any man want to have anything to do with this creature?

'It's DI Gilchrist, Mrs Rabbitt. I need to speak to you urgently.'

There was a silence, then: 'Now is not convenient.'

'Would it be more convenient for me to get a warrant for your arrest and stick you in a police cell overnight?'

More silence. 'I'll come down,' Mrs Rabbitt said.

'Great,' Gilchrist said. 'Be quick about it.'

'The deal Richard Rabbitt offered you to avoid the divorce payment. Was it to do with drugs?'

'Why should I tell you?'

'Because you don't want to become a person of interest to the police just when circumstances have conspired to change your life for ever. Because we'll be looking very closely at how that came about. Very closely.'

'He thought he'd fallen in the butter with what Farzi was offering. Marijuana production on a massive scale legally, first medicinally, then, when cannabis was legalized over here, recreationally.'

'And you saw an opportunity there.'

'What do you mean?'

'Well, your friend Sophia. She's linked to the Albanian mafia, right?' Gilchrist put up her hand. 'Don't pollute this air with denials.'

'What is this Albanian mafia racist shit you want to peddle?'

'Mrs Rabbitt. You're a tough cookie, I can see that. I don't know what hardships have shaped you into what you are. But I also know there are people in your community who are far tougher. Who feel absolutely nothing about the destruction they will wreak for and on others.'

'What are you talking about? I have no community. I am for myself.'

'So you don't know about any Albanian gangsters approaching your husband?'

'All I know is that we dropped Richard off at the end of the drive and went into Brighton to the casino.'

Gilchrist's phone rang. Sylvia Wade. 'Ma'am, the divers have found something significant in the lake over near the drive to the big house. A bundle of clothes. Shirt, jumper and red trousers. Wrapped round a hand sickle. So we were right about why he stole Donald Kermode's clothes. Immersion in water won't help us with DNA unfortunately. But, ma'am, a sickle as the murder weapon?'

'Maybe.'

'Oh, and there is an upper set of dentures in a trouser pocket.'

'I hope that will put Bilson's mind at rest.'

'I haven't heard from him, ma'am.'

'I haven't either.' Gilchrist stepped away into a corner and lowered her voice. 'OK, I'll go down to the pond now. Tell DS Heap to join me there. And please hurry those techies up with the phone and the laptop.' She glanced at Mrs Rabbitt. 'Oh, and there's Rabbitt's computer to collect from Plumpton Down House.'

'Ma'am.'

'And dig out from Kermode's statement exactly what clothes got stolen – it's time we prepared some kind of public statement. I'm surprised the story hasn't broken properly yet.'

The portly constable Gilchrist had met on the first evening of this case was standing by his car when she drew up beside the lake. She couldn't remember his name, so simply said: 'You have the evidence?'

He nodded. 'It's bagged in the back of the car, ma'am.'

'Show me the sickle, please.'

It had a worn wooden handle about eight inches long and a curved, almost semicircular metal blade that in a straight line from hilt to tip would have measured about a foot. It was sharp in the inside edge. 'Is that iron?'

'I believe so, ma'am. That probably means it's quite old – they tend to be other metals these days.'

'Do you know what they're for, constable?'

'Harvesting and reaping usually, ma'am. I know the sickle as a reaping hook, but my grandfather on my mother's side, who was an agricultural labourer over Glynde way, used to call it either a rip hook or a slash hook.'

Gilchrist turned it over in its plastic bag. 'So to slit somebody's throat with this you'd need to be behind them?'

'I would think so, ma'am.'

'Is the pathologist Frank Bilson on his way?'

'I wouldn't know that, ma'am,' the constable said. 'Would you like me to find out?'

At that moment, Gilchrist saw a police car pull up at the cattle grid and Heap climb out of the back. 'No,' she said. 'That'll be fine for now. Get these things off to the lab.' She looked at the constable. 'And thanks.'

She met Heap halfway along the iron fencing. 'And?' she said.

'Nothing to report yet, ma'am. DI Mountain was very happy to do the initial interview of Abbas. Customs and Immigration are with her because of all the passports we found stashed in his flat belonging to the people they were enslaving. She also sends her regards and her congratulations on sorting out the muddle of all those swimming-related murders back when we first encountered her.'

'I like her. I'm looking forward to sitting down for a chat with her over a drink or two at some point.'

Heap nodded.

'I think Liesl was going to be paid off with drug money,' Gilchrist said, 'especially when cannabis is legalized over here.'

'Legalization is not going to happen any time soon,' Heap said. 'The government would rather throw good money after bad fighting a drug war it can't possibly win. It doesn't seem to care because too many *Daily Pustule* readers and editorials equate lateral thinking on drugs with liberal-lefty ideas. They want safe streets but won't do the one thing that would lead to them.' He saw Gilchrist's look. 'Soap box immediately stashed away, ma'am.'

Gilchrist's phone rang. The chief constable. 'Uh-oh,' Gilchrist said to Heap, showing him her screen. 'Good morning, ma'am,' she said cheerfully.

'What the hell are you up to?' Hewitt said sharply.

'Haven't we already had this conversation?' Gilchrist said and immediately regretted the flippancy.

'That's what I thought,' Hewitt said. 'So I'm not best pleased to be having it again.'

'Well, acting on information received in Brighton we made a dawn raid on Said Farzi's property in Plumpton Down, in conjunction with Customs and Immigration, and not only found what might well prove to be a slavery operation but also found what might be the biggest illegal drugs manufacturing operation in the county. That's what I've been up to. Ma'am.'

'But why was your colleague who is meant to be handling that side of the Downs in this investigation sitting in my office on Brighton seafront five minutes ago, while you, who should be investigating the death of a student in Brighton, are over in cow-pat land?'

'Mostly llama pats round here, ma'am, actually. Ma'am, we now have two people of interest in Morocco.'

'No.'

'No what, ma'am? I haven't asked a question yet.'

'What are you doing about that young man in your actual bailiwick?'

'As I keep saying, I think what happened to him there is linked to what is going on here. And that is definitely linked to Said Farzi in Morocco.'

'We could send Detective Sergeant Donaldson to Morocco, if you insist,' Hewitt said.

'Don Don to Morocco? He couldn't handle a drone attack that turned out to be his own district's drones, so how is he going to handle something that requires a bit of brain power?'

'That's no way to talk about a fellow officer.'

'He was a fellow officer until his brain got frazzled by steroids. Now he's a lumbering disaster and should be dismissed from the force before he does something terrible or allows something terrible to happen because of his ineptness.'

'I hope you have chapter and verse for these assertions, Sarah, otherwise I'm astonished by your attitude. Now you are not going to Morocco on some wild goose chase but you are, as instructed, going to focus on the death of this poor young man in horrible circumstances in Brighton. With immediate effect, Donaldson will take over complete control of the operation on that side of the Downs, including the drug bust.'

'And take all the bloody credit for it, no doubt,' Gilchrist muttered. She took a long breath. 'Ma'am,' she said, then the call ended. She looked at Heap. 'Let's go to see Mark Harrison and Reg Dwight, see what they know about Said Farzi's operation.'

THIRTEEN

'Nothing at all,' Harrison said at the door of his small farmhouse. 'Never met the guy or had anything to do with his stables. I don't smoke the stuff so don't even know who the local suppliers are. We all know Nimue smokes but I can't imagine for one second Farzi was her supplier, given their mutual hostility.'

He ushered them into his home, ducking beneath a beam as he led them into his main room. 'I thought you were here for my recipe for ostrich egg omelettes.'

'We're not, but you intrigue me,' Gilchrist said. 'You can really use ostrich eggs for omelettes?'

'For sure. Ostrich eggs are just as edible as chicken eggs, if a bit more glutinous. Problem is, they're the size of around twenty-five chicken eggs so you really need a very big pan to cook them in and a few friends round to eat one. Makes for a very companionable occasion. If I say so myself, my omelette parties are famous. Or maybe infamous.'

'Ostrich eggshells look pretty tough,' Heap said.

'Damned right. You either use a hammer – which can get messy – or drill into them. You should try one.' He pointed into the kitchen at a huge bowl with several huge eggs in it. 'Take one of those when you go – or does that constitute a bribe?'

'Depends if we're going to arrest you or not,' Gilchrist said then flushed as she realized how unprofessional she was being. *Gawd, hormones over professionalism again.*

'And are you?' he said, an attractive smile on his face. 'Is that why you're here?'

'Do you have farm implements here?' Heap said.

'Don't have much use for them. The usual tools I suppose.'

'Hand sickles?'

Harrison shook his head.

'What about the implements you use when you're slaughtering your ostriches?'

'Oh, I wouldn't have a clue how to do that. I call someone in from over Forest Row way and he brings his own kit. I can't even watch. Too squeamish.'

'OK then,' Gilchrist said. 'That's all we need. If we find we have more questions, we'll be back in touch.' She rooted in her pocket and handed him a card. 'And if you think of anything, then please call me.'

Harrison looked at the card in his hand. 'And if I don't?' he said.

'Don't what?' Gilchrist said.

'Don't think of anything. Can I call you anyway?'

Gilchrist flushed but didn't say anything.

'Where is your flock?' Heap said quickly.

'Just round the back of the house,' Harrison said. 'Wanna see?'

'Sure,' Gilchrist said.

He led them round to a large, high-fenced enclosure. 'I've only got the three. It's all I need really.' He stopped and looked around. 'Fuck. He's got out again.' There were only two, rather drab-looking ostriches in the pen. 'I've got to make the fence higher,' Harrison said as he pointed down the field at a huge, black-and-white ostrich heading at speed towards Nimue Grace's wood. 'He goes a bit potty sometimes. I don't know why.' Harrison looked over at the police car. 'Couldn't give me a lift down there, could you? I'm going to have to bring him back. Let me just grab my tranquillizer kit.'

As they were heading back down the drive, Gilchrist said: 'How are you going to catch him?'

'With difficulty.'

'Can we help?'

'It's kind of a tricky process because there's a risk of being disembowelled. If he kicks out and catches you in the belly with that long, sharp toenail that's you done with.'

'How do you avoid that?' Heap said.

'Gotta get close enough to him to grab his neck and force his head down. He can't kick out then. I'll inject him with the tranquillizer then. Of course, it's equally tricky when I let go of his neck before the tranquillizer takes effect. Not so much the kick as his wings. He'll bat at you with them because he's disoriented and he can do it powerfully enough to break some of your bones.'

When they parked by the lake they could see the ostrich

between the trees at the edge of the wood. Gilchrist and Heap accompanied Harrison towards it. It seemed to be grazing. It watched them with one of its big eyes as they approached.

'What's that?' Gilchrist said, pointing out something lumpy a few yards in front of the ostrich.

Harrison shrugged and led them closer. He stopped about ten yards away from the lump. 'Shit.'

'Shit indeed,' Gilchrist murmured as she peered at a bearded man, lying on his back, dead and disembowelled.

An hour later, Gilchrist called Nimue Grace. 'This is just a heads-up that we have another dead person in your wood. We haven't been able to identify him yet – he had no ID on him. We don't think the death is suspicious.'

'Sounds suspicious to me.'

'The only odd thing is that he has no identification, so we're not sure if he has anything to do with Richard Rabbitt's death or has something to do with Farzi's operation – you know, a man who ran away during the raid this morning. That would explain the lack of ID. Except he's not a person of colour. Olive complexion. Maybe from somewhere round the Mediterranean but I've no idea really.

'What does he look like?' Grace said quickly.

'You think you might know him?'

'That depends on what he looks like.'

'Dark scrubby beard, dark curly hair, receding. About five foot nine. Skinny.' There was silence on the other end of the line. 'You recognize that description?'

'Perhaps. I don't know.' Grace sounded subdued. 'Does he have a tattoo on his neck of a bird?'

Heap bent over the body and nodded.

'Sounds like you know him,' Gilchrist said. 'If you could help us to identify him that would be great. You wouldn't have to look at the body or anything. We can take photos.'

'OK, come on over with the photos.'

Grace was standing by the gate to her garden when Gilchrist and Heap arrived. She looked as subdued as she had sounded. She greeted them and held out her hand.

'Should you be sitting for this?' Gilchrist said.

Grace gave a little shake of her head, her hand still held out. Gilchrist showed her a photo of the dead man's face on her phone. Grace looked at it then offered the phone back to Gilchrist. Gilchrist scanned her face. 'And?'

'His name is Antonio. Antonio Urraca though he should have been called Cuco.' She gestured behind her. 'Look, let's go and sit at the table, shall we? There's food if you want it. I have stuff to tell you.'

She led them to the long, battered oak table on the flagstone terrace outside the French windows.

'I had a relationship with Antonio. He seemed to be the kind of person I could trust and rely on but it was all show. He's the second man to pretty much destroy me.'

'Does he live in the area?' Heap said. 'Did he?'

'Well, he lived with me almost as soon as I met him. I was very vulnerable and very lonely. His ex-partner was my secretary in the days that I still needed one. She had a young daughter, Tiffany, and they would come with me to exotic places when I was working – I was taking small budget films abroad. When they had nowhere to live they stayed here, rent free, food provided, for what was supposed to be three months and turned out to be fourteen months.

'Then Antonio turned up to see them. He and his ex weren't an item or anything. He offered to help with the orchard – pruning and all that sort of thing. One thing led to another and he stayed. It was a massive mistake but I was stuck with it and I tried to make it work.'

'What did he use to prune with?' Heap said.

'Oh – no English tool was good enough for him. He had two or three sickles he'd brought with him from Spain.'

'Do you know where they are?'

Grace shrugged. 'He got it in his head to restore the water-cress beds down in the other half of the wood. There's a falling down lean-to in that half of the wood. I think he stored his tools there.' She saw something in the look Heap and Gilchrist exchanged. 'How did he die?'

'Well, don't laugh, but he seems to have had a fatal encounter with an ostrich.'

Grace did laugh. 'Perfect,' she said, shaking her head.

'Where is he based?' Gilchrist said as Heap texted Wade to check out the lean-to in the wood.

'No idea but I'd heard he was in the neighbourhood recently.'

'You were together a long time?'

'Too long but no, not really. A few years. And I paid for him too, of course. He never worked while we were together, he just spent my money. All my money. I was such a fool. At least we never had children together – he couldn't, thank God.'

'Why was he here now?'

'Tiffany's wedding in Lewes. Reception somewhere snooty. I'm not sure if it has happened or not.'

'You weren't invited?'

'When I kicked him out and stopped the money supply none of them were ever in touch again. Oh, except I got an email from Tiffany's mother saying she'd never liked me.'

'Where was your ex staying for the wedding?'

'Staying with his friend Will in Hurstpierpoint, probably. Look, I've tried to be very discreet and private in recent years. I feel very uncomfortable about exposing myself like this so I hope you'll be discreet.'

Gilchrist nodded. 'Of course. Did Antonio make any attempt to contact you recently? Did you see him?'

'No and no.'

'When was the last time you did see him?' Heap asked.

Grace thought for a moment. 'It must be two years ago now.'

'Did Antonio know Major – Mr – Rabbitt?'

'Yes. But there's no reason why he should have anything to do with Rabbitt's murder.'

'Did they get on?'

'Nobody got on with Rabbitt. He was an utter shit.'

'Where does this Will person live? And a contact for Tiffany's mum would be useful.'

'Will lives in Hurstpierpoint, the other side of Ditchling. Hang on. I'll get the address for him and the bitch.' She went into the house and handed Gilchrist an address scrawled on a piece of notepaper. 'Anything more for now?'

'It seems odd that Mark Harrison said he didn't recognize him if you were together for a good while.'

'As I said, I was very discreet. And Tiffany and her mother were still living here, so if anyone gave it any thought it would be a bit confusing.'

'Are you OK, though?'

Grace nodded. 'I never fed you,' she said absently.

'Next time,' Gilchrist said.

'What are you thinking, Bellamy?' Gilchrist asked as they drove back down Grace's drive.

'I'm thinking we mustn't let Nimue Grace's charisma blind us to her status as a potential suspect.'

'You think I'm doing that?' Gilchrist huffed.

Heap gave her a quick look. 'No, ma'am – I think I'm doing that.'

'You were right, though. She *is* a bit of an enchantress. One man found dead in her lake. A second man found dead who is her former lover. A young kid filming at her lake beaten to death – although I don't think that's connected to Nimue. And here we've been acting all pally with her.'

'Hard not to, ma'am.'

'True. But she is definitely a person of interest.'

'What's that Oscar Wilde quote about parents: "losing one parent is unfortunate, losing two is careless" – or, in our world, potentially criminal. Two victims linked to her. But do you think, ma'am, if we keep aware of that, the best way of investigating her is to take advantage of her apparent friendliness?'

Gilchrist looked at him. 'That's a bit devious, isn't it?'

'It's a bit more complicated than that for us, ma'am, because we do actually like her.'

'True,' Gilchrist said. 'What was that Grace was saying about the names?'

'His name translates as magpie but *cuco* means cuckoo – you know, taking over someone's nest.'

They were heading for the far end of Hurstpierpoint so it took a little time to get through the traffic on the narrow high street, especially as the supermarket had a big delivery van outside.

They went over the mini-roundabout, past the church on their left, to find the address they had been given was one of a short terrace of whitewashed workmen's cottages opposite a veterinary surgery. They parked on double yellow lines and knocked on the door. Nothing. They peered through the windows either side of the door. It was dark and quiet inside. Heap knocked on the next-door neighbour's door, while Gilchrist crossed the road to ask about Will in the vet's.

By the time Gilchrist had finished with the receptionist, none the wiser but touched by all the injured little creatures in reception, Heap had tried every door on the terrace.

'Only one person in,' he reported. 'Knows Will well. Antonio she has met. Hasn't seen either of them since Sunday last.'

'The day Rabbitt was probably murdered.'

'We're thinking it was Farzi, aren't we, for Rabbitt, ma'am? Business deal gone wrong?'

'We are – and this death is just an unfortunate coincidence.'

'Except it begs the question what was Antonio doing loitering in the woods. Keeping an eye on what we were finding in the lake?'

Bilson phoned. 'You have need of my services again, Sarah?'

'You're sounding chirpier.'

'I must apologize for my moroseness the other day. A major shock to my system. It was a major misdiagnosis during a routine check-up at the hospital. I thought my days were numbered. By that I mean – since I know all our days are numbered – the diagnosis I received fell into the category of "don't start a long novel". Hence my unseemly oddness.'

'Frank – I had no idea. That must have been horrible for you.'

'Not the nicest thing but one rebounds. And here I am, eager as a ferret faced with a trouser leg to get on with it.'

'We have an unusual death, but I don't want you laughing.'

'Why should I laugh? Even though I would think you would welcome that.'

'The victim was killed by an ostrich.'

Bilson laughed.

'I've been told that if they are threatened, they respond violently,' Gilchrist said. 'This one either ran over the victim or kicked him to death. The victim seemed to have been disembowelled, actually.'

'Well, the male ostrich is pretty formidable. Around nine feet tall and probably weighs 330 pounds. You will have heard of people being killed by stampeding cattle. Imagine, grotesque as the idea is, something that big and heavy and fast stampeding over you. You wouldn't stand a chance. Or you said he might have been kicked to death?'

'That's why we need you to ascertain cause of death.'

'Well, in Africa, ostriches have been known to kill a lion with a kick. Their legs bend forward at the knee not back. That gives a kick extra power. They kick and they slash. The male is quite capable of disembowelling. Each foot has just two toes and the main toe is like a hoof but with a long, sharp claw at the end. Funny how every animal seems to know that disembowelling is the most effective way to deal with an enemy.'

'So we're assuming it's accidental death,' Gilchrist said.

'Unless someone hired the ostrich to do it.'

'Very funny, Frank.'

'I thought so. I'll be at the lake in five minutes.'

Gilchrist thought aloud: 'Or unless someone killed him to make it look like an ostrich did it?'

Bilson laughed. 'Did you ever think there'd be a time in your career you'd be saying those words, Sarah?'

She joined in his laughter. 'I didn't, but the longer I spend out in the country the more I realize it's even weirder than Brighton.'

Sylvia Wade phoned soon after to say two sickles had been found in the lean-to. 'Also, ma'am, I ran that student, Joe Jackson, through the computer and checked him on Facebook and Twitter and Instagram and—'

'Steady, Sylvia, don't go all Cambridge Analytica on us,' Gilchrist said.

'It's all out there, ma'am. I was trying to see if he'd posted any footage of his film that might help us. But he hasn't. And it isn't on his computer either. We've unlocked it now. One odd thing so far. The last website he was on was that of the Bank of England. Specifically a click through about exchanging old money. There's also an automatic email from the Bank saying that if he brought old money in it would be processed by the Bank of England – if they were willing to take it. They recommended posting it as the queues at the counter in the Bank of England could be very long and he would probably be queuing for at least an hour.'

'It never occurred to me the Bank of England would have counters,' Gilchrist said. 'It's not like anyone but the government could have an account there, is it?'

'I don't know, ma'am. But that's odd, isn't it?'

'Very. Look, check locally first to see if Joe Jackson went into any bank to try to change old money. Plus phone the Bank of England, see if he did send them a pile of old money.'

'Ma'am,' Wade said.

Gilchrist frowned and turned to Heap. 'Do you think this is somehow linked to his death?'

'I don't know,' he said. 'I can't think how. Except it's usually a good idea to follow the money.'

Before long Wade came back. 'NatWest Pavilion branch on the street beside the Pav reports that he brought in £1,000 in old notes four days ago for conversion into new money.'

'Bingo.'

'But he didn't post them to the Bank of England, ma'am. They were hand delivered. Ten packages containing not £1,000 but half a million pounds in old denominations.'

'Half a million pounds?' Gilchrist tilted her chair back. 'Where is a student going to get that sort of money, new or old?'

'Maybe he found something in that crappy tenement block he shared with the other students?' Wade said.

'Did he deliver it himself?' Heap said.

'The signature they have for who delivered it is illegible but the spelled out name below is Ronald Biggs. Is he one of his housemates?'

Heap laughed. 'Someone's taking the mickey. He's one of the Great Train Robbers from back in the Sixties.'

'This is making less and less sense,' Gilchrist said. 'What has the bank done with this old money?'

'Nothing yet, ma'am – it's still being processed.'

Gilchrist spent the next ten minutes trying to do some processing herself. She was interrupted by Bilson calling back.

'The ostrich is innocent. Release it immediately.'

'What? But we saw it career into the wood then we found it a few yards away from the dead man.'

'Sarah, didn't your training tell you not to confuse coincidence with correlation? How close did you get to the dead man?'

'Not very – his guts were spilling out of him.'

'Indeed they were and indeed he was disembowelled. But not today. In fact – and you really should have spotted this by the state of the guts – not yesterday either. I would hazard that he was killed on Sunday last and I would further hazard that he was killed earlier than Richard Rabbitt.'

'With that sickle?'

'Quite probably.'

'Left-handed or right-handed?' Gilchrist said.

'Now ordinarily I would scoff at such a question, as you know, but in this instance, with this rather unwieldy weapon, that can be determined. Uninterestingly, the Spanish gentleman's assailant was right-handed.'

'Would the killer need to be particularly strong for either attack?'

'Both attacks were from behind so the element of surprise would be a powerful advantage offsetting any physical shortcomings.'

'As always, Frank, I'm obliged—'

'Though now I think of it, perhaps they are not so unwieldy in the experienced hand. You'll remember that Paulus Hector Mair, the Renaissance expert on fighting methods, has a whole chapter in his combat manual on fighting with sickles?'

'Of course I remember,' Gilchrist said. 'What do you think I am – a dunce? Goodbye, Frank.'

FOURTEEN

Gilchrist and Heap called next on Nimue Grace. She didn't open the door. Instead, she shouted through a half open window beside it. The curtains were closed.

'You two can just fuck off!'

Gilchrist did a double take. 'What's wrong, Ms Grace?'

'What's wrong? My phone is ringing off the hook and my orchard and garden are swarming with journalists trying to door-step me and photographers trying to pap me. I'm surprised you didn't run into them on your way up the drive. Half of them are from the *Daily Pustule* competing with each other for the story.'

'What story?' Heap said.

'I trusted you,' Grace said.

'We don't know what you're talking about,' Gilchrist said.

The door suddenly opened but Grace wasn't there. 'Well, come on in for a minute for fuck's sake,' she said from behind it. 'I'm not going to let them photograph me in my dressing gown as if I'm Cherie Blair bringing in the milk or something.'

Gilchrist and Heap stepped over the threshold and Grace slammed the door shut behind them. She was, indeed, in a long dressing gown. Her face was drawn, her jaw clenched.

'You,' she pointed at Heap, 'were supposed to be my Sir Galahad. My protector. And you've fucked me.'

Heap looked truly anguished.

'I'm sorry, Ms Grace, I'm completely in the dark.'

'Don't Ms Grace me. I at least expect men to call me by my first name when they've fucked me.'

Heap turned scarlet.

'Why are journalists calling you?' Gilchrist said. 'More to the point, why are you blaming us for that?'

'Because every fucking one of them start their slimy questions with "police sources tell us". That's why. You've given them *everything*. The name of the guy who was the reason I left Hollywood. The acid attack. The next-door neighbour drug dealer who wanted to make me his mistress. I'm surprised they're not asking about the Spanish guy who took all my money and ended up dead. But give it bloody time.'

She covered her face with her hands. 'I mean: fuck! They're not going to give up until they get the full story. And that means harassing me here, doorstepping all my friends from the past twenty years and what little family I have and getting that fucking creep Bosanquet to sell his braggart story of his nights of passion with Naughty Nimue Grace. There will be drones overhead all the time, paparazzi hiding in the trees – so I'll never be able to go in the garden or orchard or down to the lake and I'll have to keep my curtains closed all the time.

'Then, *all* this shit will be piled on top of me where my private life is more important than my acting career and my acting will be washed away in the flow of it.' She looked at them fiercely. 'You promised me!' She sounded in true pain. 'And I trusted you!'

Heap started to speak.

'Not another fucking word from you.' She pointed at Gilchrist. 'Or you. If you ever want to talk to me again, talk to my lawyers.'

She stood behind the door again, opened it and gestured for them to go. They stepped outside and turned. 'Why do I never fucking learn that I can't trust *anybody*?' Grace said quietly as she slammed the door.

Gilchrist and Heap didn't speak until they got in the car. 'Let's get some local coppers to flush out people on her land at least,' Gilchrist said. 'I'm not sure there is anything we can do about the drones.'

'Donaldson,' is all Heap said in response.

Gilchrist called the local community policeman and Lewes police station to organize shifts for a couple of officers to guard the perimeter of Grace's property. Then they drove back to her hotel in silence. In the car park, Gilchrist said: 'Come and have a drink in the bar, Bellamy. Please. Don't leave me feeling like this.'

They settled in the bar by the log fire – the weather was on the turn. Gilchrist had a large Sauvignon blanc but instead of his customary beer, Heap ordered a double Laphroaig. He saw Gilchrist's raised eyebrow. 'I'll leave the car here and walk home,' he said.

'It wasn't that. This has really got to you, hasn't it?'

'She's right, Sarah,' Heap said. 'She shared with us her most fiercely kept secrets and tomorrow, when the first editions come out, it's going to be out in the world for everyone to gloat over and comment on.' He saw Gilchrist start to speak and he continued: 'I think I know what you're about to say. It wasn't us it was Donaldson. But it was us. We didn't care for her privacy as we had promised.' He took a sip of his drink. 'And now we have to make amends.'

Gilchrist nodded and glumly chinked her glass against Heap's.

'So how can we? She's right about the shit storm I'm sure – she knows more about this tabloid stuff than we do and what with the internet and all the social media as well, we can't close that sewer door.'

'Can the police commissioner do anything – an injunction or something like that – to prevent the tabloids printing the story?'

'Maybe,' Gilchrist said. 'But that would just pique interest and you can't control the internet.'

'Let's go after Bosanquet. See if he's involved with what has been going on here. Find a way to shut him down before he can make her life even more difficult.'

'We go to Morocco? I told you Chief Constable Karen Hewitt won't sign off on that.'

'It doesn't have to be us,' Heap said quietly, relishing a bigger sip of his whisky.

'You mean Jimmy Tingley? And if you do mean Jimmy Tingley, what else do you mean? We can't just keep using him as our guided missile.'

Jimmy Tingley was ex-SAS and the best friend of Bob Watts and had helped them out unofficially and sometimes not entirely legally over recent years.

As if he hadn't heard her, Heap went on: 'Then we see to Don Donaldson.'

'See to him how?'

'Report him to Disciplinary. Get him demoted or kicked out altogether.'

'Bellamy, you know we can't do that. That goes against the entire Us versus Them ethos of the police. We don't rat on our own.'

Heap emptied his glass. 'Lovely smoky smell and taste this. Peaty.' He looked at Gilchrist. 'I'm not asking you to do it, Sarah. I'm going to do it. I'm not one of the gang. I'm not signed up to this tribal thing. I'm not like the others – they know it and I know it. I don't mind that. I'm comfortable with who I am. But Donaldson has been given a long enough leash and I think it's time somebody hung him from it.'

'Don't lump me in with the gang,' Gilchrist said quickly.

'I wasn't but you still have more to lose than me.'

Gilchrist, mollified, studied him over the rim of her glass.

'Has this got anything to do with the fact that you like Nimue Grace?'

'You mean that I have a crush on her because she set out to enchant me and succeeded?'

'I wasn't going to put it like that, but since you're the one saying it . . .'

'Underneath all that charm and charisma I see a vulnerable, lost woman who needs our help.'

Gilchrist nodded slowly and put her glass down.

'And faced with women like that, good men like you are doomed. Oh, dear.' She shrugged. 'Oh, well, at least there's one positive outcome from all this.'

'What's that?'

'You've been calling me Sarah for the past half hour without it sounding odd.'

Oddly, there was nothing in the next day's papers about Nimue Grace and the murders. Over the rather nice breakfast in Pelham House, Gilchrist got an animated call from Bellamy Heap.

'Good morning to you, Bellamy. It's not like you to be so excited.'

'You obviously don't know me then, ma'am. Remember that thing Bilson said: coincidence is not the same as correlation?'

'Vaguely,' Gilchrist said, chewing on another piece of toast.

'On my walk home last night I was going through the options. Said Farzi was somehow responsible for the death of Rabbitt, Antonio and, somehow linked, Joe Jackson. Or the Albanian hard mob did two of them and poor Joe was a separate thing altogether. Or, unlikely, Nimue Grace killed the lot or her ex, or and or and or – so many possibilities.

'Kate was fast asleep when I got home and I was buzzing so I glanced at that pamphlet, the Hassocks blockade, that has been staring us in the face throughout the investigation. The guy who wrote it lives in the cottages near Ms Grace. He gave her a copy to get a blurb.'

'I remember the pamphlet. Burning cars blocking a street on the cover.'

'Some years ago, back in the day when Hassocks still had three banks on the high street and before the sorting office for Royal Mail was closed down, there was an armed bank robbery of all the banks, the sorting office and the sub-post office in the village. Multiple armed robberies, rather. Very organized. They blocked off either end of the high street with cars across the road first, then two men hit the bank at the Ditchling end of the high street; two others hit the sub-post office in the middle of the high street at the same time as two more hit the bank across the road from that. Four in the sorting office and two in the bank opposite. Around ten men in total, not including the two getaway drivers stationed at either end of the town. Balaclavas, sawn-off shotguns and baseball bats. It was like the Wild West – as they got away in two different directions they set fire to those cars blocking the road at either end of the high street.

'It made all the nationals, of course. Especially as they just disappeared. The initial assumption was they had reached the A23 and either gone south towards Brighton or north towards the M23 and London – or who knows where.

'The following day a burned-out car was discovered in the National Trust car park at Ditchling Beacon and a couple of weeks later an abandoned car was found in the multistorey car park at Gatwick.'

'They got away clean?' Gilchrist said.

'As far as anyone knows. Certainly the money was never recovered but nor did it appear in circulation. The money from the banks that is, where the numbers were traceable. The sub-post office money was not traceable anyway so it's impossible to say what happened to that. Or exactly what got stolen from the sorting office, although they were, apparently, selective in there.'

'And they were never caught.'

'Never,' Heap said.

'So what are you thinking?'

'Well, the guy who wrote the pamphlet is making connections with the Great Train Robbery.'

'Same people, you mean?'

'No, no. That too was very carefully planned and executed, although the Great Train Robbery was disastrously managed at the end when it came to fingerprints. Until then, they were very professional. They stopped the train where they had multiple escape routes onto motorways. They were London thieves and could have got to London in a couple of hours. Or anywhere for that matter. But they did a very clever thing. They didn't really go anywhere. Knowing the police would be pretty quick to establish road blocks they went no more than twenty miles to a farmhouse they'd rented earlier. And they holed up there for a week.'

'You're saying that maybe these robbers in Hassocks did the same thing around here?' Gilchrist said.

'That's what this historian is suggesting.'

'Does he suggest where they might have holed up?'

'No, but he found that Plumpton Down House was empty at the time. Theoretically.'

'And they stashed the money there? And never spent it?'

'Well, if it has only been found now, none of it would be usable. The new plastic currency has replaced the old money. There's a new £50 note.'

'Why would they not have spent it, Bellamy?'

'The robbers had been put away for something else.'

'What – all of them?'

'All the ones who knew where the money was.'

'So Joe Jackson stumbles on the money at the lake. How?'

'The white containers, ma'am,' Heap murmured.

'We're talking about those blooming white containers?'

'I think we are, ma'am.'

'You've reverted to ma'am, by the way.'

'Yes, ma'am. Sorry, ma'am.'

'That's OK – but please don't do it twice in the same exchange. So, Joe Jackson was one of the filmmakers down at Grace's lake. The white containers were full of money. Old money, so not county line drug dealers. Not illicit cannabis growing in vineyards. Something else – this robbery.' She tapped her teeth with her pen. 'This whole thing could be about something else.'

'Not all of it but we probably will have to look in other places too,' Heap said.

'So, bank robbery, the culprits go away for a long stretch and while they are away the Bank of England replaces the old currency with new stuff. Richard Rabbitt and/or Joe Jackson stumble upon it when the water is particularly low.' Gilchrist rubbed her cheek. 'Yet, Bellamy, you say nobody has any idea who did the Hassocks robberies?'

'I didn't quite say that, ma'am. I said that nobody was brought to trial for it. A professional robber called Graham Goody was suspected of masterminding this – he'd been involved in the Brink's-Matt when he first started out. He was nabbed at his villa on the Costa del Crime for drug smuggling just a couple of months after the Hassocks blockade. We need to check if/when he has been released.'

'But what about all the others? They all got nabbed for this or that for long sentences?'

'As I said, maybe they didn't know where the money was stashed?'

'So they accepted that they had worked for nothing? I don't buy that. They'd come looking for Graham Goody, in jail or out. And they wouldn't take no for an answer. Who are his known associates?'

'I'll find out, ma'am,' Wade said.

'And when did Goody get released?'

Heap was working on his iPad. 'He didn't. He's still inside. In Lewes actually.'

Gilchrist smiled.

'Well, that's handy. Make an appointment for later today.'

'Ma'am.'

Sarah Gilchrist got to Lewes Prison before Heap. As she was waiting in reception, DI Mountain walked in. They had encountered each other briefly on Gilchrist's last investigation.

'How are you, DI Gilchrist?'

'Getting there.'

'How are you getting on with DS Donaldson?'

'You know him?' Gilchrist asked.

'Our paths have inevitably crossed.'

'Well, what do you think of him?'

DI Mountain looked at Gilchrist intently. She seemed to be weighing something up.

'Honestly?'

'Well, yes, of course honestly.'

'He's an arrogant pig who doesn't know his arse from his elbow. But I assume you already knew that.'

'I did already know that.'

'He's not much of a team player, is he?'

'As you say – hasn't taken you long to suss that out?'

'It was obvious from the get-go. The report you made was quite exposing for Nimue Grace. You expected him to keep it confidential?'

'Where is he now?' Gilchrist said.

'In hospital. Had some kind of attack – found in a corridor at

Haywards Heath unconscious on the floor – so he's being checked out. Bruising under his chin, no other signs of a bad fall apparently.

'An attack? You mean like a seizure or something?'

Mountain shrugged. 'Nobody knows. But the docs advised him to take the rest of the week off. Then, I hear, he's either going on suspension for inappropriate dealings with the press or being called back to Gatwick to be on the alert for the latest drone attack. He's the whizz on drones apparently. Hard to believe he's a whizz at anything but there you go.'

She looked beyond Gilchrist. 'Here's your sidekick.' Heap approached and shook her hand. Mountain nodded to both of them. 'Let me just go ahead and set this up. Won't be a mo.' She called back over her shoulder. 'Job well done, DS Heap. The drinks are on half the local force next time you're in the pub.'

Gilchrist looked at Heap. 'What was that about?' Heap shrugged.

'Mountain was just telling me Don-Don was found in a corridor earlier today, unconscious on the floor.' Gilchrist thought for a moment. 'Know anything about that?'

'No,' Heap said. 'I hadn't heard.'

'That's not what I meant.'

Heap shrugged.

'That drink culture is hard to stamp out. Is he all right?'

'Bruising under his chin, no other signs of a bad fall apparently. They don't know if he had some kind of seizure. Docs advised him to take the rest of the week off. Then his suspension will come through with luck.'

'Then he's out of the way. Excellent.'

'But it wasn't a seizure, was it, Bellamy?'

'Depends what you mean by a seizure.'

'You don't think it's going to be that easy, do you? He's going to be out to get you.'

Heap was thinking back. He hadn't exactly been looking for Donaldson but he'd found him, in a quiet corridor between offices.

'So you're trying to get me suspended, Junior G-Man,' Donaldson called as they approached each other from opposite ends of the corridor. 'Punching above your weight, ain't you, Boy Detective, taking me on?'

'We'll see,' Heap said, trying to move past him. 'You're not supposed to leak confidential information to the press.'

'Why don't we see now?' Donaldson said, knocking the sheaf of papers out of Heap's hand. 'Just you and me.'

'That didn't end so well for you last time, if you remember,' Heap said. Some years ago they'd had a tussle in which the then newly arrived Heap had floored muscle-bound Donaldson.

'Yeah, well, I know what a sneaky git you are now, don't I?'

'Outside then, when I've delivered these papers,' Heap said, gesturing to the scattered pages on the floor. He took a step back and bent sideways with a little twist of his waist to the left. As he extended his left arm towards the papers he clenched his fist, then came back up suddenly, twisting back to the centre and curling his left arm and punching upwards with the clenched fist. The upper cut, given double the force by delivering it from so far down, caught Donaldson just under the tip of his chin.

Donaldson's head snapped back as his whole body crumpled. Heap stepped forward and clasped his arms round Donaldson's waist to take his weight and guide his fall. When Donaldson was almost on the floor, Heap moved his hand to cradle his head and lower it, almost tenderly, to the floor. He looked at him for a moment, ensuring his air passages were open, then picked up his papers and carried on down the corridor.

He looked at Gilchrist now. 'I know. And it won't be with fists this time. Not with his glass jaw.'

'So it was you.' Gilchrist shook her head. 'Bellamy Heap. What will become of you?'

FIFTEEN

Graham Goody was a tall, broad-shouldered man in his fifties. He was good looking and confident. In the interrogation room, he gave Gilchrist the once-over, and nodded at Heap and DI Mountain.

'I understand why you're here,' he said. 'But what do I get out of this? If I had nicked all this money you say someone has now nicked from me, what do I have to gain now that it's all gone?'

'Somebody is murdering any person who these days might conceivably be inadvertently linked to the money. One of your colleagues?'

'I repeat, what's in it for me?'

'Well, if you fessed up to the robbery and named your colleagues that could go well for you.'

Goody threw his head back theatrically and laughed loudly. 'Do you think I'm slow or something? If I admit to armed robbery, even if no one got hurt – which they didn't – they wouldn't just add another long sentence to my existing one, they'd throw away the key. Armed robbery is treated as a beast of a different colour to the drug-smuggling charges I'm in here for. Rightly or wrongly. And as for giving up my colleagues in this alleged crime . . . dream on.'

Gilchrist leaned forward. 'There's a killer on the loose out there – two, possibly three deaths and counting. And it's possible all the deaths are linked to the money you allegedly stole in Hassocks fifteen years ago. You help us get him and it *will* help you substantially. Looking at your sheet and other stuff that unofficially you're linked with, violence has never been your thing. Ever. The threat of it, sure, but you've never gone through with it.'

'True enough,' Goody said.

Heap nodded. 'Now either that's because you were too much of a wuss and got your oppos to do the stuff you were too sensitive to do yourself or because you genuinely didn't agree with violence.'

Goody looked at Gilchrist and gestured with his head towards Heap. 'He's a bit lippy for one so small.' He gave Heap a hard look. 'Then again I knew a Scottish nutter about your size who could go through an entire room. They used to say the only way to stop him was to kill him. Which is eventually what happened, of course.' Goody looked up at the ceiling. 'I'm opposed to violence. *Not* because I'm a wuss, Detective Sergeant – I have no problem standing up for myself – but on a job it's counterproductive.'

'So will you tell us who you think this man might be?'

'I will not – Marquis of Crimesbury rules and all that. But I will tell you what you should already have thought of. Who has broken out of prison recently?'

Gilchrist nodded. 'OK. That's not going to get you much but thanks. Can we get you something in here in return?'

'You kidding? Since drones were invented – God bless you, guv'nor, whoever you are who invented them – every high-security prison is like an open prison. I can get whatever I want, pretty much whenever I want.' He chuckled. 'I wouldn't be surprised if whoever did escape was able to do so with a rope ladder dropped over the prison wall by a drone at exercise time.'

'Mr Goody,' Heap said, 'might I ask you a slightly different question?'

'Be my guest. You two seem relatively intelligent and intelligent conversation is hard to find with this bunch of thickos in here – that was the most cruel and unusual punishment the British legal system could provide for me, bunging me in here with a load of retards.'

Heap looked at Gilchrist. 'Ma'am, with permission – this has just occurred to me.' Gilchrist nodded, wondering what he was going to say. Heap surprised her with: 'When you were running your drug operation in Spain, I imagine you got your drugs from Morocco. Did you have dealings with Said Farzi?'

Goody sat back. 'Let me look you up and down, Detective Sergeant – as you'll realize it won't take but a moment. Said Farzi. Is he involved in this?'

'You got your drugs from Morocco?'

'Well, it was a bit more complicated than that but for marijuana, essentially, yes. Cocaine was something different and that came a different route. I understand now the Albanians have pretty much taken it over in the UK. Ruthless bastards.'

Heap nodded. 'The harder drugs came over from South America in one direction and Afghanistan in the other, but the cannabis was Moroccan home-grown.'

'He knows his stuff this detective sergeant.'

'My name is Bellamy Heap,' Heap said. 'Was Said Farzi a major player in this?'

Goody gave a big, toothy grin. 'Now can I get a deal on this kind of info? Marquis of Crimesbury rules don't apply to this geezer.'

'Because he's a different skin colour?' Heap said.

Goody frowned. 'No, you numpty, it's because he's an untrust-worthy sleazebag. And I draw the line at human trafficking, slavery and prostitution. Call me old-fashioned but a bit of armed robbery would be as far as I would want to go, if I were, in fact, that sort of person.'

'You can confirm he's involved with all those things?' Gilchrist said.

'You hadn't noticed? Last time I heard he was planning to do the dirty on that film star lives next door to him – what's her name? Unpronounceable first name, last name Grace. The one with the great body who's also a bit of a culture vulture. When I say do the dirty, I don't mean that kind of dirty – well, actually, that too, if he could. Can't say I blame him. Sure your Stormy Daniels-type looks worth a go-around but there's something about being with a beautiful woman with brains – well, as long as they shut up for the duration. There's a time and a place, after all.'

'What was the other kind of dirty he wanted to do?' Gilchrist said calmly.

'Force her out of her home, grab that lake and wood off her.'

'How would he do that?' Heap said.

'Have we made the deal and I missed it?' Goody said.

'No, but we will,' Gilchrist said. 'You have my word.' Goody just looked down at the table. 'Any information about Said Farzi that is substantive will definitely make for a reduction of your sentence.'

He looked up. 'You're not in a position to make that deal, though.'

'I'll get somebody who is. Within the hour.'

'Get me Bob Watts.'

Gilchrist frowned. 'Bob Watts is no longer chief constable.'

'I'm aware of that. But he's police commissioner.'

'Police commissioners have no operational input.'

'I know that and I know they've become something of an expensive joke. Politics, eh? But I trust Bob Watts. Get me Bob Watts.'

Gilchrist texted Sylvia Wade to get hold of Watts and bring him to Lewes Prison. She showed Goody her phone. 'Done. So are you saying Said Farzi is a criminal?'

Goody looked at her for a long time. 'Hello?' he said. 'Time for you to wake up and smell the shit, Detective Inspector. When you look at what criminal slime the tide has washed up here in the past decade, hidden among all the good people who have immigrated, well, he's the slimiest.' He made a zipping mouth gesture. 'But I won't say any more until Bob gets here.'

'Bob. You're on first name terms?' Goody gave a little smile and a sideways nod.

Gilchrist's phone rang. 'Sarah, it's Bob. I got your message. I'm at Nimue's. I'll be there in ten minutes. But why do you want me?'

'A prisoner called Graham Goody wants to see you to work out a deal.'

'Graham? I'll be there in five.'

Goody had clearly heard the Bob Watts end of the conversation. He mimed applause. 'Nimue – that was the first name I was trying to remember of that movie star. He's a sly one that Bob Watts. You've always got to watch the quiet ones, Detective Inspector.'

'So I understand. While we're waiting, perhaps you could say more about Said Farzi?'

Goody laughed. 'I think you know better than that, Detective Inspector. I'm sorry – what was your name again? Forgive me, I see a beautiful woman in my current circumstances and any rational thought goes right out of the window.'

'DI Gilchrist.' She gestured to Heap. 'And this is DS Heap.'

'Bellamy – yes, I remember.' Goody nodded to both of them. '*Gusto*. And I can see that it doesn't matter how small DS Heap is – he has the stuff. I'd be wary of going up against him. A bit like Bob's friend Jimmy Tingley.'

Gilchrist frowned. 'You know Jimmy Tingley too?'

Goody gave a very wide smile. 'Now then, DI Gilchrist, your first name wouldn't be Sarah, by any chance?' He glanced across at Heap. 'Down, there, Detective Sergeant, your boss is safe.' He looked back at Gilchrist. 'He's your Rottweiler, yes?'

'He's my colleague and my friend.'

'Just as Bob Watts was your colleague – your boss, indeed – when you made the beast with two backs together at that infamous police conference.'

Heap was on his feet. Gilchrist coloured but held out a warning hand. Goody looked up at him. 'I'm sorry, Detective Sergeant – and you too, Detective Inspector Sarah Gilchrist. I was trying to be witty in a worldly kind of way but I misjudged my audience. Please blame it on my low-life environment rather than entirely on me.

'Round here, what I just said would be wittier than Oscar Wilde – supposing anyone here knew who Oscar Wilde was. Or, indeed, what Shakespeare play I was quoting.' He looked at Heap. 'Please sit down. I know you couldn't do anything here to defend your boss without it wrecking your career. I wouldn't want that. If you want to take a pop at me when I'm out I'll be happy to oblige.'

Heap resumed his seat just as Bob Watts was ushered into the room.

'Bobby Boy!' Goody said, standing carefully.

Watts stayed by the door. 'Graham.' He turned to Gilchrist. 'How can I help here, Detective Inspector?'

'Bobby! No need to be so formal – everyone in this room knows the shared history of you and the lovely detective inspector, also known as Sarah.' Goody gestured around. 'And what's said in this room, stays in this room.'

Gilchrist flushed. 'Mr Goody has knowledge pertaining to Said Farzi, a person of great interest in the ongoing investigations around the deaths in Plumpton and his cannabis estate. We're willing to make a deal to reduce his sentence in return for useful information but he won't take my word for that. Hence he asked for you.'

Watts nodded to her and turned to Goody. 'You have my word, Graham.'

'Fair enough.'

'Perhaps you should explain to DS Heap and DI Gilchrist how we know each other.'

'Must I?' Goody said.

'Just to remind you . . . and me too.'

Goody sighed.

'OK. Bob saved my life in Bosnia back in the nineties. Both of us in the military. I got surrounded by a gang of those fascist Serbian bastards. Bob rescued me.' He showed his hands. 'That was it.'

'That wasn't it,' Watts said. 'Captain Goody here was protecting a dozen Muslim women and children the Serbs were hell-bent on raping and killing – not necessarily in that order. He was doing a pretty good job too. Me and my men just happened along to mop up at the end.'

Heap looked at Goody. Goody caught the look. 'I was just trying to get all of us out alive.'

Heap nodded. 'I respect that. I was just wondering where you went so wrong.'

Goody looked at Watts but Watts's face remained impassive. Goody raised an eyebrow at Heap. 'Life can get really boring, you know. Bit of excitement never did anyone any harm.'

'Except the people in the banks and post offices you scared the shit out of,' Heap said.

'Well, that would be true enough, young Detective Sergeant Bellamy Heap,' Goody said. 'But I imagine, if I had been involved, that for the rest of their lives these people have a story to tell. Probably the only story they have to tell.'

Watts stepped forward. 'Time to tell us about Said Farzi, I think, Graham, as per the deal.'

'Sure. How's Jimmy, by the way?'

'He's being Jimmy.'

Goody smiled. 'Send him my best.'

'Will do. Said Farzi?'

'Well, of course my information is about ten years out of date.'

'You seem to be aware of his current movements from what you said earlier about Ms Grace,' Gilchrist said.

'Well, I may be within prison walls but they are pretty porous. Would that they were more so.'

'Tell us about ten years ago.'

'Ten years ago, Said was working for his father up in the Atlas Mountains. They were growing high-grade marijuana and had a whole distribution route worked out down through Spain. I was one of their distributors. Getting the stuff into Spain was so fucking easy it was ridiculous.'

'Through Agadir port?' Heap said. 'Via Gibraltar?'

'He does know a thing or two, this DS Heap,' Goody said. 'But, no, that isn't as easy as it's cracked up to be. I got it into Spain without it ever leaving the Moroccan mainland.'

'Come again?' Watts said.

'You obviously don't know your Morocco as well as I might have assumed, mate. Spain has two cities actually in Morocco – Ceuta and Melilla. On the North African coastline, surrounded by the rest of Morocco on every side, but free ports that are part of Spain and, therefore, the European Union. The euro is their currency. And both are about a hop and a skip from mainland Spain. Get the stuff into those city states and you're in Europe. And there's a casino in Ceuta if you want to wash the odd bit of money clean.'

'And Said's family got it into those cities for you?' Heap said.

'Well, we did that together. But Said was always nagging me for a job or for an opportunity to strike out on his own. And then he realized that it wasn't just drugs you could get into Europe through Ceuta and Melilla. So he did strike out on his own, into people smuggling. This was before the whole refugee thing. He made it two-way traffic, importing kidnapped Eastern European white girls into Morocco and on to the brothels of the Middle East for who knows what kind of depravity? Not a nice man, you will have gathered.'

'Go on,' Gilchrist said.

'After I was pinched I didn't hear much about him for a couple of years then the next I hear, through these walls, is that his father is dead and he's now running the drug operation. How his father died I have no idea. I'd like to think it was from natural causes but when I heard that Said was living in England, just down the road from this prison and had bought a farm, I wasn't so sure.

'I heard he had various income streams. He came to see me once – just the once – a couple of years ago. Which is how I know about Ms Grace. He wanted the same thing as you lot. Wanted to know if I had done the Hassocks blockade job and, if so, if he could help me sort the money. See, if I had done it, I'd know enough to partly pay off the gang with the untraceable money from the sorting office and the sub-post office but leave the bank money sitting somewhere until everything had quietened down.

'What I wouldn't know would be that I was going to be nicked for my tiny drug operation – tiny – pretty much a hobby, really.

And that while I was inside, the Bank of Fucking England would replace the old Houblon £50 note with two new ones in succession. Then replace the £10 and £5 notes with fucking plastic – thereby giving a whole new meaning to laundering money since now you actually can.

'They got it from the surf-loving Aussies, I'm sure you know, who first thought it would be a good idea to have waterproof notes for when you want to keep your money with you as you hit those waves. Doesn't stop you and your money being chewed up by a shark, of course. In the water or on dry land, if you get my meaning.'

'Not entirely,' Gilchrist said.

'Well, I know you folk are savvy so you don't believe that old thing about "honour among thieves". You'll know it's a total load of bollocks. The Great Train Robbers got royally screwed by everyone. The Krays, the Richardsons, every chancer in town wanted a piece of that pie. And got it. I read a book about it a few years ago by a writer, local to here funnily enough. The guy kept saying: "But the mystery is, what happened to all the money?" There's no fucking mystery, excuse my continuing bad language. It's obvious: other thieves took it off them. That's what thieves do – they lie and cheat and, above all, steal. Off anybody. That's how one of the Great Train Robbers ends up selling flowers on Waterloo Bridge. Not that that is exactly poverty row given the mark-ups on fresh flowers.'

'Said Farzi came to see you,' Gilchrist said. 'When was this?'

'Yeah, sorry, I'm rambling. Couple of years ago.'

'Did he say what he was up to?'

'As I said, he was into having it off with this actress then having it off with her property and land. He said he'd told her he'd buy her house off her but she could stay there for services rendered until he got bored with her – he didn't say that last bit to her, of course.'

'Did he say how she responded?' Heap asked quietly.

'I hear he didn't get anywhere with any part of his plan,' Goody said. 'I imagine she told him to shove it up his arse. Do excuse my language, DI Gilchrist. It's being stuck in here, you see.' He turned to Watts. 'But you're obviously getting in there with the actress. Good for you.'

Watts looked puzzled for a moment then said: 'It was a policing matter. You in touch with the boys in Henfield much?' Goody shook his head.

'What boys in Henfield?' Gilchrist said.

'For some obscure reason a whole gang of ex-SAS have settled in Henfield,' Goody said. 'Keep each other company, I suppose. They can talk about things they can't talk about with anyone else.'

'You were in the SAS?' Gilchrist said.

Goody nodded. 'Didn't Bob already say that?'

Gilchrist frowned. 'I thought it was just regular army you were talking about. So that's how you know Jimmy Tingley?'

'Yeah – that's how I know the Secret Fart.' He saw Gilchrist's look. 'Silent but deadly, he was. Probably still is.' He grinned. 'We all had nicknames, darling. Do you want to know what Bob's was?'

'Is there anything more to tell us about Said Farzi?' Watts said hastily. 'Contacts here or in Morocco? The location of their plantations in Morocco?'

'I think knowing the location of his drug plantations in Morocco would take even you way above your pay grade, Police Commissioner. If I were you, I'd focus on how he is finding a more efficient way to service the UK marijuana market.' Goody smiled and looked down at the table. 'Home grown is always best.'

'Oh, we know about that,' Gilchrist said. 'We've already rolled that operation up. Do you know a Major Richard Rabbitt?'

'Never met him but I hear he's been murdered down at his lake,' Goody said, keeping his eyes down.

'He lives at Plumpton Down House. Do you know that?'

The corners of Goody's mouth crinkled into a smile. 'I've heard of it. And I read that too.'

'Do you know Stephen Faber?' Heap said, looking up from his iPad.

Goody looked across to the detective sergeant. 'I'd rather not say.'

'Does he favour red trousers?' Heap said.

Goody laughed. 'If I were to know him, I could imagine he might be the kind of person who would.' He looked across at

Watts. 'I imagine him to be the kind of person who pretends to be a cut above what he is.'

'Like the late Major Richard Rabbitt?' Watts said.

'I wouldn't know,' Goody said. 'As I indicated, I don't know that man.'

'Could you see such a man as Stephen Faber – if you knew him – being a killer for the sake of money?' Heap said.

'How have you come upon that name?' Goody said.

Heap smiled. 'As you indicated might have happened at the start of our conversation, this man escaped from Wandsworth Prison a few weeks ago, using a rope ladder dropped into the exercise yard from a drone. He got over the outer wall and dropped onto the roof of a waiting removals van.'

Goody mimed applause. 'Well tracked, DS Heap. I laughed out loud when I read about that escape. The old methods remain the best.' He saw their looks. 'That chancer Ronnie Biggs, the least important of the Great Train Robbers, and three others, escaped from Wandsworth in the same way back in the sixties.'

'Could you see Stephen Faber as a killer?'

'Well, I don't believe I'd be breaking any Marquis of Crimesbury rules to say he's probably a fucking psychopath. He's ex-military – not us, Bob, but he might as well have been.'

'I thought before you said you wouldn't be willing to break the rules,' Gilchrist said.

'I've reconsidered,' Goody said. 'Must be the benign influence of you people. Yeah, Faber has a temper on him. So, let me get this straight. Major Rabbitt, surveying his estate, stumbled on the money and nicked it before Faber could get to it.'

'Actually, we think it was someone else who stumbled on it,' Gilchrist said. 'But if you're anti-violence why would you have Faber in your team? Allegedly.'

'Didn't realize, did I, until it was too late? Although, actually, he behaved himself, aside from a bit of GBH on a stationary car.' He saw their looks. 'Long story. Allegedly. So how did they stumble on it?'

'Very dry summer. The lake unusually low.'

Goody nodded.

'How many containers had money in them?' Gilchrist saw Goody's look. 'Allegedly.'

'Three. They were with a load of others.' He looked at Watts. 'I think the others had been used as support for some kind of Bailey bridge across a wide stream on that side of the lake.'

'A temporary bridge,' Watts explained to the others.

'So Faber thinks, naturally enough, that Rabbitt, as owner of the lake, nicked our money and kills him in the course of interrogation. Throat slit, I heard.'

'How did you hear that?' Gilchrist said.

Goody raised his eyes. 'I told you. These walls are porous. And crime gangs are putting their own guys into prisons as warders these days.'

'You're saying that some of the warders here are actually criminals?' Heap said.

'I wouldn't dream of saying that,' Goody said. 'But it only takes one. So who do you think took the money? That kid in Brighton that got beaten to death?'

Gilchrist gave a little nod. 'But he didn't have it either. He'd sent it to the Bank of England.'

Goody thought for a moment. 'But would Faber know that? Is he after someone else?'

'You kept saying Rabbitt owned the lake. He doesn't. It belongs to Ms Nimue Grace.'

Goody looked at Watts. 'You need to get hold of some of those guys in Henfield because, if Faber is still looking for the money, he's coming for her next.'

SIXTEEN

Nimue Grace watched a big, bulky man walk up her garden towards her home. He wasn't trying to hide. He was quite up front about it, in fact. He didn't look like a journalist, he looked more like someone who was ex-military.

His gaze swept from side to side as he came. He saw her watching him through a gap in the curtain at a small window but didn't respond until he got within twenty yards. Then he stopped and gave a little wave. She didn't respond; just kept looking at him.

'I'm a security expert,' he called. Grace didn't catch the name he gave.

She opened the window a little. 'What do you want?'

'To protect you.'

'Well, you're a dollar short and a day late if you want to do that,' Grace said.

'You're still alive, aren't you?'

'Someone thinks my life is in danger?'

'The police do. They called me as a matter of urgency. I have some friends in the same line of business coming over soon to put a ring of steel round you that nothing will penetrate. Check with DI Gilchrist and DS Heap, if you don't believe me.'

'I can't – my power is down. The phone is dead. The internet too.'

'What about your mobile?'

'Getting a signal here is really iffy.'

'Bummer. When did your power go down?'

'Ten, fifteen minutes ago.'

'Then we don't have much time,' the man said, resuming his walk towards the house. 'He must be here already.'

'Who?'

'The man who might be a threat to your life.' He had reached the window.

'But why would anyone want to kill me?'

'We think he's after something that belongs to him and you know where it is.'

'What might that be?'

'That's above my pay grade. If you'd let me in I'd be able to do my job a lot better.'

'Of course,' Grace said. 'But, first, I didn't catch your name and, second—' she paused to point at his trousers – 'what is it with the military and ex-military and red trousers?'

The man smiled for a moment. 'I can't speak for the trouser colour, except to say I like it. I've got half a dozen more of these. And my name is Jimmy Tingley.'

Grace gave him a little smile, then dropped the curtain closed. The man stood there, unsure what to do, until he heard movement to his left and a male voice saying: 'That's funny. I thought I was Jimmy Tingley.'

Jimmy Tingley was expecting a fight but Stephen Faber just looked at him and the half dozen hard men from Henfield who were in a semicircle around him. Faber dropped to the ground and sat cross-legged. The back door of the house opened and Sarah Gilchrist and Bellamy Heap stepped out to arrest him.

In the house, Bob Watts sat with Nimue Grace at the kitchen table. 'It's over,' Watts said.

'Thank you for all you've done. Keeping the story out of the papers at least for a day or two. Advising me on suing the force for leaking my private information. And now, bringing your former colleagues to my aid.'

'Sarah and Bellamy are not to blame for the tabloids getting on to you.'

'Of course they are. If they'd been more careful with what I told them, nobody would be any the wiser.'

Watts shook his head. 'They were leading a murder investigation so anything you told them which might be relevant – and the things you told them seemed very relevant to the identity of a potential murderer – needed to be noted. Then, they were obliged to share this information with another officer. He is most likely to have been the police source for the tabloids.'

'They shouldn't have trusted him, then, should they?'

'They didn't, but they had no choice. They have done their utmost to protect you in every way. And Bellamy may well lose his stripes or face suspension for exacting his own justice on the man who betrayed you.'

'What do you mean?'

'He was so angered that you had been betrayed – and he and Gilchrist *do* feel responsible, even though they shouldn't – that he confronted the detective sergeant who had sold your information to the tabloids and taught him a lesson.'

'You mean little Bellamy Heap beat him up?'

'Little Bellamy Heap is not unlike my friend, Jimmy Tingley, in that regard. There is much more to him than meets the eye. But, yes, that's what I mean. Quite what the chief constable will do about that I don't know.'

'My Sir Galahad,' Grace murmured.

'Pardon?' Watts said.

Grace shook her head. 'What will happen to the man who did sell my information?'

'The way things can work in the police service he may just get a slap on the wrist. And, knowing the Neanderthal he is, I doubt he will learn the lesson Bellamy taught him. But if I have any say he will be disgracefully discharged from the service.'

'And this man Faber?'

'A ruthless, violent man. He escaped from Wandsworth prison a week before the murder of Richard Rabbitt. Came for the money that he knew was stashed in your lake.'

'He killed Rabbitt, Antonio and Joe Jackson?'

'The first two probably. The third maybe not. The whip marks on Joe's face suggest a different culprit. But that's what Sarah and Bellamy will be up to next, ascertaining that.'

'Not you?'

'Although, as you can see, I often blur the lines, my brief is not operational so, no, I won't be doing any of that.'

'You blur the lines. You're not as square as you appear, are you?'

'It's been my observation, Nimue, that people who appear *square* rarely are whereas those who try hard to be – what's the opposite? – *hip,* although that used to be *hep*, often turn out to be pretty conventional and old-fashioned. Anyway, I like jazz very much.'

'Me too. But that doesn't mean either of us are hip.'

Watts smiled. 'Jazzers came up with the term *square* in the 1940s to describe anyone who didn't like jazz. They equated it to boring old classical conductors rigidly wielding their baton to make a square shape when an orchestra was playing a conventional four beat rhythm.

'But back in the old days – the thirteenth century – *square* was a good thing. It comes from old French *esquire* and means someone who is honest and upstanding. That meaning carried on – it gets into phrases like *fair and square* and *a square deal* – until the jazzers came along and turned it into something pejorative.'

'Is this Encyclopaedia Britannica stuff what I'm going to have to listen to when we go out to dinner?' Grace said.

'Are we going out to dinner?' Watts said.

'Well, I bloomin' well hope so,' she said.

'It won't be for a few weeks, I'm sorry to say. Jimmy Tingley and I have to take a little trip.'

Grace tilted her head. 'More blurring of the lines?'

'A couple of things to sort out in Morocco and then on to Canada.'

Grace's eyes widened. 'Said Farzi is in Morocco, I understand. What's the other thing?'

'A low-life pretending to be a man who needs to be taught a lesson.'

Grace gave an odd little smile and Watts noticed her eyes fill with tears. 'Two more knights errant. Is there something in the air round here?'

'There are a lot of decent men in the world, Nimue – I'm talking about Tingley and Heap, not myself – though I admit you sometimes have to sift through a lot of dross to find them. But, actually, for Said Farzi, we're going a bit mob-handed.' He gestured out of the window. 'Those boys out there are bored stiff living off their army pensions in Henfield. There are only so many clay pigeons you can shoot down in a week.'

'What are you going to do to the other one?'

'Whatever seems an appropriate response to his behaviour. Unless you have a view.'

Grace shook her head and looked down. 'Thank you,' she whispered.

Stephen Faber did a deal. He agreed to name all the men involved in the Hassocks blockade in return for a reduced sentence and the reduced charges of manslaughter. Gilchrist and Heap were fine about the first but insisted to Chief Constable Hewitt they questioned him first to see if they could figure out whether the two, possibly three, killings were murder or manslaughter.

When they went into the interview room they saw a man who was all angles. Big, thick angles. Big but sharp nose; broad but sharp shoulders; big but sharp knuckled hands. He spread his hands when he said: 'Ask me what you want. I've got nothing to hide.'

'You killed Antonio Urraca first. Then Richard Rabbitt. Then Joe Jackson.'

'I only recognize one of those names.'

'Which one?'

'Richard Rabbitt.'

'How do you know that name?' Heap said.

'It was on a leaflet in Plumpton post office for a magic lantern slide show in the village hall. Whatever a magic lantern show is. It described him as owner of Plumpton Down House and Estate.'

'So you came looking for him.'

'I came looking for the money we'd left in his lake.'

'But first you killed Antonio Urraca.'

'The man with the beard? That was an accident. Urraca was his name? I *thought* he was a foreigner, especially when he opened his gob. I'd come on him lurking in the wood and asked him if he was the owner of the lake. He was an arrogant bugger. Bit bolshie. Got my goat up, frankly. Anyway, wrong bird as to ownership. I asked him if he'd taken our money. He told me to ask somebody with a foreign-sounding name. Nim-something. I ran out of patience.'

'So you killed him,' Heap said.

'No, no. To be strictly accurate, the sickle killed him. Bloody lethal weapon, that is. I had it held against his stomach and he suddenly tried to break away from me and the point punctured him and, as he twisted, started to rip his stomach. I thought I'd better finish the job to put him out of the misery he'd caused himself. It was assisted suicide, you might say.'

'How long after that did Richard Rabbitt come along?'

'Which one was he?'

'The man with the dentures?'

'Guy with the dentures!' Faber laughed loudly and long. 'That was so fucking weird. I was down by the lake washing off the sickle and I heard a car draw up and somebody get out. I see this bloke, looking a bit the worse for wear, weaving his way past the lake on the drive. I wondered if it might be, what-sisname, Rabbitt? I climb over the wire fencing and go onto the road. He sees me and asks what I'm doing. I says someone is injured and needs help in the wood.

'He says: "a woman?" I go along with that. "Yeah," I say. "Is she naked," he says. I go with that too, though why he would think that I don't know. "Starkers," I say. So he follows me into the wood and when we get near to the island I point across to the other side to the white containers. "What?" he says. "Where is she?" "Those white containers," I say. "You've had three of them. I want the contents." Rabbitt squints and, ignoring what I just said, says: "I can't see her. Where's Nimue?" And I realize that's the same name the foreign bloke was saying.

'I persevere. "I want the contents of those three containers back. You've stolen them." He looks at me and says: "You said Nimue had collapsed." "Who the fuck is Nimue?" I say and I hit him in the Adam's apple with the webbing between my thumb and my first finger. Not hard. Really, not hard. And this set of teeth comes out of his mouth and hits me in the chest. Fuck me, never seen that before.

'Now this is where I hold my hand up because I persevere with the questions while he's still choking. I thought he was trying it on. "You won't tell me?" I says for the third time. He shakes his head more vigorously and I think he's resisting. It's only after I realize he's saying he can't speak. So my bad that I didn't twig that and instead I got cross.'

'You killed him.'

'Well, again, *kill* is putting it a bit strong. I flipped him, sure, and put the sickle to his throat but that fucking sickle! It has a life of its own. He struggled, still gagging, the sickle cut into him.' Faber shook his head. 'Blood went everywhere. I was covered after I'd dumped Rabbitt in the water. Then this other man comes along in a tracksuit with *Muscle Beach* written across his pathetic chest. Real jerk. Whistles while he walks for fuck's sake. I get out of the way and he strips off totally – which is not a good look for him – then shouts: "Here I come, Nimue," and wades in. That name again. I steal his clothes, although I leave the woman's knickers he's wearing, dump my blood-soaked stuff and the sickle and take off.'

'To Brighton to beat a young student to death.'

'What? No. To find out who the fuck this Nimue is. Turns out she owns the lake. So I head her way.'

'To kill her too,' Heap says.

'To get the fucking money!'

* * *

Gilchrist and Heap came out of the interview room. 'He didn't know about Joe Jackson finding the money. So I think we can stay with our supposition that Joe's death was down to Said Farzi's man, Abbas, getting carried away when persuading Jackson to quit his flat.'

Gilchrist's phone rang. Chief Constable Hewitt. Gilchrist smiled at Heap. 'Good news, ma'am.'

'We're going to Morocco?' Tingley said as he and Bob Watts headed towards Gatwick.

'A bit of unofficial police work to do.'

'What kind?'

'The usual. Shut somebody up, then track someone else down.'

'Shut somebody up permanently?'

'No!'

'But we're off the books?'

'We are.'

'Good job I'm retired or I'd be getting peeved at not getting paid for my work. So just to clarify, we're not shutting up this person permanently?'

'No way.'

'We'll see.'

Ouarzazate was a two-hour car journey through the Atlas Mountains from Casablanca airport. Watts found it exhilarating. Tingley sat beside him, occasionally sipping at a hip flask and more regularly glugging water.

'You've been here before, I'm guessing, by your lack of interest in this landscape,' Watts said.

'Many times. Further up in the mountains. Some bad vibes.'

'It's the snow on the peaks with the hot desert below that impresses me.' Tingley offered him the flask. Watts took a sip. 'Nice.'

'So you say this actor takes a punching bag with him wherever he goes.'

'Yeah – sounds like a total idiot, right?'

'A total dick, I think you're too cultured to say. How was Graham?'

'He was Graham. You ever thought of going to the Dark Side?'

Tingley looked at him. 'Are you kidding? I *live* on the Dark Side.'

'Yes, but not robbing banks and all that.'

'All that is trivial compared to what I do.'

'In a good cause every time.'

'So I tell myself. But I don't think that's going to save me.'

The hotel was like a compound – high walls and, inside, blocks of red sandstone buildings in neat squares. There was a huge pool on a big terrace with a bar. In the corridors there was movie memorabilia dating back to the 1950s. Papier-mâché statues of pharaohs, a balsa wood Roman chariot, huge film posters of sword and sandal epics in many languages.

Watts and Tingley were sharing a big room. 'I'm going for a recce,' Tingley said.

'I'll come with you,' Watts said.

Tingley shook his head. 'I'm damned. You're still on the side of Light.'

'So are you, Jimmy,' Watts called after him as Tingley walked out the door.

Tingley watched Bosanquet at the bar for an hour. Saw him go to the bathroom a couple of times. The second time he hadn't cleaned himself up very well – the plug of cocaine hanging from his nose was visible from where Tingley was sitting. Tingley nursed his beer, his cigarette packet and lighter, as always, set out in a neat line on the table by his drink.

The guy was tall and Tingley could see that he had once been well muscled but now it was mostly lard. Clearly it had been vanity muscle, not real muscle, punching bag or no punching bag. The guy had a supercilious, self-satisfied look about him which Tingley despised. Tingley noted that he favoured his right leg, just a tiny bit. But it was the tiny bits with which men like Tingley operated most effectively.

The guy downed a few beers with a changing roster of people. He was trying it on with a couple of women. One was interested, the other not. Tingley nursed a second beer, smoked another cigarette. When the big guy excused himself to go to the bathroom for a third time, Tingley followed.

Tingley waited outside the bathroom in the wide corridor. A

huge, fake Egyptian throne was placed a few yards away and giant posters of Italian biblical epics he'd never heard of were framed along the walls. He was looking at a *David e Golia* poster featuring a chubby Goliath and a camp-looking David when Bosanquet came back out of the bathroom, wiping his nose.

'Hey, big man,' Tingley called after him. 'You are that big man from Netflix, aren't you?'

Bosanquet turned and looked Tingley up and down.

'I'm a Netflix star, yeah.'

'I heard you always travel with a boxing bag – hang it up wherever you are. You a keen boxer then?'

'Can I help you with something?' Bosanquet said. 'Only I'm kind of busy here. Lot of people outside want autographs. Is that what you want?'

'No, thanks. I just want a moment of your time to confirm or deny that when you don't have your boxing bag to punch you punch women. Or arrange to have acid thrown at them.'

Bosanquet frowned. 'Say what?'

'I wondered if you knew what it was like to try to punch a man.'

'Hey,' Bosanquet called down the corridor. 'Can we get security along here?'

'Me, for instance.'

Bosanquet put on the sneering, supercilious look of the stupidly arrogant.

'You? I fart in your face and you'd blow over.'

Tingley laughed. 'I must remember that one. But, yes, I mean me. Are you ready? I mean that left knee is looking a bit wonky. Probably all that blubber you're carrying. Self-satisfaction fat we call it back home. But I think your days of being self-satisfied are over.'

Bosanquet gave him a hard stare.

'Ha!' Tingley said. 'Actors can't do the thousand yard stare because, well, they're acting. You should really put your hands up by the way because I'm not a punching bag or a defenceless woman.'

'I have no idea what you're talking about but you're really asking for it—'

'I really am.' Tingley held out his hands. 'See, I've even put my gloves on so I can hit you harder without hurting my knuckles. Although mostly I'm going to be using my feet to mess you up.' He pointed down at his shoes. 'Steel-toe caps. It's a bugger getting through airport security but great for teaching bad, bad men a lesson. So why don't you try to give me what you gave to Nimue Grace and no doubt others?'

'Nimue? That bitch? She set you up for this? She murders a child and thinks I'm the bad guy?'

Tingley let that last remark pass, largely because he didn't understand it. 'No, this is all me. Nimue doesn't give you another thought except when she's scraping shit off her shoe.'

Tingley kicked Bosanquet hard on the right shin and followed it with a tight roundhouse kick to the side of his left knee. The bad knee. That's all it took. Bosanquet was jerking back in pain on his stiff right leg when his left leg collapsed underneath him and he went down. Heavily. Tingley looked at the stupid *David e Golia* poster facing him, trying to decide whether to finish Bosanquet off with a kick to the head.

'No,' Bob Watts said, coming out of the shadows behind the fake throne.

Tingley looked from him to Bosanquet, lying unmoving on the floor. 'OK,' he said, stamping down hard on the actor's right knee. Tingley shrugged. 'If they ever remake *Ironside* in the next year he's in clover.'

'That was a bit harsh,' Watts said as they walked away.

'Oh, come on. He deserved cutting down to size just for travelling with a punching bag. Any guy who travels with a punching bag who isn't a professional boxer is a first-class dick and major poser. He deserved much more than he got for that alone. Just call me soft-hearted.'

'I'll try. Here we go: Jimmy Tingley is soft-hearted.' Watts shook his head. 'No. Doesn't sound right.'

'Fuck off.'

'Permission to disobey and pour you another drink back in the room.'

'Bosanquet said an odd thing though. He said Nimue Grace murdered a child.'

'That's something to investigate when we get back,' Watts said. 'By the way – CCTV?'

'Disabled on that corridor and from the terrace a couple of hours ago.'

'OK. Let's go and see if the boys from Henfield have located Said Farzi. Where he's concerned, I won't try to pull you back from doing whatever you want to do.'

Nimue Grace walked with Gilchrist and Heap to the edge of the lake opposite the island as dusk was moving in. The evenings were getting chilly now. She looked out over the placid waters.

'I had such plans for this place for my children. I wanted to make it an idyll for them.'

'It already is,' Gilchrist said.

'No, I know, but tree houses and canoes and camping.'

'*Swallows and Amazons*?' Gilchrist said.

'Never read those books,' Grace said. She pointed to a small inlet a few yards away. 'I wanted a short pier here to dock the canoes. I wanted rope ladders between trees. Everything.' She shook her head. 'But none of it happened except for that shitty tree house on the island.'

'It's still beautiful for you without your children,' Gilchrist said.

'Maybe,' Grace said. She looked up at the darkening sky. 'The moon, the stars, the night clouds drifting by disdain all that we are.'

'That's bleak,' Gilchrist said, shivering slightly.

'I *am* bleak,' Grace said. 'Haven't you realized? What's there for me not to be bleak about?'

'Pretty much everything,' Heap said quietly.

Grace gave him a look that kind of flared. Had it been a fantasy movie there would have been lightning bolts shooting from her eyes. Then: 'I had a child. I mean inside me. Bosanquet's. I aborted it. I don't regret it. But there isn't a day I don't think about what might have been.' She gave them her brilliant smile but it faltered. 'Let's go to the pub,' was all she said.

The Half Moon was quiet so they had the pick of the tables. Gilchrist and Heap went up to the bar. Grace took three tries to be satisfied with a table. She finally sat with her back to the room facing the wall. She caught Gilchrist's puzzled look. 'I know you're thinking I'm a diva but downlighting isn't flattering for anybody and, when the paps can pop up at any time or anyone with a mobile phone can be an amateur pap, people like me have to be careful. "Nimue's misery" or "Time for a facelift Nimue?" or whatever crap headline they'll slap on a crap photo of me looking haggard because of the lighting.

'I hardly ever come to pubs – very sad as I love a country pub, but it's just too much. I was in the Bull in Ditchling not so long ago with Francis and a gay friend and this bloke was really giving me weird looks. Freaked me out.'

'Different worlds,' Gilchrist said. 'Where is Francis, by the way? We haven't seen her – him? – since our first visit.'

'I couldn't afford Francis. I really do struggle financially, unbelievable as that might sound.'

'Jimmy Page used to play acoustic sets in this pub way back,' Heap said, carrying drinks from the bar. 'He had the house down the road here – the one with the moat? – and would bob in here every now and then with his guitar.'

'I was going to buy that house,' Grace said. 'When I was looking for somewhere here to buy. The actress who taught me to play chess told me how wonderful this area was. Some mega-selling American romantic novelist owned that Jimmy Page house at the time. I decided against because it seemed too vulnerable – too near the road and so on.'

'Your privacy is important to you,' Gilchrist said.

'The most important thing,' Grace said. 'Isn't it for you?'

Gilchrist laughed. 'I don't have much to be private about.'

'Well, I'm the same but when you're under tabloid scrutiny – and judgement – all the time it becomes a rather different story. It becomes their story, not the truth. Scum that they are.'

'I can only imagine,' Gilchrist said.

'There's a painting on the wall by the bar from the 1970s,' Heap continued. 'All the regulars. Jimmy Page is in it.'

'Are you a heavy metal fan, Detective Sergeant Heap?' Grace said. 'Do you play air guitar when you're alone?'

'Neither of those things, Ms Grace. Just interested in cultural history.'

'Then did you know that James Wilby used to live nearby – across the road from here, I think. Camilla used to live here too. I think her family had the house James eventually bought. I met her once. Very engaging. She said that in her privileged childhood she regarded that bridleway across the road as part of the family garden, she went riding there so often.'

'You've worked with James Wilby?' Heap said.

Grace shook her head. 'I was never offered a Merchant Ivory film – oh, I know he's done other stuff but that's what I most think of him doing. I was busy earning wheelbarrow loads of money doing crap, big-budget Americana.' Grace sighed as she looked out of the window at Plumpton Hill. 'There's something about the Downs that is quite magical.'

'Like your lake, Ms Grace,' Heap said.

Grace laughed and raised her glass. 'To my lake. And new friends.'

EPILOGUE

Gilchrist and Heap gave Nimue Grace a lift home from the pub. She waved them off, her heart-melting grin on her face, as they drove back down her drive. New friends? Maybe – she liked them well enough – but only if she hung around. She flicked on the lights in her cottage and took a big key from a hook by the front door. She unlocked the stripped wooden door Sarah Gilchrist had thought was for the loo at Grace's party.

That had been careless of Grace, leaving it unlocked. She opened it now and flicked on the light switch just inside the door. She walked gingerly down the rickety steps. She loved the smell of apples down here, even the sickly sweet smell of apples that had rotted.

She looked at the chute and the broad barrel full of apples beneath it. She looked at the three white containers against the far wall. She looked at the huge pile of money on the table in the middle of the room.

She thought about Joe Jackson. When he'd been filming and come across the containers, he'd seen immediately that three of them were full of money. Honest lad that he was (dim lad that he was), he'd brought them to Grace, assuming they were hers.

She had known immediately where the money had come from. She'd already read the pamphlet she'd been given about the Hassocks blockade.

She persuaded Jackson that he should see what the procedure was for getting the money converted into usable currency in return for a cut of the money big enough to fund his short film and one more after. She'd promised she'd star in that second one, if she liked the script.

She'd been relieved to hear that his death was nothing to do with that. Just coincidence. Abbas getting carried away as he tried to persuade Jackson to move out of the flat in Said Farzi's apartment block.

But now she had to figure out a way to get the money converted without drawing attention to herself if the Bank of England was now alerted about the old money from those Hassocks robberies.

But she was confident. She was on a roll. After all, two people who had been horrible to her were dead and others were about to get their comeuppance. She was confident that before she had to sell this place because she was skint she would have figured out a way to access these two million pounds. She was a wizard with that sort of thing. She was, after all, the Lady of the Lake.